I have had the pleasure of immersing myself in Patrick Alexander's three novels based on the complex twentieth century history of Miami. Starting with his first book, *Death by Water*, he takes us on a suspenseful and, at times, rollicking journey through the back stories of North America's "last frontier" – South Florida.

From the land boom of the 1920's to the Cuban influx starting in the '60's, he weaves an intricate tale of love, lust, power and greed – with a murder or two thrown in for good measure. You can quickly determine from the flowing prose that Patrick is skilled in the language arts and has a solid foundation in classical literature.

As a lifetime resident of Miami, and former Mayor of Coral Gables, I can assure the reader that there is much truth and reality cleverly buried amid the fictional plotlines and characters. Each book is a quick, enjoyable read that leaves the curious reader asking for more.

Don Slesnick

DEATH BY WATER

By

Patrick Alexander

Published by Lanehouse

Miami, Florida, USA

ISBN-13: 978-1727765236
ISBN-10:   1727765230

DEATH BY WATER

THE CUBAN CONNECTION

VOLUME ONE OF

THE GREENHAVEN TRILOGY

BY

PATRICK ALEXANDER

Also by Patrick Alexander

Marcel Proust's Search for Lost Time

The Booklovers' Guide to Wine

Recollections of a Racketeer

The Nigerian Letter

Proust on Twitter

Death on the Eighth

Dead Naked

As always – to Jude

My love and inspiration

And to Andrés Pruna

And all his comrades in the 2506 Brigade

IV: Death by Water

Phlebas the Phoenician, a fortnight dead,
Forgot the cry of gulls, and the deep sea swell
And the profit and loss.
                    A current under sea
Picked his bones in whispers. As he rose and fell
He passed the stages of his age and youth
Entering the whirlpool.
                    Gentile or Jew
O you who turn the wheel and look to windward,
Consider Phlebas, who was once handsome and tall as
    you.

T.S. Eliot: The Wasteland

Table of Contents

One: 636 Canal Drive, Greenhaven, August 2011

It was not the size of the alligator in the family's swimming pool that so caught Mrs. Doyle's attention, it was more the quality of the suit worn by the partially devoured body floating face down, just below the surface. "Saville Row" she noticed. "Wool, pinstripe. Who on earth would wear a three piece, wool suit in South Florida in August?"

"Honey" she called to her husband, who was still unpacking the trawler. "There's an alligator in the pool. "

"Is it the same one?" He called back.

"I don't think so. It seems bigger than the last one." For some reason she lowered her voice, perhaps so that the neighbors would not hear or else so as not to offend the large reptile, "Also it seems to have eaten somebody."

"Not the gardener?

"No. Nobody we know."

Raymond Doyle heaved the last of the suitcases off the deck of the boat and onto the wooden dock. He still needed to remove and empty the ice chests and then hose down the decks. It never ceased to amaze him, how much work, preparation and clean-up was involved in just a simple little three day cruise up the Intracoastal. Carrying two of the suitcases, he walked across the lawn from the boat-dock to the main house, where his wife stood beside the pool.

Rather selfishly, he had to admit, Raymond was relieved that the body in the pool was not the gardener. Jose had been with the family for almost five years and knew exactly how they liked things arranged. He was reliable, honest, hard-working and an undocumented Cuban immigrant which made him far more affordable and avoided all that bothersome paperwork.

1

Placing the suitcases on the coral deck, he stood beside his wife and looked down at the body. "What's he doing in our pool? And where's the damned alligator?"

"The alligator's resting on the bottom. Look, over there. Probably digesting that man's leg. A postprandial nap maybe."

The Doyle's pool was about forty feet long and perhaps twenty feet wide. It was an infinity pool surrounded with coral and limestone pavers. Raymond had been looking forward to relaxing in it when he arrived home, holding a vodka martini in one hand and good cigar in the other. It was a favorite spot to unwind while watching the sun slowly sink between the palm trees on the far side of the canal. Obviously, that was now out of the question. An eighteen foot reptile however well-fed and sated, was not the sort of company he enjoyed sharing his pool with - not to mention a one-legged corpse.

"I suppose we ought to call the police" Margaret suggested.

"Or the SFFWCC first maybe."

"What?"

"The State of Florida Fish & Wildlife Conservation Commission." Raymond pointed at the body, indicating the torn and shredded trouser leg and the missing limb. "Best to deal with the alligator before he consumes the rest of the evidence."

In the decade that the Doyles had been living beside the canal in Greenhaven, they had found alligators in the pool on several occasions, particularly when South Florida was having an unusually dry season. The alligators would move east from the Everglades and swim in the canals, quite often climbing into the neighborhood swimming pools, especially if the owners were away.

Raymond and Margaret loved their home and loved living beside the canal which was large enough to accommodate their fifty foot trawler. The canal offered easy access both to Biscayne Bay and the Atlantic Ocean beyond. When the kids were still living at home, they always loved watching the large, gentle manatees that, even today,

2

still like to congregate around the dock - but there was no way of avoiding the fact that the alligators were a terrible nuisance. Just this past year, the Rodriguez family, on the other side of the canal, had lost two small dogs, Yorkshire Terriers - or Yorkshire terrorists as Raymond called them. Maria Rodriguez was convinced the alligators had carried the Yorkies away in their jaws and now wouldn't even let her children play in the back yard.

"At least we don't have to listen to their constant yapping" Raymond had said. "Or their damned kids yelling and screaming all the time."

ooOoo

Police Sergeant Jorge Gonzalez interviewed Raymond and Margaret in their living room while three uniformed officers removed the body from the pool and laid him, face up, on the coral deck while waiting for the coroner's team to arrive. Another officer, armed with an all-black, vicious looking Kel-Tec KSG shotgun stood nervously at the edge of the pool just in case the alligator decided that the first leg was just an hors d'oeuvre before the main course..

"So you left here last Thursday noon, spent three nights up the coast with some friends near Palm Beach and you returned home about an hour ago."

Raymond had just given his wife a gin and tonic and was pouring himself a large martini. "Are you sure I can't offer you something Sergeant?" He asked.

Gonzalez shook his head. "Thank you, no, Mr. Doyle. Now, just to confirm; the gentleman in the pool, was not in the pool when you left on Thursday?"

Raymond shook his head.

"And neither of you know him or recognize him from somewhere else?" The policeman wrote down their negative answers in his notebook. "And the alligator" he continued. "May I assume that this particular reptile is previously unknown to you and was not in the pool when you left last Thursday?"

"I think that's a fair assumption to make sergeant." After draining half his glass, Raymond was feeling more relaxed. Navigating his fifty foot trawler along the narrow part of the canal which traversed the Alhambra golf course, with the danger of errant golf balls whizzing overhead was always nerve-wracking. But having to maneuver under that damned final bridge, with barely a foot to spare on either side always left him tense and irritable. Finding a half consumed, though well-dressed stranger in his swimming pool had done little to relieve the tension.

"What will happen to the alligator?" Margaret asked. "Last time the Fish and Wildlife people took it away in a van"

Like her husband, Margaret had not had time to change out of her boating clothes and was aware that her blouse was crumpled and stained with salt water and her white shorts were no longer quite so white.

"Depends whether it's guilty or not" Gonzalez answered. "If the autopsy shows that the alligator killed the floater, then it will be euthanized. To me it looks as though the deceased was pulled into the pool by the alligator grabbing his leg and he probably died from a combination of shock and drowning. We can't release a man-eater back into the wild; we'll have to shoot him." He closed his notebook and replaced it in his breast pocket. "That's why we have to wait for the coroner's report."

"And if he rules a different cause of death?"

"If the deceased was already dead when the alligator found him; well that's different" he answered. "The alligator was just doing what comes naturally and so Fish and Wildlife can truck him back into the Everglades, tag and release him."

"So then all we have to do is find out what a dead body was doing near our pool."

"Exactly" said the Sergeant, rising to his feet. "And now, if you'll excuse me, I must go and see how the coroner is progressing."

Two: Greenhaven Police Station, 2011

As Greenhaven's first Haitian-American Police Chief, Philippe Lacroix felt it important, at all times, to project an image of dignity and command. At six foot three, he was already an impressive man and, with skin as black as his immaculate and always pressed uniform, his piercing brown eyes and deep voice, power sat easily on his broad shoulders. This image of authority was further enhanced by his regular, and carefully stage managed, interviews and photo opportunities with both the local and national press. Seldom a month passed when Chief Lacroix did not organize some law enforcement ceremony to be held in the Community Meeting Room of the City Museum; recognizing an Officer of the Month, or addressing a Neighborhood Watch Committee. Such events were always well covered by the Greenhaven TV Network, the Greenhaven Gazette and even by the Miami Herald.

George Attwood, the museum janitor had worked with Chief Lacroix for several years and knew exactly how the Chief liked the room to be arranged. He knew how many chairs to set out and where the podium should be positioned. He also knew where to place the U.S. flag so that from whatever angle the photographer chose to shoot the Chief, at least part of the Stars and Stripes would be included in the photo. George was even aware, with the Chief's discrete encouragement, of the movement of the sun through the seasons of the year so that the position at the podium would best catch the noontime light through the east facing window and thus display the Chief's photogenic profile to best advantage. Projecting an image of dignity and command required a certain amount of conscious preparation.

George himself was no stranger to image manipulation, having spent his career as professor of French literature at the local university. Keeping students amused and alert during discussions of Marcel Proust's use of visual metaphors in *A la recherché du temps perdu* required no small amount of stagecraft.

"I hear we have a man-eating croc on the loose" George said as he moved Old Glory behind the podium.

"What do you mean?" the Chief asked.

"I was playing golf with Sergeant Anna Hartman, earlier this morning" George said. "She told me some guy had been pulled into a swimming pool and killed by a crocodile."

"That's about the best example I've heard of why a police officer should not discuss his or her work with unauthorized members of the public" Lacroix said. "And why members of the public should not listen to gossip."

"So it's not true?"

"In the first place it was not a crocodile. It was an alligator. You've lived here long enough George to know the difference, and so has Anna."

"Crocs have long pointed snouts and can live in salt-water. Alligators have rounded snouts and need fresh water to survive" said George proudly. "I work in a museum so I know stuff" he added with a smile.

"Secondly, the alligator did not kill the victim. Anna has not seen the coroner's report yet. It only arrived on my desk about an hour ago. The victim was already dead when the alligator found him. He died as a result of multiple blows to the face and two bullets to the back of the head. Probably soft nose bullets which expanded inside the skull resulting in a large exit hole which removed the lower jaw and all the teeth. His hands had been removed, probably with a machete, and his face was so pulverized that there is no way we can get an I.D."

"Oh," George said, visibly shocked. After a pause he said. "So the alligator's not guilty: free to go?".

The Chief nodded. "The Florida Fish and Wildlife boys are already trucking him back to the Everglades. Meanwhile, we have a murder investigation to take care of. I'll be talking to Channel Seven at noon and we'll be asking for the public's assistance in trying to identify the deceased."

"Here at the museum?"

"Yes. After the awards ceremony. Since we will have the media here anyway, this is the perfect opportunity to catch the public's attention and hopefully alert some witnesses."

"Then let me slightly adjust the podium" George said. "To better catch the angle of the noontime sun."

ooOoo

Anybody stepping into the Tenth Hole Diner, the clubhouse of the Alhambra Golf Course, could be forgiven for thinking they had stepped into a time-warp and they were now back in the mid-20th century. From the floor-mounted, soda-fountain stools, matching Naugahyde booths and Formica countertop - everything screamed 'The Fifties.' As for the music – every single disk in the ancient juke-box had been recorded long before Elvis Aaron Presley ever walked into the Sun Record studios.

Charles Wilson, affectionately referred to as "Chili Chuck", the owner of the Tenth Hole Diner, was widely known throughout Dade County, both for his flaming-hot Chili ("best Chili in town") and also for his unique collection of music from the '40s and early '50s. Chuck's father had started the restaurant back in the 1920s when the golf course first opened and Chuck had taken over after his father's death in 1954. As a teenager Chuck had built a large collection of 45 rpm disks of his favorite artists like Glen Miller, Bing Crosby and Perry Como. As a hormonal young man he'd also had short-lived crushes on Doris Day, Dinah Shore and each one of the Andrew Sisters, individually, – all of whose records he had collected. For a couple of years, before taking over the Tenth Hole, Chuck had served in the Korean War and that experience added people like Jimmie Osborne and Wilf Carter to his collection with such timeless classics as *"Goodbye Maria (I'm off to Korea.)"* With some of the money his father had bequeathed him he bought a Paul Fuller designed Wurlitzer jukebox and proudly installed it in the Tenth Hole where it still has pride of place. With the addition of a few more artists such as Jimmie Davis, Vaughn Monroe and Ernest Tubb, the jukebox had reached its full capacity of 150 disks and Chuck simply stopped buying any more records.

A week after Chuck's final purchase, Sun Records in Memphis released *"That's Alright (Mama)"* by Elvis Presley – just too late to ever make it into Chuck's jukebox. Not only did Chuck never buy a record by Presley or, heaven help us, one of those British boys; he also never bought an LP record or, Lord forbid, a compact-disk thingy. Nobody was allowed to touch or 'mess with' Chuck's pride and joy and he would lovingly polish it each evening before closing for the day.

On a shelf beside the jukebox was a large bowl containing ten dollars' worth of nickels for customers to use in the machine. In the thirty years that the bowl had sat there, Chuck had never had to replenish it, not once. Every nickel was still accounted for, either in the bowl or in the machine. "That's just how folks are in Greenhaven" Chuck liked to say. Nonetheless, he would still count all the nickels each evening after the staff left, just to be sure. "Can't be too careful" was another of Chuck's favorite expressions, as was "Can't trust nobody, these days."

Mike Smith ran the other half of the Tenth Hole – the Pro-Shop. The two halves of the building were separated by a glass wall with a connecting glass door. In reality, more than just the glass wall separated them, though that was an appropriate metaphor. The real separation was a frosty silence between the two managers. Chuck ran his half of the Tenth Hole as an efficient diner with the Best Chili in town; Irish Mike ran his half as an efficient golf pro-shop with the best prices south of the Mason-Dixie line. While Chuck was often described as 'a stick-insect in khaki shorts', Irish Mike was more like 'Santa Claus without the boots'. Mike's shorts were kept in place around his ample girth with a pair of bright green suspenders and his reading glasses hung slightly below his bushy white beard on a bright green cord which matched has favored footwear – emerald green Crocs.

But the two men, working in such close proximity had not spoken to each other for at least thirty years, certainly longer than anyone could remember. Some sort of woman trouble was what people said, though few could remember the details, or cared much.

ooOoo

Vera Lynn had just finished singing '*I'll be with you in Apple Blossom Time*' when Sgt. Anna Hartmann joined George Attwood and Raoul Gomez at their table in the Tenth Hole,

"Apple blossom time?" she said, pulling out a chair. "Have you any idea how hot it is out there? Apple blossoms would just shrivel-up and die in minutes. It's like an oven! So what's good for lunch, George?"

George pointed up at the 'Today's Special' list on the wall next to the kitchen. "Check it out" he said.

The exact same 'Today's Special' list had been fastened to the wall, with no changes, since George had first eaten there, almost thirty years previously. In fact nothing had changed since Charles Wilson had taken over the Diner from his father during the mid-fifties.

She laughed. "I guess a bowl of hot chili is just what I need when it's 90° in the shade. You know George, I've lived in South Florida almost ten years and I still can't believe how hot it gets in the summer."

"Most people can't believe how hot it gets in the winter" Raoul grinned as he rose to his feet.

9

"You're not staying for lunch Raoul?" Anna asked.

"Nope. I'm having a fence installed around my front yard" he said. "That new dog of mine, Jose Marti, keeps leaping over the hedge whenever he sees a lady dog in the street. He'll just get run over if I don't fence him in."

"I didn't know Raoul had a dog" Anna said, after Raoul had left the Diner.

"He found it two days ago. Tied up with an old rope outside the Pro-Shop when he came to work. Had a note on him which said 'My name is Jose-Marti. I need a kind home'. It was mutual love at first sight."

"Jose-Marti. What a funny name."

"Cuban National Hero" George explained. "Helped liberate Cuba from the Spanish."

"I thought that was Teddy Roosevelt and our City Founder, Ray Connolly."

"That was a couple of years later. The Spanish American War. But it was Jose-Marti who had started the rebellion but then he was killed, 1895 I think, just before the Americans joined in. So he's a big hero to the Cubans."

"I guess that's why Raoul couldn't resist keeping him."

After Darlene had taken their order for two bowls of chili and a shared basket of fries, George said. "Looks like we've got a big-time gangster, murder mystery to solve in little old Greenhaven. Here's your chance for promotion to detective Anna."

"Why do you say 'gangster' George?"

"Pin-stripe suit. Stands to reason. Must have been a gangster. Who else would wear a woolen three-piece suit in South Florida in August?"

During Chief Lacroix's television briefing on the mid-day news, he had described the deceased as best he could without showing a photograph. They had debated whether to show the man's face on T.V. but decided it was so brutally disfigured that not even his own brother would recognize him. As the weeks passed without any leads and the weeks became months, so the whole case became an unsolved mystery for the Greenhaven and Dade-County Law enforcement agencies who referred to it, if at all, as the 'Three Piece Suit Case'. DNA samples had been carefully taken from whatever evidence remained at the scene. There was a machete, presumably used to remove the hands; there were shards of broken glass which proved to be from an expensive Baccarat crystal Champagne glass. There were a few unmatched fingerprints lifted and several samples of blood. Everything was carefully bagged and labeled but with little further progress, the evidence eventually remained undisturbed in the evidence–locker.

"Well, I guess the Chief is keeping that case for himself. Meantime he's got me working on the butt-cases."

"Butt cases?"

"Yes. Come on George, you must have heard about all these illegal butt jobs. It's the latest fad to sweep South Florida. It's stories like this that help us maintain our reputation as the weirdest State in the Union."

"Butt jobs?"

"Yes. Ladies with big butts. They get them injected with industrial silicone and fix-a-flat and then they turn toxic and usually die – which is how I start getting involved when they're brought to me as possible homicide cases."

"You've got to be kidding me. Somebody is going around stabbing ladies in the butt with fix-a-flat! Like those KGB assassins with poisoned umbrellas?"

"No. These aren't assassins. These women actually pay to have this done. It's called Buttock Augmentation Surgery."

"Get away!"

"No seriously. It's a Cuban thing. What is it with you guys wanting everything bigger?"

"What do you mean? I'm not Cuban."

"No. But you're a guy. Guys want bigger and bigger breasts so, look around you – OK, not in Greenhaven maybe – but in South Florida, on the beach, in the clubs, all you see is big, plastic boob jobs. And now, apparently, guys are wanting bigger and bigger butts. So that's the new fad among the Cuban women and all these clinics are opening-up to offer butt jobs. There's even a popular song about them by one of our local singers."

"You've got to be kidding me."

"You must have heard it on the radio." Anna leaned close to George and quietly started to sing.

> *"Esa jevita esta enterita, y tiene tremeno culo*
>
> *Esta tan linda, esta tan rica y tiene tremendo culo"*

"What does that mean?"

> *"That girl is gone and she has such a huge ass.*
>
> *She's so cute, she's so rich and she has a huge ass."*

"You mean that's a real song? They actually play that on the radio?"

"All the time. It's by a guy called Pitbull. He's probably the most popular singer in Miami."

"Unbelievable! And these butt jobs, are they legal?"

"Sometimes, if they're licensed and run by certified plastic surgeons. But half of them are run by guys with a turkey-baster, a bicycle-pump and some fix-a-flat from the nearest Home Depot."

"How did you get involved in this Anna?" George said. "You certainly don't look like you need any augmentation."

"And what in Heck's name exactly do you mean by that remark Mr. Attwood?"

"Nothing my dear. I mean, you're already most perfectly proportioned, in all respects, and if only I were a younger man the only augmentation I might possibly propose would be a wedding ring."

Anna looked at him suspiciously. "They all said you're a slick talker Attwood but they never said how slippery you were." She relaxed and smiled.

"I've been working on Medicare fraud for over twelve months now. You know Miami is ground-zero for Medicare fraud in the nation. South Florida Medicare fraud is bigger than the rest of the whole US combined. Anyway, part of my research into these phony clinics along Eighth Street, billing the government for billions of dollars led me to this whole new sub-culture of butt-jobs. So, while you are so concerned with dead gangsters and innocent alligators – the real police are dealing with more serious problems – like Cuban butt-jobs."

"Tremendo culo" George smiled. "I must remember that."

Three: Havana, Cuba, August 1958

Oscar Enriquez was determined not to cry. He blinked his eyes fiercely and clenched his jaw as he climbed the stairs to his room in order to pack his suitcase. Stupid school; why couldn't term start a week later? Even a day later. If Groton started its new academic year, just one single day later, then Oscar would not have to return to the United States until tomorrow and so would be able to go to El Capitolio and listen to his brother's speech to the Senate.

Oscar worshiped his brother Carlos who was ten years his senior. Carlos had graduated early from Groton, the Massachusetts school that Oscar was now attending, and then gone straight to Harvard. Following a Harvard degree in International Relations, Carlos had then earned a law degree at the University of Havana. Just twenty four years old, he was one of the youngest Senators in Cuba's history and, as a member of the Partido Ortodoxo was becoming increasingly recognized for his opposition to Batista's corrupt and autocratic rule. Despite the fearsome power of the secret police, the Bureau for the Repression of Communist Activities or BRAC, Carlos was able to voice his opposition because of the Enriquez family's immense wealth. As owner of Cuba's largest sugar plantation, not to mention several prestigious cigar factories and an internationally acclaimed criollo stud farm, the family patriarch, Don Carlos Enriquez Sr., was one of the most powerful men on the island. His eldest son was untouchable.

Although eschewing violence and armed insurrection, Carlos planned to give a speech to the Senate, sympathizing, if not supporting the aims of the MR-26-7 party, (26th of July Movement). Don Carlos had warned his son that this was a risky move and that 'he would be crossing the Rubicon'. There could be no stepping back after such a speech.

Led by two upper-middle-class brothers and an Argentinian doctor, the MR-26-7 party was ensconced in the mountainous jungles of Oriente's Sierra Maestra and in the mountains of Escambray where it was organizing armed rebellion against Batista's government. For over two years they had been attacking military barracks, blowing-up bridges and ambushing government soldiers. Just the year before, they had even attacked the Presidential Palace. Under 'Operación Verano', Batista's forces were desperately trying to destroy the rebels, using the national air force to bomb villages and jungle camps while torturing and executing anyone suspected of aiding the guerrillas.

Although Carlos was not a member of the MR-26-7 party, he shared many of their views and certainly shared their hatred of the corrupt Batista regime. The previous year, in 1957, Raúl Chibás and Felipe Pazos, two of the leaders of the Partido Ortodoxo to which Carlos belonged, had met with the leaders of the MR-26-7 and between them had produced the *Sierra Maestra Manifesto*, in which they demanded that a provisional civilian government be set up to implement moderate agrarian reform, industrialization, and a literacy campaign before holding multiparty elections. Even though the manifesto was widely published internationally by the *New York Times*, CBS and Paris Match, because the Cuban press was so heavily censored, Batista was able ensure that the manifesto received no coverage in Cuba.

That was to be the subject of Carlos' speech. He planned to read the *Sierra Maestra Manifesto,* on the floor of the Senate and thus communicate its contents to the Cuban people. This was the speech that Oscar so wanted to witness. He had heard it already when Carlos was rehearsing it at their family mansion on the corner of Calle 69A and Avenida Quinta in Miramar. Though he was only fourteen, Oscar understood the significance of the speech and knew that his brother was about to make history. But he would not be allowed to witness it – because his father insisted that he return to school.

It was so unfair!

The two Castro brothers, Fidel and Raul, like the two Enriquez brothers came from wealthy landowning backgrounds, unlike President Fulgencio Batista who came from humble and impoverished stock. With little formal education, Batista had left home at the age of fourteen to work as a day laborer in the sugarcane fields; the Castro brothers on the other hand had attended the elite Jesuit college of Belén before going to the University of Havana. Carlos of course had both Harvard and the University of Havana in his resume. Although settled in Cuba for several generations, the Enriquez bloodlines were pure Castilian, and the Castro brothers too had pure Spanish blood, from Galicia. Batista however was of mixed race and included African and even Chinese blood in his parentage. He was a mongrel – a mutt.

But it was the low-born, uneducated, half-breed who had all the power. It was the despised Batista who sat in the presidential palace, and the well born and well educated Castro brothers who crouched like beasts in their jungle lair. Batista had ruled Cuba for almost thirty years, first as chief of the Armed Forces, twice as democratically elected President and finally as a U.S. backed dictator. But he was no tin-pot tyrant: Cuba was the second wealthiest country in Latin America with a gross domestic product equal to that of Italy. Not only were wages higher in Cuba than elsewhere in the Caribbean but there was also a thriving middle class that filled the schools and universities with writers, painters, lawyers and intellectuals, all of whom shared a contempt for their vulgar and uneducated leader. The reality was that, although low-born and with little formal schooling, Batista was a voracious reader, self-educated and with a sophisticated intellect. Indeed, later in life, Batista became known for his extensive library and his valuable art collection. But because of his mixed blood and humble beginnings, the land-owning 'Castilian' elite always despised him and treated him as a vulgar upstart.

Although he may have harbored a certain aristocratic disdain for the low born and supposedly ignorant Batista, Senator Carlos Enriquez opposed him for reasons other than pure snobbery. Batista was a cruel and corrupt despot who was destroying his country and selling it to the Americans. Although the Enriquez family were sufficiently well established and wealthy enough to retain control of their family plantations, Batista was handing over control and ownership of most of the island's sugar industry to 'Yanqui' corporations. Even President John F. Kennedy admitted "At the beginning of 1959 United States companies owned about 40 percent of the Cuban sugar lands—almost all the cattle ranches—90 percent of the mines and mineral concessions—80 percent of the utilities— practically all the oil industry—and supplied two-thirds of Cuba's imports."

Even more humiliating, Batista effectively handed over control of the tourist industry to the American Mafia. From just across the Florida Straits, Meyer Lansky and Jimmy 'Blue Eyes' Alo in Miami, and Santo Trafficante in Tampa, owned and operated all the hotels and casinos in Havana. They also controlled all the prostitution and sales of drugs and liquor on the island. Some twelve-thousand Cuban women worked as prostitutes for the Yanqui tourists. The noble and historic island nation of Cuba, once the crown jewel of the Spanish Empire, had become a cheap and sleazy playground where the ugly American came to get drunk, get laid and throw up over its once proud people.

Oscar Enriquez's big brother wanted to regain his nation's dignity; he wanted to cleanse the island of all the foreign mobsters and halt the endemic corruption that, he believed, pervaded every level of Cuban society and was destroying the national soul. By reading the *Sierra Maestra Manifesto* during his speech to the Senate, Carlos would be striking a democratic blow in favor of regime change, while offering an alternative to the violent and destructive acts of the MR-26-7 movement. Carlos had wanted his kid brother to be present when he made his speech but he agreed with his father that it might be too dangerous. He might be provoking Batista too far, and his henchmen might want to take revenge on the family. Oscar would be better off back at school, safely away in America. Even Don Carlos Sr., the father, planned to take his wife and most of the servants out of Havana to the Enriquez finca, the family's primary estate, in the northern foothills of the Sierra del Escambray near Santa Clara in Las Villas province.

At the airport the two brothers hugged each other. "Good luck tomorrow bro" Oscar said. "I want to read about it in the *New York Times* – 'Young Senator gives them hell!'"

"If anyone asks what motivates me, I'll say it's my kid brother." Carlos grinned. "I'll see you at Christmas bro. Who knows, we might even have a new government by then."

In the event, none of those things occurred. Carlos' speech was not reported in the *New York Times*, nor in any other newspaper. In the Senate chamber of El Capitolio, the next day, Carlos' voice could scarcely be heard as PAU members and government supporters yelled insults and banged on their desks throughout the speech. Not only was it not reported, it was not even heard.

Nor did Carlos and Oscar reunite at Christmas – in fact, they were not to see each other again for twenty-two years. Instead of returning to Cuba for the Christmas break, Oscar flew down to Miami to stay with a classmate's family. Events in Cuba were unravelling fast and Don Carlos thought it too unsafe to bring Oscar home. Castro's rebel armies had left their stronghold in the Sierra Maestra and were now moving west, towards Havana. One by one, the cities of Las Villas province, the ancestral home of the Enriquez family, were being over-run by the forces of MR-26-7.

Don Carlos Enriquez had never been a supporter of Batista or his PAU supporters, but, as a close friend of Ramón Grau, he had always been a supporter of the nationalist Partido Auténtico. But, despite his loyalty to the Auténticos he was also tolerant of his son's membership in the more radical Partido Ortodoxo despite its more left-wing sympathies. But never would he approve of the unruly, bearded rebels or their anarchist, irreligious and sexually promiscuous lifestyle. He was all in favor of democratic elections but he was very suspicious of the communist sounding goals of the MR-26-7 guerillas. The final straw came on December 30 when, fresh from their victory at the nearby city of Santa Clara, the rebels came storming into the Enriquez finca demanding horses for their soldiers.

Don Carlos was proud of his stud farm and he raised horses that were sold to U.S. breeders as well as to Europeans and South Americans. The leader of the rebel forces who had just won the battle of Santa Clara was an Argentinian, and so should have been well aware of the superior quality of the horses that he was demanding.

"When will I be paid for the horses?" Don Carlos asked.

From his position in the back of the dusty jeep, the young Comandante looked surprised by the question. Languidly he removed the large cigar from his mouth. "Your payment will be the honor of serving the People. This is your contribution to our glorious revolution." The man's arrogant, Argentinian accent was infuriating. "You should be proud to be playing such a momentous role," he added with a sneer.

Don Carlos pointed to one of his grooms who was standing close by. "This man is one of 'the people'. How will he benefit? If you take away all the horses, he will be without a job. How will you justify that senor, whatever your name is?"

Sitting in the backseat of a jeep, unshaven and wearing a beret on his head, the young man slowly rose to his feet and unholstered his sidearm. "My name is Doctor Ernesto Guevara" he said. "But most people call me Che." Pointing his pistol at the groom, he said. "If this man has no job and does not work, then he is a parasite."

The blast of the gun was so unexpected that even Don Carlos flinched, but Guevara's face was expressionless. The groom sprawled, motionless in the dust, blood gushing from the eye-socket where the bullet had entered while Guevara calmly re-holstered his weapon. "There is no place for parasites in our revolution' he said.

While his men rounded-up the horses, Guevara leaned back in his seat. He waved his cigar in farewell to Don Carlos. "On behalf of the People," he said. "On behalf of the Workers, I thank you for your contribution." The spinning wheels of the jeep kicked up dust and made Don Carlos cough.

Four: Greenhaven 2013

"Do you think George and Lady Sanders are having an affair?" Margaret Doyle suddenly asked, as she watched the two of them going out through the door of the Greenhaven Country Club. It was the winding down of the City's 'Meet & Greet' where the citizens of Greenhaven had an opportunity to meet and mingle with their elected representatives and to hear what an honor and humbling experience it was for their public servants to represent them.

Mayor Thomas Biddle Adams was there along with most of the city commissioners and State Representatives. The citizens were represented by most of the leading local retailers, realtors and, as the City Manager, Ken Kerman phrased it, 'leading citizens of class'. Or, as George less decorously described it, 'the usual collection of wife beaters and bed wetters'.

"What on earth made you ask that" said Maurice Mayhew. "I don't think Catherine would be attracted to a fellow like George. Not that there's anything wrong with George, of course. I don't mean that at all. I just don't think he's her type."

"Anyway he's gay," said Harriet Brownmiller. "So she's not his type either."

"Really?" said Margaret. "I had no idea."

"Now, now Harriet." Don Westlake interrupted. "You know that's not true. George was once well known as a ladies man."

"Must have been before my time." Harriet sniffed.

"It was the big U.M. romance back in the day" he continued. "I remember it well. I'd just joined the faculty myself when George came back after spending a year lecturing at the Sorbonne. Brought back a beautiful young bride from Paris. Eloped apparently. Word was her aristocratic family were furious. She was supposed to marry some French Marquis not run-off with some penniless American professor."

"When was that then?"

"Oh. I don't know. Must have been early '70s. Yes. I joined the faculty in '73 so it must have been '73 or '74, still a few years before the Mariel boatlift from Cuba.. Forty years ago now. Can't believe it's been so long. They were definitely the 'It' couple on campus. The beautiful people. She was absolutely gorgeous, with a

French accent to die for. They had a daughter too. Beautiful little girl. Mathilde. She was almost like the university mascot. Everybody loved her."

"I had no idea George had a daughter. How come we never see her?"

"Chloe took her back to Paris with her. They got divorced when the daughter was about ten years old. Chloe got custody and took her back to France. Poor George never really recovered."

"How sad" Margaret said. "I had no idea. After such a romantic marriage, why on earth would they get divorced?"

Don Westlake shrugged. "These things happen. The surprise is that so many marriages actually survive and don't end in divorce."

"Well there wasn't much of a surprise about George's divorce," Maurice said with a chuckle, winking at Don. "Old Don here is being discrete. Fact is, George got caught bonking one of his students. Big, big scandal that was. George was lucky to keep his job. Good thing that he was tenured."

"My goodness," Harriet said. "Who would have guessed! So how did he get caught? Come on Maurice, give us the scoop. We don't often get juicy gossip in Greenhaven."

"He took her to Miami Beach" Maurice explained. "Back then, in the early '80s South Beach hadn't been properly discovered. It was mainly old Jewish retirees, crack addicts and hookers. The buildings were all dilapidated and definitely not hip or trendy. But a lot of young Europeans had discovered the beach itself and the really cheap hotel rooms. So you'd get all these gorgeous young French and Italian girls lying topless on the beach, almost naked and soaking-up the Florida sun. And that's where randy George used to take certain young students for an afternoon frolic in the sand. He knew that nobody from Greenhaven would dream of going to such a run-down place, so he felt safe."

"So what happened? How did he get caught?"

21

"I'm coming to that" Maurice said, obviously enjoying his story. "Although South Beach hadn't yet been discovered by the developers and the public in general. It had been discovered by some of the more edgy advertising people. Beautiful naked girls on the beach, crumbling but sun-kissed buildings. Lots of the New York agencies were sending camera teams and models down to South Beach for glamor shoots with urban decay and grunge in the sun. Word was slowly getting-out."

"And...?" Harriet was getting impatient.

"And," Maurice continued, grinning mischievously. "The *New York Times* decided to run a story about fun in the sun. It was a black and white photo essay in a Sunday supplement. You know, shots of little old Jewish ladies on Medicaid with their walkers, shuffling past hookers and crack dealers lounging in the dark doorways of decrepit and crumbling art-deco buildings. And of course, lots of shots of beautiful, topless Europeans on the beach."

Maurice paused, looking around with a smile and then lowering his voice. "And there of course was George; caught in flagrante delicto. Nibbling on a nipple so to speak. Not only was she one of his students, she had even baby-sat for them. And now Chloe had to see her in the *New York Times*, wearing nothing but the skimpiest bikini bottom, on the beach with her husband."

"What happened?"

"Oh. She was out of there immediately. Packed her bags and by Monday evening, she and her daughter were back in Paris; never to return."

"George never got over it," Don Westlake said. "Never forgave himself. His philandering days were over. I don't know that he's ever been in any relationship since then. All he wants is to try and reestablish a relationship with Mathilde, his daughter."

"And Chloe?"

"No hope there. She remarried long ago. Got a couple more kids from what I hear. She's never forgiven George for that terrible and public humiliation. But no. George is not gay Harriet. And he's not having an affair with Lady Sanders. He just works for her at the museum."

"That's another thing that's always made me curious." Margaret said. "After such a distinguished academic career and all those books he's written – what's he doing as a Museum janitor?"

"I'm afraid it's one of those sad but all too common South Florida stories," Don explained. He invested all his life savings, his pension, everything with Bernie Madoff - you remember, the Ponzi swindler. Took him for every penny he'd got."

"But I thought Madoff's victims were all Jewish."

"Oh no. Nothing prejudiced about Madoff. Bernie doesn't have a bigoted bone in his body. He would swindle anybody, whatever their religion: Jewish, Catholic, Seventh Day Adventist, Sunni, Shia – they are all equally precious in Bernie's eyes. George had been mentoring a Jewish book-reading group on Miami Beach. They met for a couple of hours every week for a year in one of the Synagogues and worked through all seven volumes of Marcel Proust's novel in twelve months. I guess while he was there, somebody introduced him to Madoff. George invested some of his savings and was really impressed with the results. His account kept growing. So he invested more and more and finally withdrew everything from his 401K and gave it to Madoff."

"But why? He's never struck me as a greedy man."

"His daughter. He was always wanting to make up to her. When he turned sixty, he retired from the university and reckoned that thanks to Madoff, he had accumulated enough money to move to Paris, establish a relationship with his daughter and give her and her family a decent inheritance. It was his way of making up for the pain he had caused."

"So what happened?"

"George left the university at the end of the academic year in May, I guess it was 2008 and spent a few months in Paris, planning his new life. Then Madoff was arrested in December and George discovered he was totally ruined."

"How awful! The poor man. I had no idea."

"Lady Sanders was an old friend, she needed help with the museum and so it was the perfect match. It gave him some income and a sense of structure, and the museum got an educated janitor. He'd had to sell his house to pay off his debts of course. So now he rents the cottage behind my house. Dorothy and I live on the golf course and George likes to play a round every morning before he goes to work. We travel a lot and George watches over the house. So it all worked out perfectly in the end."

"Except for the daughter," said Margaret.

"That's improving," Don said. "They're in closer contact finally. She actually came over for a visit with her two children last July. George spent the whole time riding them around the golf course in a golf cart and letting them drive. They loved it. Can't wait to come back."

"Who can't wait to come back?" Ken Kerman asked, joining the group. "I hope you're talking about tourists and city visitors. I've just been looking at the numbers and our hotel occupancy is down again. Second year in a row."

Ken Kerman, the city manager, took his position and his responsibilities seriously, and he liked people to know that he did so. A short man with rather wide, almost feminine hips, he moved with a ponderous waddle while appearing preoccupied with weighty civic matters. And he was right to be concerned; city revenues had been declining, hotel occupancy was down for the second year in a row and yet another restaurant had closed just last week. Tourists were all flocking to sexy South Beach and the new, hip galleries of Wynwood.

Greenhaven was regarded as old fashioned and stuffy. Much of the problem, the City manager believed, was that the mayor and the commissioners were also old fashioned and stuffy and the city would never modernize as long as they remained in power.

Mayor Thomas Adams, scion of an old and illustrious family, had been born in Greenhaven and lived there all his life. He was serving his third term as mayor and was considering the possibility of running again in the next election. Nothing would ever change with Adams as mayor; he hated change and wanted Greenhaven to remain the way it had always been. As for that fossilized old crustacean, Commissioner Alfred Connolly II, he fought every modern improvement that Ken Kerman tried to introduce. Connolly had fought Kerman bitterly, and successfully against permitting outdoor seating for downtown restaurants and cafes. As the grandson of the City's founder, Ray Connolly, he vociferously attributed the decline in public morality to the introduction of the 'right-turn on red' law. He also blamed the increase in sexual promiscuity on the new European style traffic roundabouts at some of the major intersections.

With Connolly and Adams in charge, Greenhaven was doomed to remain stuck in the past, becoming increasingly irrelevant. Ken Kerman was determined to bring some new blood into the city. Ideally, he would like some energetic candidate with vision, like Dr. Orestes Martinez, to run for mayor against Tom Adams, but in the meantime, he was hoping to attract some wealthy developers to invest in the city. Kerman knew that Maurice Mayhew's law firm had done some work for the big Korean developer, William J. Park, whose glittering condominiums, hotels and golf courses littered the local landscape from Palm Beach to Key West. He needed Maurice to introduce him to Mr. Park so that he could propose the hotel development project.

"I'm afraid we weren't doing anything as weighty as discussing declining city revenues Ken" Maurice said. "We were just exchanging some juicy gossip about George."

"George?"

"Attwood. George Attwood, you know. The museum janitor."

"Ah yes. Lady Sanders' friend. Indeed." Placing his hand on Maurice's arm, Kerman gently lead him aside. "When you have a moment Maurice," he said. "I'd like to discuss a hotel project that I think might be of interest to your client William Park. Why don't you come to my office later?"

Moving back into the group, ignoring the women with his usual lack of social grace, Kerman addressed Don Westlake. "Are you up for reelection next year Don?" he asked.

"Afraid so Ken," Don replied. "It's that time again. If I'm to stay on the Commission, I'll need to do my dog-and-pony show again. Hope I can count on your vote Ken," he added with a smile. "Oh. And by the way Ken. What do you hear about this fellow Orestes Martinez, maybe running for mayor against Tom?"

"I've heard the rumors Don, but I've not heard anything official. Mind you, he could prove to be a big asset; he's got billions behind him. He owns one of the biggest health-care organizations in the nation. If he decides to run, he could bring a lot of energy into the city, not to mention money and investments."

"But he's a Cuban" Harriet Brownmiller said. "He's not from Greenhaven. He should be running in Hialeah or Miami, not here in Greenhaven.

"I agree," Margaret Doyle joined in. "The Cubans are taking-over everywhere. It's hard enough trying to get a maid or a gardener who speaks English these days. The last thing we want is a Cuban mayor."

"Even in Publix you can't find anyone who speaks English," Harriet said. "Just this morning I was trying to find some English marmalade for Herbert's breakfast muffin and nobody had a clue what I was talking about." She rolled her eyes and gave an exaggerated shrug. "Que?" she said. "'Que Senora? No comprende!' I mean it's like we're not even living in America anymore. No. The last thing we need is a Cuban mayor. I'm sure I'll get into trouble with all the politically-correct people, but Greenhaven is one of the last Anglo cities we have left. We should fight to keep it that way."

Five: Las Villas, Cuba, January 2, 1959

The day following the 'liberation' of the horses, Guevara returned in his jeep to Don Carlos' finca accompanied by two other jeeps, filled with armed guerillas. Don Carlos was out in the paddock at the side of the main house, helping his men dig a grave for the dead groom whose body lay in a simple wooden coffin inside the house. Despite his age and his poor back, Don Carlos felt it incumbent on him to physically participate in the digging, as a sign of respect for his murdered employee.

Climbing out of the grave and leaning on his shovel, he glared at the insolent young man reclining in the back seat, smoking a cigar.

"I have no more horses, Senor Doctor," he said. "You took my whole team with you yesterday."

"I am aware of that comrade Enriquez. But it is not horses that I have come for today." Guevara took a long pull on his cigar and then slowly exhaled a long plume of smoke. "Today we are here for horse power."

Rising to his feet, Guevara sprang over the side of the jeep and pointed to the gleaming, polished motor car standing on the driveway facing the main entrance. "I noticed it yesterday while I was here. If I'm not mistaken" he said. "That's a Hispano-Suiza, J12 – about 250 horse-power I believe. We take control of Havana tomorrow. I think we should arrive in style."

Although he was incredibly wealthy, Don Carlos was not materialistic; he was not terribly attached to possessions. Ideas and values were of more importance than mere things. But his Hispano-Suiza was the exception. It was a 1938 model and he'd owned it for 20 years. He loved the car with a passion. It was the biggest, fastest and most luxurious car that Hispano-Suiza had ever made and it was his pride and joy. His chauffeur, Miguel, had been in charge of the car for the past ten years. He made sure that the bodywork was polished daily and that the engine was always in perfect working condition. Thanks to his care, the car was still like new; still as immaculate as it was when it arrived in a wooden crate at the Havana docks in 1939, twenty years previously. And now it was to be taken away by a group of ignorant, bearded bandits who knew nothing about cars. They would destroy it.

"You should take my chauffeur, Miguel." Don Carlos finally said. "He has the keys. He knows this car and will look after it for you." Turning to Miguel, he nodded. "Go with them Miguel. Drive them to Havana or wherever they want to go. Just look after the car."

As Miguel walked towards the car, Guevara called out to him. "Stop. Give me the keys."

Silently Miguel gave him the keys.

Turning towards Don Carlos, Guevara grinned. "I don't need a chauffeur. I like driving myself. I like to drive very fast. We have no room for chauffeurs in the revolution. They are parasites."

Turning to address the chauffeur he said. "You're out of a job, Miguel. No job. No work. You're a parasite." There wasn't even a pause while he simultaneously spoke and pulled the gun from his holster. Miguel fell to the ground without even knowing he was the victim. ".32 bullet to the right side of the brain" Guevara said as he re-holstered his pistol. "Exit through the left temporal lobe if I'm not very much mistaken." Turning to Don Carlos he grinned apologetically. "Medical training I'm afraid. Once a doctor, always a doctor."

Stepping over Miguel's dead body he strode towards the gleaming motorcar and climbed behind the wheel. With his cigar clamped firmly between his teeth, he grinned at Don Carlos and waved a farewell gesture. "Hasta luego!" he shouted. The wheels of the large car suddenly spun, kicking up gravel as it lurched abruptly forward and then roared off, followed by the three jeeps.

Impotently, unmoving, Don Carlos stood rooted beside the grave, watching the trails of dust kicked up by the vanishing vehicles. As the women appeared from the house, Don Carlos pointed at Miguel. "Take him inside and prepare him for burial," he said.

Climbing back into the grave he resumed digging.

ooOoo

Carlos Jr. was out in the streets of Havana on New Year's Day, January 1, 1959. It was crazy. Total chaos. People firing guns in the air but very little violence. There was the occasional spilling of blood when the crowd recognized a Batista policeman but on the whole the atmosphere was joyous. Gradually the news spread, mainly originating from Venezuela's Radio Caracas, that Batista and his cronies had fled during the night. Many had flown to the Dominican Republic, others to Texas, Tampa and New Jersey - but most had gone to Miami, including Meyer Lansky and the rest of the *Norteamericanos* gangsters. When word got out that the Cuban army had already surrendered to Che Guevara after his victory at Santa Clara, the remnants of Batista's police and military forces, discreetly slipped out of their uniforms and joined the revelers in the streets.

Despite the apparent chaos and the breakdown of all formal authority, order was somehow maintained by bands of bearded young men, some sporting insignia of the MR-26-7 and others claiming allegiance to the DRE, *Directorio Revolucionario Estudiantil*. There was lots of drinking, singing and dancing throughout the heart of the old city, but very little looting. Carlos felt the thrill and excitement of the moment and reminded himself of Wordsworth's lines at the time of the French Revolution.

Bliss was it in that dawn to be alive, But, to be young was very heaven!

29

He was worried however, about his parents, especially since the Enriquez finca was so close to Santa Clara, the site of the final and decisive battle. He had been unable to get through on the phone and assumed that, in all the upheavals, the lines must have been cut. There was nothing he could do but listen to the radio and wait for news.

Late in the afternoon of New Year's Day, Radio Caracas announced that Fidel Castro now controlled Santiago de Cuba at the Eastern end of the island, and that his brother Raul controlled the North Coast. Word quickly spread that the rebels, now referred to as the Army of Liberation, were in control of the whole island.

Later that night, Major Che Guevara arrived in Havana and, very quickly, he and his men took control of all the key locations in the city. Guevara immediately installed himself in Fortaleza de San Carlos de la Cabaña, the giant 18th century prison-fortress which dominates the whole city from across the harbor mouth. This became his headquarters for the next six months and it was in 'La Cabaña' that Guevara supervised his secret tribunals and it was here that any surviving Batistianos or enemies of the revolution would spend their final unhappy days.

While student leaders of the *Directorio Revolucionario Estudiantil* took control of the Presidential Palace. Comandante, Major Camilo Cienfuegos, took control of Batista's military headquarters in Campamento Columbia, less than a mile south of the Enriquez mansion in Miramar, By January 2, the streets of the capital were firmly under the control of uniformed and bearded but remarkably disciplined members of the MR-24-7. The citizens of Havana were amazed. Fearing scenes of raping, looting and indiscriminate killings, they had been dreading the arrival of the guerilla army. In the long, tumultuous history of their nation, they had never known an occupying force to be so civilized and respectful. The Castro brothers were expected to arrive within the week after making their slow victory tour across the island from Oriente Province.

Already the Batista dictatorship had been replaced by an experienced, provisional government under the leadership of President Manuel Urrutia who immediately returned from exile in Venezuela, and José Miró Cardona who was appointed Prime Minister on January 5, 1959. They quickly assembled a government from members of the Partido Auténtico and the Partido Ortodoxo of which Carlos Jr. was a member. The American ambassador, Earl Edward Taylor Smith from Newport, felt comfortable with the new government and reassured President Eisenhower back in Washington that these were experienced politicians who would be able to keep the young hot-heads under control. The important thing was that there was not a single communist among them.

As an indication of the responsible stability of the new regime, Comandante Cienfuegos ordered the boisterous, student leaders of the DRE to be expelled from the Presidential Palace so that President Urrutia could be installed.

Despite becoming an international icon of the Revolution in later years, Che Guevara initially kept a low profile, preferring to work behind the scenes and allowing his fellow Comandante, Camilo Cienfuegos, to garner the public acclaim. From his office in Batista's old seat of military power, Campamento Columbia, Cienfuegos was appointed Chief of Staff of the Cuban Army. For a while, his was the friendly, public face of the Revolution.

Already, on January 2, the previously banned rebel newspaper *Revolución* appeared on the streets, sporting a photo of 'the glorious Major Cienfuegos' and 'the incomparable Che'. Soon the smiling, bearded portrait of the handsome, valiant guerilla leader was on posters and newspaper front pages everywhere and many young women in Havana - and elsewhere murmured Camilo's name as they fell asleep. He was seen on Havana Television, releasing caged birds at his military headquarters and telling the viewers: "these too have a right to liberty!" Even after the arrival of Fidel Castro in Havana, he still remained the romantic hero of the new era of Freedom. At a rally soon after his arrival , Castro interrupted his speech to ask Cienfuegos "¿Voy bien, Camilo?" (Am I doing all right, Camilo?). When Cienfuegos roared back "Vas bien, Fidel" (You're doing fine, Fidel) the crowd went crazy and "vas bien" quickly became a slogan of the revolution.

As a Senator, Carlos Enriquez was unsure of his position within the new regime. The government was only provisional and the Senate was not in session. Would the provisional government continue to hold power or would the MR-26-7 leaders take power for themselves? What about the Communists, would they demand a role? Although he was a member of the Partido Ortodoxo in opposition to Batista, as a Senator he worried that he might still be perceived to be a member of the *ancien regime*. Even more worrisome, Carlos still had no news of his family; he considered driving to the Santa Clara finca but was unwilling to leave Havana in such a state of turmoil. He had tried contacting Camilo Cienfuegos directly by phone but emphasizing his Senatorial title had no effect on the new military bureaucracy and he was unable to get through.

The Enriquez family finally arrived back in Havana on Wednesday, January 7th, the same day that the US government recognized the new Cuban government of President Urrutia. It was also the day before Fidel Castro's own triumphant arrival. Don Carlos arrived at the family mansion on Avenida Quinta, in a dusty old bus that was used for moving farm-workers around the estate. He could have used one of his other cars but decided that keeping a low profile was more important than comfort.

"We must leave at once" Don Carlos said to his son when they had finally reunited. "We must get out now, while we still have time." Don Carlos had been visibly shaken by his encounters with Guevara and the casual murder of his two servants. "These people are animals," he said. "Worse than animals. Animals do not kill for sport." Carlos saw that his father had physically aged during the week since he had last seen him and agreed that the sooner his parents were safely in Miami with Oscar, the better."

Through the rest of the Wednesday and throughout Thursday, the mother and father packed all their most precious possessions into suitcases. While the mother packed her best clothes and jewelry, the father visited his bank and withdrew as much cash as was available. He also packed a briefcase with certificates of stocks and bonds as well as certificates of deposit. Who knew how long they would have to support themselves in Florida before all this madness ended. It could be weeks. Months even.

Carlos meantime visited various airline offices in downtown Havana to buy plane tickets to Miami. At each airline, the story was the same. Flights out of the country had been terminated. When Castro had heard about Batista and his cronies looting the treasury and flying out of the country, he was furious. Understandably, for two days and nights following Batista's departure, American gangsters and Batista's henchmen had all been fleeing Cuba by air. Castro immediately ordered the airports closed. Now, it was impossible to leave the country without an exit visa. But of course, nobody knew how to get one or even where to apply. In fact, Carlos suspected that simply applying for an exit visa was enough to get you arrested.

When Carlos returned home with the news, his parents were devastated. Don Carlos, once such a proud and imposing paterfamilias had become, overnight, a frail, little old man. "What will become of us?" he sighed, putting his arm around his wife's shoulders. "Those brutes will murder us all."

Six: Miami, Park Tower, 2013

"Maurice Mayhew and Kenneth Kerman" Mayhew said to the young oriental woman behind the reception desk. "We have a two o clock meeting with Mr. Park." After confirming their appointment in her computer, the receptionist handed them two printed name tags which already included their photographs along with their names.

"That's very impressive" Kerman said. "How on earth did she do that?"

Smiling at the woman, Mayhew said "that's why they use such beautiful girls. They know that you can't resist looking at them, so they position the hidden camera just behind her." He winked at her as he said, "That's why so many of the faces on the photographs seem to be drooling." The woman returned his smile with a blank expressionless stare. "Mr. Qiu will be here shortly to take you to Mr. Park's office," she said.

The two men were standing in the vast atrium of Park Tower on Brickell Avenue in downtown Miami. In Brickell's Shanghai-like canyon of twenty-first century, steel and glass sky-scrapers, Park Tower stood head and shoulder above the rest. Not only was it taller than all the others, it was also much flashier. The plate glass cladding that soared sixty-five stories up into the blue, south Florida sky, was tinted green. "The color of money" as Park never tired of telling the visiting journalists.

The atrium lobby was six stories high and the walls were hung with outsize Velazquez-style portraits of seventeenth century Spanish grandees and conquistadores, in heavily gilded rococo frames. The shining floors were a pale blue marble and the towering lobby roof was supported by dark basalt pillars carved to resemble the mysterious stone heads on Easter Island.

"This is most impressive" Kerman said, looking around wonderingly, like a mediaeval peasant on first entering Chartres cathedral.

"Wait till you see his office" Mayhew said.

Mayhew's law firm did consulting-work for the William J. Park corporation and Ken Kerman had asked Maurice for an introduction to Mr. Park on behalf of the City of Greenhaven.

"What's in it for me?" Mayhew had immediately asked.

Maurice Mayhew's avaricious reputation preceded him and so Kerman had already prepared his response. "If we can persuade Mr. Park to take on the restoration of the Palace Hotel for the City, you will have an exclusive on all the legal work - at standard rates of course."

"Of course, of course" Mayhew said. "I would always be generous to the city."

Despite coming from a wealthy background, Mayhew was well known locally for his embarrassing financial greed and his even more embarrassing meanness. His Greenhaven Country Club dues were two years in arrears and in restaurants or in a bar, Mayhew was always in the men's room when the bill was being settled or else, after ostentatiously slapping his pockets, he'd say "Good Lord. I must have left my wallet in the office." This was especially embarrassing for his wife, Jane, a highly respected history professor at the University of Miami. Kerman assumed this is why she seldom accompanied him to social events; the two of them were seldom seen out together. Kerman had no idea what Mayhew did with his money. Some people had suggested a drug habit, but he displayed none of the usual signs of a junkie. Others suggested fast women, which was certainly possible. He and Jane showed none of the mannerisms of a close couple; he also had wandering eyes and, some said, wandering hands. A more likely explanation in Kerman's mind was slow horses. Kerman's father had been a hopeless gambler and Kerman recognized all the signs - for example, Mayhew lighting his cigarettes with match-books from the local Seminole Indian Casino.

In any event, the possibility of earning a commission from the city had proved effective and within just a couple of days, Kerman was on his way to meet the famous William J. Park. They were escorted in a private, glass elevator to Park's penthouse by a taciturn Korean body builder in a tight, dark suit. The name badge showed 'Mr. Qiu' and his profession was 'Security'. They rode to the 65th floor in silence.

35

They found themselves standing inside a clear glass tube in the center of a vast, oval office which covered the entire top floor of Park Tower. Except for the north facing wall which was paneled in oak with a display of Spanish Colonial maps, the rest of the room was made entirely of glass, with views to almost every point of the compass. To the east they could see across the colorful display of sailing boats on Biscayne Bay, to the Atlantic Ocean beyond. To the west they could see well beyond the church spires of Greenhaven, towards the Everglades, and to the south, the view reached almost as far as Key Largo.

With a slight hiss, a glass door slid open and Mr. Qiu ushered them into the center of the room, where they were greeted by their host.

"What a view huh? What an incredible view. Have you ever seen a greater view than this? Never. Of course not. There is no view as incredible as this. It's the best. It's my view. I created it. I look at it every day. It's so incredible, I share it with my friends. I have lots of friends. Good friends. Wonderful people, the best. They all love me. And they love this view. I show them it and they all say "Billy"' that's what my friends call me. They say "Billy, this is such an incredible view, it's huge. How do you get such a view?" And it's not just friends, business people too, CEOs, celebrities, they see the view and they're like "Mr. Park sir, how do you get such an incredible view? And I tell them "I built it", that's what I say. I say "I built it" because I did. That's why it's such a great view, such an incredible view. Because I built it. That's why it's so great. Everything I build is great. It's the best. Lots of people don't get it. They don't understand. Haven't got the vision. Maybe they're just dishonest. Whatever. No view. So sad."

Rising from his chair behind a large, ornately carved, mahogany desk, William J. Park advanced towards them, his arms gesturing at the various impressive vistas through the glass walls while his hands, small for so large a man, emphasized each point that he was making. Head of a sprawling Korean, multinational conglomerate engaged in development projects on four continents, for the past few years Park had focused his attentions on South Florida. His hotels, condominium towers and golf courses stretched all the way from Key West to Palm Beach. All his developments were easily recognizable, not just because they were larger and flashier than the competition but also because his name, PARK, was always prominently displayed atop the buildings in large gold letters.

Although he maintained a three-story, penthouse apartment in Tallahassee, Florida's State capital, in which he liked to lavishly entertain State Senators and Representatives, most of his time was spent in a sprawling, luxury mansion on Miami Beach. Having been banned from so many South Beach nightclubs for grabbing women in an inappropriate manner, Park had finally built his own night club on his own property. His parties were the stuff of legend, Roman legends. There was never too much alcohol, never too much flesh and no behavior was considered inappropriate.

Solidly built, Park stood at six foot three - or at six foot two without in-soles. Always conservatively dressed in a dark navy blue suit with red silk tie and starched white shirt, his face had a permanent tan and alternated rapidly between the two extremes of warm bonhomie or barely repressed fury. His eyes however, never changed expression; they remained forever small, cold and calculating.

"Mr. Kerman, I assume. Mind if I call you Ken. Maurice here has told me so much about you and your wonderful city. Beautiful city. Doesn't have one of my buildings in it yet, but it's still a beautiful city. Greenhaven. Great name Greenhaven. Very classy name. Well of course it is. Classy city. I like classy cities. You know I've got a Park Tower on Park Avenue in Manhattan and I've another Park Tower in London, on Park Lane and I'm in the process of building another next to Parc Monceau in Paris. See, that's what the Park brand is all about. It's about class. That's why I've got to be really selective about the projects I agree to put my name on. Very selective. Got to represent class. I get people all the time you know, wanting to work with me. Wanting my name. Big people. Big names. Huge celebrities. CEOs. You can't imagine. All the time. You wouldn't believe. But I got to be tough. Got to make a deal that works for me, not something stupid and lame. That's for losers. 'Mr. Park, sir' they say. 'This is such a great deal, you'll love it' but you know, I look at it like a deal maker. I mean that's what I do. I make deals and if it doesn't have class, then it's no deal. I have to be tough, I'm sorry."

"I'm very relieved to hear that Mr. Park. At Greenhaven, we take our reputation for good taste and integrity very seriously."

"Call me 'Billy', Ken. Please, no formalities here. Everyone who knows me, and you'd be amazed at how many people know me, and respect me too I might add, will all agree that I tell it like it is. You'll get no B/S from me, they'll tell you. No phony formalities. It's all straight down the line. I say what I mean, I'm a straight shooter. Always have been. Ask anyone. So call me 'Billy' and come and sit down and enjoy the view. Incredible isn't it. Never get tired of it. So tell me what you're prepared to give me if I agree to restore this old hotel of yours? What's the deal? What are you offering? I checked it out you know, the moment our boy Maurice mentioned it to me, I was onto it. That's how I am. Sent Mr. Qiu here over to Greenhaven to check-out the property. Said he couldn't get in, all bordered-up, shuttered, he said. Isn't that right Mr. Qiu?"

Standing silently beside the elevator with his hands behind his back, Mr. Qiu nodded his confirmation.

"From what Mr. Qiu could see, he said the building looked very old and shabby. No glitz. No style. No class, he said. Needs a serious workover. Big challenge. Huge challenge, he said. But you know what Ken, I like you. I can see you're a man I can do a deal with. Maurice says you're a great guy. And, to be honest, Greenhaven is my kind of place. It's got class. I like that. OK. So we're agreed. I'll come over next week with some of my people; the best. I have the

best people. Top architects, the best engineers, designers. You have
your people show them around, answer their questions, give them full
access. And then later, you and me Ken, we get together and we
work-out a deal. OK? Good. Now, let me offer you a drink."

Park turned in his chair to snap his fingers. "Mr. Qiu, bring us all
a pitcher of Park Pimm's. You'll like it. It's one of those classy old
English drinks. We serve it in my hotel in Singapore, The Park
Straights. You'll love it. Everybody loves it. It's incredible."

Seven. Havana, January 9, 1959

On January 9, eight days after the fall of Batista, dressed
smartly in a white linen suit with a matching Panama hat, Carlos
drove just a few blocks south from the family mansion in Miramar to
Batista's old military head-quarters at Campamento Columbia in the
suburb of Marianao. Driving a bright red Jaguar XK120 convertible
with an official Senate decal and flashing his Senator's ID, Carlos was
able to get through the outer perimeters of the armed camp with no
problem. But after parking his car and climbing the steps to the main
entrance he was stopped by guards casually sporting M1A1
Thompson sub-machine guns.

Without being in any way arrogant, even at a young age
Carlos was able to convey a sense of power. The fact that he was tall
with broad shoulders and an athletic build conveyed obvious strength,
but his easy and friendly smile annulled any sense of threat. It was the
eyes which gave him his authority; the steel blue eyes were piercing
and unblinking. Women felt he was undressing them while men felt
he could see deep into their souls. Even the young guard who stopped
him, did so respectfully.

"I am here to see Comandante Cienfuegos."

The guard looked at a clip board with a list of names. "I don't
see your name here comrade."

Carlos pointed again to his Senate identification. "I am a Senator," he said. "This is official government business."

The guard shook his head and brushed away the proffered card. "Not here you're not" he said. "We have no Senators here. This is the Revolution."

There was a silence while the two men looked at each other. Carlos had immense charm and even without speaking, his eyes conveyed his innate decency. "Listen comrade." The young guard finally said. "Don't take it personal. I wouldn't let you in whoever you are. Even the American ambassador can't get in. Believe me. He's tried. Do you know how many people want to see Comandante Camilo? Hundreds. Everyone wants to see him. And it's my job to make sure they don't."

Carlos reached into the inner pocket of his suit and pulled out a pen. Removing a small pad from another pocket, he leaned over to rest it on the official's table and wrote a short note. Tearing it from its pad, he handed it to the guard. "Please have this message delivered to him immediately." The man looked at it skeptically and read it aloud. "'Congratulations on the battle of Santa Clara. Was it as good as the battle of Harvard Yard?'' The guard, young and bearded, lean and wiry; weary beyond his years but with a burning glint of energy in his eyes, looked up from the note and glared at Carlos. "You're fucking with me," he finally said.

"Trust me" Carlos said. "He will want to read this and will be very upset if he learns that it wasn't delivered."

After a hurried consultation with his colleagues, the note was given to a young, un-bearded conscript who scurried-off upstairs. Obviously, if the wrath of the Comandante was to be felt; better it should be felt by the young and untested. That is how lessons are learned and revolutions survive.

"Stand there and wait." The command was clipped, direct and unequivocal. Carlos moved to a completely exposed position at the top of the steps. He was instructed to stand 'at ease' with his arms by his side, and to 'wait'.

The bearded young guerillas, lounging around the entrance in their olive-green uniforms, with their bored and contemptuous faces, were obviously waiting for a little entertainment and he knew they were watching him closely. Carlos – after twenty-four years of privileged existence, suddenly understood the arbitrary meaninglessness of life. These guys might shoot him, and watch his body tumble lifelessly down the wide entrance steps and not even care or know who he was. He was not a person; he was a Senator, a wealthy bourgeois – a *gusano* – a worm. He was a parasite and could be killed, shot or clubbed to death if that is what the Comandante ordered.

Carlos was not stupid, nor naive. When he set off that morning he had no illusions about his chance of success. In driving his fancy car and wearing his elegant clothes he knew he was taking a risk. He well understood that the secret of survival in times of political uncertainty and unrest is to keep a low profile and to stay below the radar. He also understood that sometimes you have to pile all your chips together, stare the croupier in the eye and place them on the Lucky Seven. All or Nothing. He was also realistically aware that his would not be the first, bullet-riddled politician's body to tumble down those very same steps. Nor the last.

The guard at the entrance desk was lighting-up a cigarette and caught his eye.

"Would you like a cigarette, comrade?" he asked.

Carlos suddenly remembered a 'New Yorker' cartoon of a blindfolded prisoner, standing before a firing squad and being offered a 'last cigarette'. "Thank you, but no," the condemned man had said. "I'm trying to quit."

"Thank you," he smiled. "I'm trying to quit."

The guard shrugged. The bearded young men clutched their eclectic collection of firearms as they lounged and crouched around the entrance. Occasionally one would glance at Carlos as though measuring the distance and calculating the angle of fire, the trajectory of the round. The round. That's what the American press called it. Not bullets or shots, but 'rounds'.

Carlos was quite sure that this bearded bunch would not refer to 'rounds', they were more comfortable with machetes. Maybe they would just club him to death.

Hearing the sound of men approaching, the lounging soldiers rose to their feet and were suddenly alert. The double doors at the end of the corridor burst open and a group of bearded soldiers, all in their olive green uniforms and boots, came striding towards them. Leading them was the young man whose face was on all the posters around town and as soon as he saw Carlos he stretched out his arms and beamed his famous smile.

Camilo Cienfuegos was actually smaller in real life than he appeared on television or in his photos. In fact, when Castro's guerillas sailed from Mexico to Cuba, they did not even want to let him come aboard their boat, the *Granma*. They thought his skinny frame would not be able to survive the physical challenges ahead. But for Carlos, apart from the beard, Camilo had not changed since they first became friends six or seven years earlier.

Carlos was in his second year at Harvard and had spent the evening with friends eating and drinking at a bar on Peabody Street. On his way back to his apartment, where he planned to complete his paper on the Balance of Power in late 19th century Europe, he heard some shouting ahead of him as he crossed the grassy center of Harvard Yard. A group of four, burly young men were standing in a circle around another man lying on the ground. Each time he tried to stand up they would kick and knock him down. "Fucking faggot!" one of them yelled. "Cuban cock-sucker!" another one shouted.

As he approached the group, Carlos could see, from the crossed-oars logo of the Harvard Crew on their shirts, that the men were all members of the university rowing club. They were large men with broad shoulders and deep chests. The man lying on the ground was much smaller and, unlike his tormentors with their short back-and-side haircuts, his hair was long, almost to his shoulders. His nose was bloody and his upper lip was bleeding from where he'd been kicked. Again he pushed himself up from the ground and again they kicked him down.

"We know Cuba," one of the men shouted. "That's where we go when we want to get laid. All the women there are hookers and all the men are faggots."

One of the other men laughed. "Maybe that ugly one we all screwed last month was his sister. She looked a bit like him, long hair and all."

"Or his mother. He looks like the son of a whore."

Carlos saw a broken branch lying on the grass beneath one of the ancient oak trees. Must have fallen during the storm the previous night. Picking it up and holding it casually by his side, he approached the group with a friendly smile.

"Hi guys" he said. "What's up."

"Found this Cuban faggot" one of them said. "He was skulking around near the freshman dorms. Probably waiting to break-in and steal something. That's all they know how to do, lazy Cuban bastards!"

While the men were talking to Carlos, the man on the ground had risen to his feet and glared defiantly at all of them.

Carlos smiled at him. "I'm here in the name of Jose Marti" Carlos said to him in Spanish, referring the Cuban national hero. "Let's give them Hell!"

Turning towards the largest of the men and speaking again in English, Carlos said. "I too am Cuban." His tree branch swung

43

upwards as he spoke and shattered the man's nose in an explosion of blood.

The face of the young Cuban lit up in a delighted smile. 'Cuba Libre!" he yelled and, displaying surprising agility he jumped up and smacked his forehead against another assailant's nose. The second man fell to the ground clutching his face as blood spurted between his fingers, but the Cuban wasn't finished with him. As the man sprawled on his back, legs splayed, his attacker repeatedly kicked and stamped on his groin until the man vomited in pain.

Carlos had already knocked the third man to the ground with second swing of his club to the side of the head. Before the man could pull himself back to his feet, Carlos hit him again, with more force, to the back of the skull. This time the man stayed, face-down, unmoving. The unrestrained violence and the unexpected suddenness of the attack had obviously disoriented the fourth man who just stood there, his mouth open, staring at the bloody carnage.

Carlos and the Cuban looked at each other and grinned.

Carlos made a mock bow and pointed to the remaining man. "Please" he said in Spanish. "Please be my guest."

The Cuban returned the formal gesture and reached-out to take hold of the tree branch.

"Gracias" he said.

The fourth man still hadn't moved. He stood rooted in shock.

Swinging the tree branch back, as though it was a baseball bat, the Cuban smashed it with all his force into the man's right knee. There was a sickening sound of bones breaking and the man suddenly bellowed in pain. After a few more blows to the head, the cries subsided and were replaced by a low moaning sound.

"Vamos" Carlos said. "Time to be somewhere else."

As they hurried over the grass away from the groaning bodies, Carlos gave his companion a silk handkerchief. "Wipe your face with this" he said. "It will take the worst of the blood off. We don't want you frightening everyone who sees you."

Back in Carlos' apartment, after pouring them both a large Scotch, Carlos introduced himself and explained he was studying International Relations and planned on returning to Cuba after graduation.

"My name is Camilo Cienfuegos" his new friend said. He too had been born in Havana, but not in the wealthy Miramar district. He was raised in the working class district of Lawton. Twenty-one years old, he was three years older than Carlos and had been independent and self-sufficient since leaving the Academy of San Alejandro without completing his studies in Fine Arts. For the moment, he was hitch-hiking around the USA, doing odd-jobs such as dish washing in restaurants.

"I don't really have any plans" he said, flashing a big smile. "Life's a party and I'm just having fun."

Carlos had a class the following morning at 9am. He left Camilo in the spare bedroom and told him not to leave the building. He was still in bed when Carlos returned at 10:30. When Camilo sat up in bed, bare chested, Carlos could see that his body was badly cut and bruised from the night before. "We need to leave town for a while," Carlos said.

In class that morning he had heard that the Campus Police were taking the 'Harvard Yard Massacre' very seriously. Apparently a group of elite members from the rowing club had been set upon and badly beaten by a cowardly gang of Hispanic thugs from East Boston. The police were making enquiries and looking for witnesses. A class mate had already asked Carlos about the bruised swelling on his right hand and the cut on his forehead. Camilo's black-eye and bruised lip, to say nothing of his heavy accent, would soon attract unwanted attention.

It was near the end of term and Carlos had no significant classes he needed to attend; so skipping town for a while was not a problem. Keeping Camilo's face well hidden, they climbed into Carlos' Chevrolet Belle Aire and set off for New York City. Camilo had some friends with a big apartment in Greenwich Village and they were both invited to stay for as long as they wished.

It was not so much an apartment, more a converted and abandoned garment factory. Camilo's friends were a mixture of restaurant co-workers, artists, musicians, poets and an endless parade of pretty girls.

Although appearing to be a wealthy and sophisticated young man-about-town, in reality Carlos had lived a very secluded life. His only sexual experience had been paid for, in a brothel, since nice girls didn't do that sort of thing. At home, his father, though loving, ran a strict and decorous household. Initially, Carlos had attended the exclusive Jesuit preparatory Colegio de Belén, but after he had twice been caught climbing over the school walls to look at the half clothed dancers at the Tropicana nightclub in the grounds next door to the school, he had been expelled. Outraged, his father sent him away to New England to complete his education at Groton. Groton school prided itself on the high moral standards which were strictly enforced and at Harvard, Carlos's only relaxation from his studies had been baseball. The dancing girls at the Tropicana soon became a distant memory.

The bohemian lifestyle that Camilo introduced him to in the Village was like nothing he could ever have imagined. There was music all the time, and dancing, and spirited discussions about politics and life and poetry and everything else imaginable until the early hours of the morning. Everywhere they went, Camilo told everybody how Carlos had saved him, and the accounts of the battle of Harvard Yard became ever more colorful and heroic. As Camilo's friend and savior, Carlos was welcomed everywhere. Every night was spent at a different bar or at a different cafe or restaurant or jazz club. And wherever they went, Camilo had friends, or quickly made new ones.

But the most amazing gift that Camilo had, was attracting beautiful women. They just flocked to him and, as Camilo's best friend, they flocked to Carlos too. As Carlos later described those two weeks in the Village to a friend, he said "I never imagined so much flocking in my life. It was Paradise. Non-stop flocking."

But even Paradise must end and, after two weeks, Carlos had to return to Boston and then to Havana. Camilo was staying in New York as he had been offered a part time job writing political articles for an exile newspaper, *Voz de Cuba*. The two friends embraced warmly and promised to keep in contact. Unfortunately by the time Carlos returned to Harvard for the next semester, Camilo had been detained by US immigration agents for working without a visa and deported back to Cuba. Carlos was disappointed by the news, if only because he had signed-up for the rowing club and was now a much respected member of the team. He had hoped to invite Camilo for a weekend visit.

They would see each other occasionally when Carlos attended the University of Havana Law School but as Camilo became more and more involved in revolutionary politics and Carlos began running for Senate, their meetings became less frequent. The last time they had seen each other was three years previously, in March 1956 when Camilo was being hunted by Batista's police. He phoned Carlos at the family home in Miramar saying he needed help and Carlos had put him up for a couple of nights in the old City at a discreet apartment he maintained for romantic encounters. Two days later, one of Carlos' friends at the Havana yacht club hired Camilo to crew for him on a sailing trip to Miami.

From Miami, Camilo had gone south to Mexico where he joined-up with the Castro brothers and the MR-26-7 group. The rest, of course, is history.

Eight: Greenhaven Museum, 2013

George Attwood was tending bar at the Greenhaven Museum and, as always, found himself explaining to Harriet

Brownmiller that each glass of wine cost five dollars - even though she was a member of the Museum's board of directors.

"It's the best deal in town" he assured her. "There's nowhere else in Miami that serves wine for five bucks; and certainly nowhere near our quality. Lady Sanders selects it herself. Personally."

Lady Sanders, the museum director, did indeed select all the wine herself. She selected it from a distributor friend at $3.25 per bottle. "That's slightly more than 'Two-Buck Chuck'" she explained. "But the label is not as easily recognized as an 'el- cheapo'."

"Oh well," Harriet said. "Let me try the Merlot."

Pursing her lips, she swirled it around in her mouth. "The odor is rather sharp" she said. "Let me try the Cabernet again."

She smiled at George as he handed her yet another glass and he noticed that she had a smear of lipstick on her teeth.

Even though the museum had been offering the exact same selection of wines for the three years that George had worked there, Mrs. Brownmiller always performed the same ritual, as though sampling each one for the first time. She managed to consume at least five dollars' worth just in 'tastes' and, what really annoyed George, she insisted on a fresh glass for each one. One of George's duties was washing the glasses at the end of the evening. The lipstick was not just on her teeth, it was also on each glass.

It wasn't as though Mrs. Brownmiller was poor. Her husband, Herbert, was a City Commissioner and they lived in one of those big, fancy mansions overlooking the golf course. According to Lady Sanders, Herbert had made his money, maintaining and stocking employees' vending machines in hotels and resorts throughout the eastern United States. His company had exclusive contracts with most of the major hotel chains.

"You mean snacks and sodas?"

"Yes. Nibbles and munchies."

"I would never have imagined there was so much money in it." He paused. "Or even that such a job existed. Yet another career path I overlooked!"

"You mean your Career Counselor at school never told you?"

"Obviously not. Janitor was all he told me about. A fine career and a noble calling, he assured me."

"So where is Lady Sanders this evening?" Harriet asked, interrupting George's thoughts.

"I believe she's in the next gallery, with the National Park people. Probably discussing alligator wrestling."

As Harriet Brownmiller strode away, determinedly clutching her glass of Malbec and in search of free food, Raoul Gomez, President of the Greenhaven Golf Association, asked for another bottle of Becks beer.

"You're pretty thirsty this evening Raoul" George said as he passed over the bottle.

"Who's counting?"

"Just one friendly golfer expressing concern for a fellow duffer."

"It's to steady my nerves" Raoul said. "To calm me down. Make sure I don't attack one of the City Commissioners or a zoning inspector."

"Why? What's happened now."

"My fence. Cost me two-grand to fence in the front yard so Jose-Marti wouldn't escape. Now those bastards in City Hall have ordered it demolished because I didn't have a goddamned permit. They've fined me two-hundred, charging me another one-fifty for a permit fee and then I have to apply for a permit with a surveyor's property plan, which means waiting around in the goddamned Zoning Department all morning while those fat-jerks sit around on their asses thinking up new ways to mess with the people who pay their wages. That's why

49

I'm having another beer. Useless, overpaid, bureaucratic assholes!"

ooOoo

The museum was hosting the opening reception for a new exhibit on 'The Everglades', sponsored by the National Parks Service and Florida State Parks. It was a prestigious event and the Governor himself was expected to attend. From his vantage point behind the temporary bar, George calculated that everybody in Greenhaven, not yet deceased, was in attendance. Mayor Adams had ceremoniously cut the ribbon, formally opening the exhibit and then had himself photographed standing next to an eighteen-foot stuffed alligator while wearing a Park Ranger hat. "The things I do for votes" he'd muttered to Lady Sanders after the two of them returned to the bar, following the ribbon cutting.

"At least you didn't have to kiss the crocodile," she replied.

"It was an alligator," George interrupted. "Rounded snout."

"Looks like the one they found in our swimming-pool a couple of years ago" said Raymond Doyle, leaning against the bar.

"Oh. Was that your pool Mr. Doyle?" Lady Sanders asked. "I was over in Europe at the time but I remember reading about it. It made headlines in the Guardian, and CNN made a big thing of it. It was a man-killer if I recall. Wasn't there a dead body as well?"

"Yes there was a dead body, but quite unrelated to the alligator."

"Apart from the fact that it had eaten one of the legs," said George.

"Well yes. There was that, but the animal was not a killer. The body was already dead when the alligator found him."

"It sounds like you must have a very busy pool Mr. Doyle" said Lady Sanders. "Were you having a party or something."

"No. No. My wife and I were not even there. We were up in Palm Beach for the weekend."

"And they've never found the killer, I hear."

"No. They haven't even identified the corpse. Face destroyed beyond recognition and hands chopped-off, so no fingerprints."

"How utterly ghastly," Lady Sanders said. "And here in lovely, respectable Greenhaven too. Do we even know why your pool was selected? I mean, what was the dead man doing there? Before he was dead I mean."

"As far as the police can tell, assuming that they're telling us everything they know of course" Raymond said. "The man was shot with a bullet to the back of the head while standing on our lawn, near the pool. After he collapsed on the grass, his hands were chopped-off with a machete and then his killers left him there. Tracks in the grass show that the alligator climbed up out of the canal and then dragged the body into the swimming pool."

"Where he chewed off one of the legs," George added.

"Simply awful," Lady Sanders said, handing over her glass. "George, be a dear please. People just didn't do that sort of thing when I was growing up. Of course we didn't have swimming pools in England, back then."

"Or alligators," George said, handing over her refilled glass.

"What about your police-woman friend?"

"Anna Hartman?"

"Yes. Doesn't she have any ideas? Any inside scoop about 'who done it'?"

"Not really. They assume that it was a professional hit. The victim must have been lured to the house under some pretext and the killers must have known the house would be empty that weekend."

"They questioned me and Margaret for hours" Raymond said. Wanted the name of everyone who knew we were leaving town. But that was the problem; everybody knew we'd be out of town. It's the Annual Trawler Fest. We go every year. It's when people who own trawlers on the East Coast all get together for a weekend. Some years it's in Miami, some years in Charleston. That year it was in Palm Beach. So it was no secret that our house would be unattended all weekend."

"Trawler Fest. Good lord" Lady Sanders said. "Who would ever have imagined? So what do you all do at these Fests? Look at each other's trawlers? Compare engines and horse power and that sort of thing?"

"Mainly drink, actually" Raymond said. "We stagger from boat to boat drinking gin and tonics, if the truth be told."

"Well that sounds more like my cup of tea" Lady Sanders said.

Nine: Havana, January 1959

"Carlitos! My friend! How good to see you." With scarcely a glance at the guards, now all standing at attention, Camilo Cienfuegos wrapped his arm around Carlos' shoulder and led him back into the building. "Come my friend. I have so much to tell you!"

Back in Camilo's large and spacious office the two men toasted each other with large glasses of rum and coke - *Cuba Libres*. Camilo opened a large humidor and the two of them each lit a Cohiba cigar before sitting back in their chairs and catching up with events of the past few years. Camilo described how, after sailing to Miami, he had hitch-hiked to Laredo in Texas and then crossed the Mexican border and joined up with the Castro brothers, Che Guevara and the rest of the MR-26-7 brigade who were gathered in the small fishing village of Tuxpan in the state of Veracruz. The plan was to sail across the Gulf of Mexico and land in the same spot on the South coast where, sixty one years earlier, the legendary Cuban hero, Jose Marti had landed to launch the Cuban war of liberation from Spain. Other members of the MR-26-7 and allied revolutionary groups, strategically placed around the island, at a signal from Castro, would simultaneously attack Batista's forces and, within days, the island would be forever freed from the heavy yoke of tyranny. At two in the morning of November 25, 1956, under cover of darkness, eighty-two revolutionaries climbed aboard the yacht *Granma* and set-off to liberate their homeland.

Granma was actually an old and battered sixty-foot cabin cruiser, built to carry a maximum of twenty-five people, not eighty-two, not to mention all their weapons and ammunition. The sea crossing took seven horrible days in the leaking, overcrowded boat. There was a lack of food, a lack of water and an overwhelming stench of human vomit, urine and other matter.

"At one point we thought we were taking on water and going to sink, so even though we didn't have much, Raul made us throw all our food and supplies overboard to lighten the load. By the time we discovered the boat wasn't leaking and it was just a plumbing tap which we'd forgotten to close, it was too late. We had no food and we were starving."

Camilo closed his eyes and shook his head at the memory.

"I made an oath on the soul of my Mother that never, never would I ever go on a boat again. Ever! I swear to God, it was worse than anything. Even the next three years in the stinking jungle was better that the seven miserable days on that stinking, goddam boat."

Arriving two days too late for the planned, coordinated uprising it also appeared their plot had been betrayed, and Batista's army and air force were waiting for them. Most of the group were either killed or captured while the twenty survivors, lost and disoriented stumbled around the coastal marshes of Coloradas Beach until they were able to regroup in the remote jungles of the Sierra Maestra mountains.

"It was a nightmare, I tell you. We had no food. We were all students and townies. We didn't know shit about living rough. We didn't even have proper boots. You know why we have beards? You think it's because it's hip and romantic? Think we wanted to become the *barbudos*, 'the Bearded Ones'? No man. It's because water was scarce and we ran out of razors."

Camilo poured them both another Cuba Libre. "Shit, I don't even want to talk about it anymore" he said. "Three damned years we were up in those mountains. Batista knew we were there and kept pounding us with his bombs and his soldiers. But you know..." he clinked glasses with Carlos. "That's what made us tough. Made us keep going, and you know what my friend? Here we are! We did it. We made it. We won!"

They both clinked glasses again, they took big gulps from their drinks, slowly pulled on their cigars and smiled at each other.

"You know another thing kept me going in the jungle?" Camilo said finally. "Harvard Yard."

He leaned forward and his voice dropped. "You know? That night in Boston. I really thought I was going to die. I knew those bastards would keep beating on me till I gave up and I knew that I would never give up. I can't." He slowly pulled at his cigar. "I wanted to. I wanted to roll over and pretend they had won. But I just couldn't. I had to keep pulling myself up." He grinned. "Even then. In all that pain I knew I was being stupid. I was out-numbered. Let them win, I thought. But no. I had to keep going."

Camilo leaned over and clutched Carlos by the back of his head, pulling him forward and kissing his forehead. "And then you came along. Out of the blue. And that's when I understood that as long as you believe in yourself and you keep standing up and you keep fighting back and you don't take any shit from anybody, then in the end it will be all right."

Camilo filled their glasses again. "And here we are man. Me – head of the goddam army, sitting in Batista's Campamento Columbia drinking Cuba Libres with my old friend from Harvard Yard." He paused and looked long and hard at Carlos. "I can't begin to tell you my friend, how many miserable nights I spent in that lousy, mosquito-ridden jungle with nothing to eat and nothing decent to drink – dreaming of sitting here like this with a friend like you."

Camilo stood up and told his adjutant outside in the vestibule that he was not to be disturbed before making sure the door was closed.

"Now my friend. There was another memory that kept me going through all that time in the jungle." He sat down on the couch next to Carlos. "You remember Greenwich Village? You remember the dancing? The salsa, the cha-cha-cha?" He puffed on his cigar and then grinned wickedly. "You remember the girls?"

Carlos raised his glass and he smiled. "Oh yes. I remember."

"So that's what kept me alive. And all these battles I've won, and all my brilliant military strategy they write about?" He leaned forwards, grinning. "It wasn't just 'Freedom' or 'Liberty' … it was Cha-cha-cha. That's what I was thinking about. That's what I was fighting for."

It was only mid-afternoon and they were both already slightly drunk but Camilo poured a fourth generous Cuba Libre. "I'm so amazed you arrived today. I'm so pleased. After three years in the jungle I've lost all my street skills. I had no idea how to find you. My 'little black book' is long gone. But you live here in Havana. You know where to go. You and me – we can discover Greenwich Village again, here in old Havana."

"For God's sake Camilo. Watch the TV, look at the papers. There's a whole city full of beautiful young ladies wanting to have sex with you. There's probably an equal number of fathers hoping that they do. Why do you need me?"

"No, my friend. Not like that. I want you and me to go out like we did before and have fun. I want to go dancing. I want to pull girls with my eyes and my moves. Not my name." He leaned forwards. "It's been six years, nearly seven since I was in Havana. You know the places to go. I want to go discretely, with you. Not with a bunch of soldiers and body guards."

"But why me? Why not Che?"

"Listen. Che's a good guy but he's not a fun guy" Camilo shrugged. "He doesn't drink. He doesn't dance or flirt. He ain't gay but he doesn't play around either. He's not fun. If he knew about you and me in the Village – he'd probably have us shot. He's really big on saying the Revolution is serious. Don't get me wrong, he's a good guy and a great comrade – but he just isn't a party guy – if you know what I mean."

That was the opening that Carlos had been waiting for. Remaining as detached and as non-judgement as he could be, he described Guevara's interactions with his father and explained that his parents, being old and frail, were anxious to leave Cuba. They were too old for all the excitement.

Carlos kept his version of events as neutral as possible; focusing on the needs for his parents to leave the country rather that the specific reasons. Nonetheless, he could not avoid mentioning the murder of the two family employees, and how that had frightened his parents.

Camilo was surprised and questioned him closely.

"That doesn't sound like Che. Certainly he has killed many people. He himself admits he is ruthless for the Cause. He would kill me, if he thought it would aid the Revolution. But just killing for a whim … that does not sound like the man I know."

"My father would not make it up. He dug the graves himself and showed me the blisters on his hands."

"You say this was December 30."

"Yes. And the second time on January 2."

"Maybe that's it. You've got to remember we had just fought the battle of Santa Clara. It was touch and go at times. It was a fierce battle. There was a lot of blood. I tell you my friend, moments like that change a man. There's a blood lust – it's the only way you can survive. Kill or be killed. We all became killers in Santa Clara. It takes a day or two before you become human again. Maybe that's why Che acted out of character."

"Anyway, my friend" Camilo said, calling in his adjunct to prepare the paperwork. "Your parents will have two exit visas, signed by me personally. They will be in Miami or New York or wherever they want by tomorrow lunchtime.. Don't worry about it. It's a done deal."

After the assistant had left the room, Camilo poured two more glasses. "But that's only two exit visas I signed," he said. "You don't get one. You are staying here to enjoy the revolution!"

Carlos grinned as he raised his glass. "You know what my friend. Maybe this was all fated after all, maybe this is part of some divine plan."

"How do you mean?"

"My family house is only about a mile north of here, in Miramar. You find yourself stationed here, in Batista's old barracks in Marianao: do you have you any idea what lies about half-way between us both?"

"What?"

"Only the greatest nightclub in the world, my friend. The Tropicana!

Ten: Greenhaven Museum 2013

Mayor Adams had left Lady Sander's group beside the bar after seeing Alfred Connolly II beckon to him from across the room. Connolly was a tall, angular man with a glittering eye, dressed as always in a crumpled, white linen suit which hung loosely on his bony frame. He had a gaunt, lined face, creased in a grim, permanent scowl of either distaste or disapproval. Adams could never decide which.

Back in the 1920s, Connolly's grandfather had owned all the land on which the city of Greenhaven now stood. That same grandfather, who had ridden with Teddy Roosevelt in the Rough Riders and who had been a close gambling and business buddy with Henry Flagler, was the founder of the city. It had been his vision and determination which had transformed this wilderness of rocky, alligator infested swamp into one of the most beautiful and elegant cities in the United States. But Connolly had achieved this by developing his land and selling it off, plot by plot, to new home owners and investors. His imperious grandson however, sometimes behaved as though the Connolly family still owned it all.

"What's this I hear about you not running, next year?" Connolly asked.

"Well I haven't yet decided," Adams said. "Laura and I are still discussing it. I mean I've been in office over ten years now. Laura wants to travel more; spend more time with the grandkids. You know how women are."

"Nonsense" Connolly said. "You're still a young man. What are you, fifty? Far too soon to be slowing down. Anyway, we need you. The City needs you. We need to fight this new threat."

"What new threat?"

"Martinez. The Cuban mafia. Follow me, we're having a little meeting in the Connolly Gallery."

As one of the major donors to the Greenhaven Museum, the Connolly family had been given their own gallery, dedicated to Ray Connolly, the City Founder. The permanent exhibit described the history of the City with a special emphasis on the Connolly family. There was a large sepia photograph of Ray Connolly himself with a fearsome scar traversing the right side of his face. The scar was the result of a savage Spanish saber slash during a wild cavalry charge in Cuba during the Spanish American War. Some rumors suggested that the saber slash was made by a young Winston Churchill, from England who had spent a few months fighting for the Spanish Crown.

There were also photographs of his sons; Ray Jr. who had died tragically in a prestigious sporting-car accident and of Alfred Connolly, the eldest son, who had sacrificed his young life, fighting alongside General Patton on the beaches of North Africa in 1940.

Early plans for the city were laid out in glass cases as were photographs of homes and hotels, swimming pools, schools, fountains and grand entrances that Connolly had constructed with his father-in-law, Alfred Nordmeyer the famous New England Banker. The Connolly gallery was the perfect place for a quiet meeting since few people ever visited it.

As the two of them entered the room, Adams saw that Don Westlake, Herbert Brownmiller and a couple of other City Commissioners were already sitting around the long conference table.

"Just a minute guys" Adams said. "We can't do this. What about the Florida Sunshine Laws? We are not supposed to meet as Commissioners, except in public."

"Oh don't wet your panties Tom," Connolly said. "This ain't no smoke filled room. Nobody smoking cigars that I can see. This is just a bunch of old friends having a chin-wag. Y'all got your glasses like I told you?"

Leaning down to one of the antique desks that was part of the permanent exhibit, Connolly withdrew a small brass key from his waistcoat pocket, opened the door and withdrew a very large bottle of Jack Daniels. He poured each man a generous portion before returning the bottle to the desk and locking the door. "You will have noticed gentlemen that this is not rum. It is not made by Bacardi and we do not mix it with Coca Cola. This is a fine Tennessee sipping whiskey. It is one-hundred percent American." He paused before finishing. "American - not Cuban."

He raised his glass and looked around the table, fixing each man with his glittering eyes. "Like this City," he said. "One hundred percent American. Not Cuban." He took a sip of his whiskey and swirled it around his mouth, savoring the warm taste. "This city is one-hundred percent American. Its founder was one hundred percent American. He risked his life fighting to liberate the Cubans from their Spanish colonial masters and then he came home and built this city with his own bare hands. I am not going to allow those spics to repay his sacrifice and his bravery by usurping his memory and his city."

"Hold on Alfred," Adams interrupted. "What's brought all this on?" Smiling, he said "Who's got your panties in a twist?"

"Martinez" Connolly said. "Dr. Orestes Martinez, that's who. Word is he's planning to run for mayor of Greenhaven. Goddam Cuban gangster! Thinks he can take over my grand-pappy's heritage – turn it into another Hialeah. They're moving everywhere these Cubans; Hialeah, Miami, North Miami, South Miami Coral Gables. They'd have overrun Miami Beach if it wasn't for the Goddam Jews. Well they ain't getting Greenhaven."

"Hear, Hear!" Herbert Brownmiller and a couple of other Commissioners banged the table in agreement.

"Got to draw a line in the sand" Brownmiller said. "Pardon my French but these fucking Cubans are taking over everywhere. My wife says she can't even go grocery shopping without a translator. You see them everywhere, swarthy fellows with shifty eyes; and their women! My God! Tight dresses and great big asses. We can't let them take over, we've got to fight them."

"That's why we need you Tom" Don Westlake said, addressing Adams. You've got a decade of experience, you have a reputation for integrity and the people know and trust you."

"But this Martinez, Rodriguez, Enriquez – whatever the hell his name is – he is a well-documented crook, like all those Cubans." Connolly had risen to his feet in anger. "He's got billions of corporate dollars behind him and he's just planning to buy this city. Lock, stock and barrel as the Brits say. He'll swamp the airwaves with ads. He'll fly Miami Herald and PBS journalists around in his helicopter and hire teams of hookers for the rest."

Connolly sat down again.

"You've got to get in the race Tom," he continued. "You have to run again or else we're going to see big-arsed Latinas dancing salsa in the streets while their sleazy, Marielito boyfriends break into our houses, rob us blind, and rape our maids and daughters. They're going to destroy our Goddam culture."

"Look, I'm sorry you fellows, but I just don't understand why you're all so riled-up. I've got to admit, I've slacked off a bit recently and I'm not as up to date as I should be. I was just telling Alfred here, Laura and I are planning a trip to Europe. Want to visit my daughter in Paris, spend time with the grandkids. I'm already cutting back on my schedule at the law-firm. Got lots of bright young associates straining at the bit, so running another four years as mayor just doesn't appeal."

Adams took a sip of his glass and tried not to react to the burning sensation at the back of his throat. "I don't understand," he said. "What's the problem with Martinez? Just because he has a Latino name?"

"He's not just Latino. He's Cuban."

"Oh for God's sake. Who cares? Jesus, look at my name. Adams." He took another sip from his glass. "I mean, apart from Eve, I've got the oldest and purest name on the planet. Pointing at them while sipping again from his glass Adams said "Brownmiller, Connolly – what kind of names are those? German, Irish? What the hell is wrong with Martinez?"

"OK Tom" Don Westlake raised his hand. "I understand what you're saying. This is a nation of immigrants, and that's our strength. Mainly Europeans on the East Coast and mainly Asians on the West coast. A melting pot. A wonderful blend of the best people in the world. No problem – I think we all agree that is what has always made America Great."

61

"Well said Don" Adams said. "With your well-known, customary discretion you have put everything in perspective - except to explain why Laura and I should sacrifice our Golden Years to protect a bunch of old fashioned, bigoted stick-in the muds!" Adams turned and raised his glass to the other men at the table. "Present company excluded of course."

Adams rose to his feet, toasted his glass to the others and then raised it to his mouth and drained it. "Fine sipping whiskey Alfred," he said. "And I thank you kindly. But now I must get home and plan next month's cruise down the Rhine with Laura."

"Martinez is a crook," Connolly said. "He is a major criminal. He is corrupt. He's disgusting and he will destroy this city. This city where you were born and raised."

Returning to the antique desk, Connolly refreshed everyone's glass, including Adams.

"While you are lounging around with your Rhine maidens, chewing your wiener schnitzels, gulping your pilsner and singing the Horst Weisel song, Jorge Martinez will have taken-over the city of your birth and will be looting and destroying your heritage."

He returned the bottle to its locked drawer.

"So what do you say to that Mr. Mayor? Or don't you care any more about your heritage?"

"Where does all this talk about looting come from? You can't accuse a man of being a crook just because he's a Cuban. From what I've read he's a very successful business man; he's developed one of the largest health-care organizations in the country. He's a billionaire. He obviously doesn't need the money. With all that wealth and experience, he could be a big asset to the city."

"But it's a different culture Tom. They don't think like us." Herbert Brownmiller said. "They don't have the same values, the same traditions that we do. Those are the values that your father died defending."

Adams sat down again. Any mention of his father always had a strong effect on him. His father had been a marine, a war hero who had lost his life during the Vietnam war on a secret mission in Laos. Even today, the nature of that mission remains highly classified. Tom had never known his father who'd been killed soon after Tom's birth and so, proving himself worthy of his hero father had always been the motivating focus of the son's life.

"What makes you say this man is a crook?" Tom asked.

"No hard proof yet, but we're sure as hell working on it. Plenty of rumors though. Suggestions of years of Medicare fraud behind him. Too much to just ignore."

"Well let's all do some more research then" Adams said. "If this man really is a threat to the integrity of the City, then yes. I will consider running against him. But I'm not running on a simple racist ticket. This is South Florida gentlemen. Whether you like it or not, we are effectively part of Latin America. Don't forget, Florida was part of the Spanish Empire for far longer than it's been part of the USA. I've been mayor of this city for over ten years. Maybe it's time for a change Maybe time for some new blood. Maybe time for some Cuban blood."

Eleven: Havana, Cuba, January 1959

Oscar missed his family and was upset when he was told to stay with family friends in Miami instead of spending Christmas in Havana. He was also worried as rumors of the revolution began to appear in the American newspapers. He had total confidence in his parents; Don Carlos would make sure that Mami was safely protected and nobody, not Batista nor the rebels would ever mess with Papi. But Carlos was a different matter and Oscar worried about his brother's speech in favor of the *Sierra Maestra Manifesto*. According to the Miami Herald, Batista was becoming increasingly repressive and violent. Carlos' speech to the Senate might have got him in trouble. Perhaps he had even been arrested and that is why Papi didn't want Oscar to come home.

Oscar had tried calling home on New Year's Eve but there was no answer and on New Year's Day he could not even get through. The international, long-distance phone operator in New Jersey said that very few calls to the island were getting through. By the end of the day the radio news was reporting that Batista's government had collapsed and by the following day The Miami Herald was filled with stories of confusion and chaos. But still no news from his family.

Oscar's only consolation was the Leica M3, 35mm rangefinder camera which his father had sent him as a Christmas present. It was an astounding gift, deliberately chosen to make-up for spending the holiday alone. Oscar had been fascinated with photographs since he was a small boy and had always owned a camera, usually Kodak Brownies, but he had never dreamed of owning something as magnificent as this Leica. Now he felt like a professional photographer and indeed, that's when his life's calling first became a reality.

The family finally made contact on January 8th. It was a very brief phone call but Oscar was told to stay in Miami and to ask his hosts to look for a suitable house where the family could stay. His father would call again in a few days when they had made their travel arrangements. Since the friends that Oscar had spent Christmas with had a home in Greenhaven, they obviously looked for a rental property nearby. After all, just as Miramar was the most fashionable residential district in Havana, so too, Greenhaven was the smartest address in Miami. The Enriquez family would feel quite at home during their temporary exile.

After using the precious exit visas to purchase plane tickets for his parents, Carlos placed them in a small document folder along with their passports and told his father to keep them safe. "This is worth more than gold Papi." Don Carlos nodded gratefully.

"Thank you my son" he said. "But I still think it would be wiser for you to come with us to Miami. You know what your Mother is like. She will worry endlessly."

"No Papi. I need to stay. For a start, I'm still a Senator, at least for the moment. I still have a role to play. The country needs protecting. Batista might still come back, the Americans might still support him. And even if Batista doesn't return, there's still the communists to worry about. My friend Cienfuegos says there's a lot more communist sympathizers in the movement than people know about. He says we should be vigilant that they don't take over the Revolution. Anyway Papi" Carlos put his arm around his father's shoulder. "Somebody needs to be looking after the family's property. If the house looks empty and if the farms and the finca are not seen to be occupied and working – then who knows what will happen?"

Don Carlos flushed angrily. "I suppose you're right. These bandits take whatever they want. The President needs to take more control. We need discipline. I don't know that Urrutia is up to the job. I shouldn't say it but we need another Batista."

"No Papi" Carlos said gravely while squeezing his father's shoulder. "You shouldn't say it and you most certainly should not let anyone hear you say it."

As though to prove his warning, Marialena, one of the maids opened the door to the drawing room and stood back to let Camilo enter.

"I'm sorry Don Enriquez, but he said you were expecting him."

"That's OK Marialena" Carlos said. "I had invited him to visit."

Instead of withdrawing from the room, the maid stood by the door, transfixed, staring in awe as Camilo strode, smiling across the large reception area.

"Papi. You remember my student friend Camilo Cienfuegos. He came to the house a few times when I was at the University."

"Of course. Of course I do. And now you are Commander in Chief of the Army." Shaking his hand, Don Carlos said. "I am honored to have you in my house, Senor Comandante and I want to say how grateful I am to you for organizing our visas. My wife is no longer young, nor in the best of health so I think she needs a little rest, away from all the excitement of Havana."

He smiled and gestured to his son. "My house is your house, Senor. Carlos will make sure you have whatever food or drink you may require. The only thing I insist on is that you do not leave without sampling our Finca Enriquez cigars. But now I must go. I need my sleep, so I will leave you young men to discuss your plans to make the world a better place. Goodnight."

After a good cigar and a couple of Bacardi rums, the two men were ready for their evening out on the town. President Urrutia had an obsessive hatred of prostitution and gambling, and one of the new government's first acts had been to shut down all the casinos. This was probably an empty gesture since Meyer Lansky and the other American mobsters had already fled the island. Nevertheless, despite the crack-down on gambling, the hotels and the clubs were still open and there was still music, there was still drinking, still dancing and, as Carlos assured him, there were still girls.

Leaving his army jeep at Carlos' house, the two friends headed south in the red Jaguar. The Tropicana Club in the Marianao district was located halfway between the Enriquez mansion in Miramar and Camilo's H.Q. at Campamento Columbia. As Carlos had said, they were fated to go there. The Tropicana had long been the most famous nightclub in the world, and its flashy, feather and sequined dancing girl atmosphere became the model for every nightclub from Las Vegas to Paris.

But the showgirls at the Tropicana had no equal anywhere in the world. Known as "Las Diosas de Carne" or "Flesh Goddesses", they had made the club and indeed Havana, the world's most voluptuous playground throughout the 1950s. Most of the other big hotels and nightclubs in Havana were owned and operated by the American mob. Meyer Lansky owned the Habana Hilton as well as the Hotel Nacional, the Riviera and the Montmartre among many others; Santo Trafficante ran the San Souci and the Hotel Capri while Vincent 'Jimmy Blue Eyes', 'Moe' Dalitz, 'Lucky' Luciano and Albert 'Mad Hatter' Anastasia all held various controlling interests in the city's many other casinos.

But the Tropicana was unique, not only for its world-wide reputation of top quality entertainment, but also because it was one-hundred percent Cuban-owned. Martin Fox with his brother Pedro had acquired ownership in the Tropicana by the late 1940s and quickly used its lush tropical setting to make it hippest club in the Western Hemisphere. By the time Carlos returned to Havana after graduating from Harvard, the Tropicana was in its hey-day and Carlos Enriquez, scion of one of the island's oldest, wealthiest and most well-connected families was exactly the sort of customer that Martin Fox worked hard to attract.

What Martin Fox did not know was that Carlos had already been attracted to the Tropicana since he was a young schoolboy. Carlos' school, Colegio de Belén, was located next door to the lush grounds of the Villa Mina where the Tropicana was located and, by climbing a tree and looking over the wall, the boys could see the half-naked dancers as they relaxed outdoors. Carlos had gone further than most boys and had climbed the walls and joined the girls to smoke cigarettes. The Flesh Goddesses had been amused by their schoolboy admirer and encouraged his advances which is why, even after being caught and punished with a caning by his teachers, Carlos continued to climb the wall. After being caught for the second time, Carlos was expelled from Belén and his father sent him to New England to finish his education.

All through his time studying law at the University of Havana and later, during his two years as a Senator, Carlos had been a regular at the Tropicana and had developed a warm and intimate relationship with the Fox family. Even though he was strongly opposed to the American mobsters and their hold on the Cuban economy, because Carlos did not gamble, he was able to stay aloof from the mobsters. What drew Carlos to the Tropicana was the music, the dancing and the girls. Throughout most of the 1950s, there were very few evenings when Carlos did not spend at least some time at the Tropicana. As he was later to confess, those carefree years at the Tropicana were the happiest years of his life.

But Castro hated everything that the Tropicana represented; the frivolous and decadent lifestyle of the bourgeois and the corruption of the American mobsters whom he called '*desfalcadores*' or embezzelers.

Meyer Lansky fled back to Florida on New Year's Day while Santo Trafficante had stayed-on in an attempt to protect his casinos but he was swiftly arrested and held in the Trescornia prison for several months. The casinos were closed and there was no more gambling on the island. But the Fox brothers stayed on, Armando Romeu and his famous orchestra stayed on, the 'Flesh Goddesses' stayed on and the show carried on.

Carlos introduced Camilo to his old friend Martin Fox who was obviously delighted to have so important a member of the new regime as a patron of his nightclub. "We are honored Comandante to have you in our club. And, as a friend of Don Carlos here, we are doubly honored. Please consider this your home from home."

"Keep it low key, please" Camilo asked them. "Be discreet. No public statements. This is where I come to relax, you understand. Not to make speeches or give interviews." Smiling, he draped his arm over Martin's shoulder. "This is where I come to be among friends."

Obviously, with his beard, his obligatory olive-green fatigues – not to mention his famous smile – there was no way that Camilo could remain unnoticed or anonymous and, if girls had flocked before, now it was a migration. However thanks to the discretion of the Fox brothers and after a few discreet words with the editor of the *Revolución* newspaper, Carlos and Camilo's evenings at the Tropicana were never the subject of public gossip; no photographs or stories ever appeared in the press.

Nonetheless, the austere members of the MR-26-7 leadership were fully aware, and disapproved of Camilo's inappropriate lifestyle. Raul Castro, stuck away in the provincial hinterland of Oriente Province received regular reports from his agents in the capital about Camilo's decadent lifestyle, not to mention his growing public popularity. Che Guevara, in his sinister, high tower, overlooking the capital knew everything that was taking place in the city below. His eyes were everywhere and Camilo's nocturnal activities at the Tropicana offended him deeply.

ooOoo

Carlos dropped-off his parents at the Jose Marti International Airport at 12:30PM on Saturday, January 10, 1959 where they were to catch a Pan Am flight to Miami. Without an exit visa, Carlos was not allowed to accompany his parents within the airport. He was allowed however to hire a team of four porters to wheel their luggage for them before leaving. As he drove away in the family Daimler he saw them, in his rear view mirror, waving farewell to him from the curb. That was his final view of his mother and father. He was never to see them again.

"Documents please." The young official behind the passport desk was dressed in the now ubiquitous olive-green uniform of the revolution. He also had a beard. But it was not yet, the bushy beard of the *barbudos*, and it had not been grown in the mountains of the Sierra Maestra. This was a beard hastily grown since the fall of Batista.

His face was expressionless as he slowly examined the two Passports and then the two exit visas before carefully placing them aside on the counter, beside the tickets. With a snap of his fingers he ordered the porters to deposit all the suitcases on the long examination tables. With another, silent and expressionless command he ordered his men to open and examine the cases. All this was done without a word or even a glance towards Don Carlos and his wife. The two of them stood nervously watching as the officials methodically emptied their cases. Don Carlos took his wife's hand and squeezed it gently. The very unfamiliarity of the gesture unnerved her and she began to tremble but fought against any open display of fear.

Clasping his hands behind his back, the officer slowly paced behind his men, looking to see what they were bringing out to display upon the table. Openly contemptuous, he held up a silk dress and some underwear from one of Donna Enriquez's cases.

"You have some fine clothes comrade" he said as he threw them back on the table.

Don Carlos held her tight, his arm now around her shoulder.

The officer had moved to another table and now discovered her jewel collection. "Well, well, well," he said. Have you been raiding the National Museum of Fine Art? Do you have documentation showing your legitimate ownership of all these fine jewels.?"

Picking up various broaches and necklaces he continued to examine them in a detached, superior manner. "Should I conclude then, from your silence, that you have no proof of ownership?"

"But they're my mother's" Donna Enriquez finally whispered. "They have been in my family for generations. They are pieces my husband bought on his foreign travels. There are little things, of no financial value, that my sons have bought me."

But again, the officer had already moved on, without listening to her. One of his men excitedly showed him a large leather briefcase, filled with cash. For the first time the officer smiled. Sticking out and then curling a short, stubby finger, he gestured Don Carlos towards him. "Just so that I don't have to waste time counting all these notes, would you like to tell me how much money we have here?"

"Two hundred and fifty-thousand US dollars" Don Carlos murmured.

"Louder. I did not hear that." The officer turned to one of his men and asked "Did you hear what the gentleman said comrade?"

Without waiting for a reply, the officer, no longer disguising his anger said "Tell us again *gusano*, you worm. Speak louder. Tell us how much cash you are stealing from the Revolución."

"Two hundred and fifty-thousand dollars" Don Carlos said. "But It's my money. It's not stolen. I withdrew it from my bank yesterday. There are records. You can check. It's all legitimate. It's not stolen. Let me give you the address of my banker. It's Jorge Hernandez. He's a fine man. He's known my family well. His family bank goes back to the first revolution. His grandfather was a comrade of Jose Marti."

But again nobody was listening. The young officer was already examining another briefcase and pulling out handfuls of documents. "Quite an international portfolio for a humble worm," he sneered. "Suez Canal shares. Standard Oil. Rothschild Debentures, Flagler's Railroad, Krupp's, Shell, De Beers. Well aren't you the man of the world? But nothing Cuban - no Bacardi?"

The officer was interrupted by one of his officials who whispered something in his ear. He gave an abrupt nod of understanding and then returned to his desk to pick up the plane ticket, passport and exit visas. He handed the documents to Don Carlos with a slight bow. "Have a good trip comrade. Your plane is ready to depart and the captain has requested immediate boarding."

Don Carlos pointed to all the suitcases and their possessions, scattered all over the tables.

"But our property" he said. "Our belongings?"

The officer shrugged. "You cannot take any of these. There is no authorization to take any of this property. The exit visa only applies to the two individuals named here." He pointed an accusatory finger. "Strictly speaking, you should not even leave the country. I should detain you until you can account for all this possible contraband."

"But we have exit visas. Look – signed by Comandante Cienfuegos himself. Personally."

"Exactly. That is why I am being so generous and understanding to you. Ultimately I report to Comandante Ernesto Guevara and his rules and instructions have been very explicit. All counter-revolutionaries, hoarders, worms, parasites and social criminals are to be detained at the border. But since you have been approved by comrade Cienfuegos, I am going to let you go. But go now, before I change my mind."

Four hours later, Oscar greeted his parents at Miami International Airport where they were admitted to the United States of America, owning no more than the clothes they stood up in.

Twelve: Greenhaven City Hall, 2013

The stone double-staircase sweeps elegantly from the first to the second floor of Greenhaven City Hall in a wide and graceful curve. Built with the local eolithic limestone, the handrails have acquired a smooth patina from decades of citizens touching them, perhaps for luck, on their ascent to the mayor's office and the city council chamber. Built in the glorious Mediterranean style of the 1920s, the building was widely recognized as the 'crown' of Greenhaven's architectural treasures. In one of her books, the renowned local historian, Jane Mayhew, had referred to the double staircase as the 'jewel in the Greenhaven crown'.

"I always feel I should be wearing a long, glamorous ball gown when I climb these steps" Lady Sanders said to Jane Mayhew as they approached Mayor Adam's second floor office for their meeting.

"Well of course, that's what Phineas Paist had in mind when he designed it with all these low risers" Jane said, in her typically pedantic manner. "At all the grand social events that he envisioned being held here, ladies in ball-gowns would be able to glide up and down these stairs effortlessly."

The daughter of an English Earl, Lady Sanders had married an American rock-musician at a young age and moved to join him in South Florida. After her husband's unfortunate and early death, she decided to remain at their home in Greenhaven rather than return to England. "Far too cold and dreary" she said. "After living in the Florida sun for ten years, it's quite impossible to live anywhere else." Financially independent, she had been appointed Executive Director of the GCM, Greenhaven City Museum and was currently planning an exhibit about the incorporation of the city in 1914. The Museum exhibit was just one of the many activities the city had planned, in order to celebrate its upcoming Centennial.

While Lady Sanders envisioned a family oriented exhibit that would appeal to people of all ages and would include fun activities for children, Jane Mayhew planned a far more academic approach. "I don't think we should be encouraging people to bring their children anyway. They always want to touch everything with their sticky little fingers" she said. "And anyway, they will get bored and start whining and distracting the adults."

"That's just my point Jane, that's why we have to make sure they don't get bored. For instance, we can get a 1914 Ford model-T in the gallery, and then we can make some period clothing, children's hats and dresses, that sort of thing, so they can dress-up and have their photo taken beside the Model-T. Oh there's all sorts of things we can do to make the experience fun. We want to get them interested in history."

"There is no reason we can't do both" Mayor Adams said. As usual he found himself in the middle of two strong-willed women. His father had been killed in the Vietnam War soon after he was born and so he had been raised by his strong-willed mother and equally unyielding grandmother. Of necessity, Tom Adams had been a peace-maker from an early age.

"Obviously we want to take advantage of having such an eminent historian living in our midst, and there is nobody who knows more about the history of South Florida than you Jane." He smiled and reached across the desk and touched her hand. "We know and value the integrity of your research and the quality of your work. Believe me, I want to take full advantage of your scholarship. I don't want any academic compromises. I've got my fellow commissioners to agree that the City will fund the publication of a serious catalog. After Miami, Greenhaven is the oldest incorporated city in south Florida and we are determined to treat this as a serious historic project."

"Thank you, Tom. I knew I'd have your full support. Greenhaven is my city; I've lived here all of my life." She kept her eyes focused on Tom and made a point of not looking at Lady Sanders. "After all, I was born here in South Florida. I'm a native. This exhibit is not only important to me, it is also very personal. That's why I don't want it compromised or cheapened. I won't stand to have it dumbed-down."

"I have no desire to dumb it down Jane" Lady Sanders interrupted. "I just want to make sure it is entertaining as well as informative. Even though I was born elsewhere, this too is my home now and I am taking this project very seriously."

Mayor Thomas Adams had known both women for many years. He had even dated Jane when they were both in their early twenties, before either of them married. Catherine, Lady Sanders, he had known since the day, way back in the eighties, when his friend Peter had triumphantly brought her back with the band following one of their wild, European tours.

"Got married man" he'd said. "Ready to settle down and have kids."

"How did that happen for God's sake. You've only been away two weeks."

Peter shrugged. "Dunno man. We were doing this concert out in some country manor near London; Knebworth House. So she comes to the dressing room afterwards and then gets in the helicopter with us back to London and then, I don't know, it was all a bit of a whirl, you know how it goes, we were having so much fun and then the next thing I know we're up in Scotland. Big concert in Edinburgh and then Kathy says 'Let's go to Gretna Green and get married.' Like it's some little village on the border with England where people run-away to get married. I don't know why, man." He shrugged. "You know what the Brits are like. Sometimes it's best not to ask. Anyway, we go into this little blacksmith's shop, you know, a smithies, and then suddenly, bugger-me, there we were, married! Mr. and Mrs. Peter Raven; except of course she isn't Mrs. Raven, she's still the Lady Catherine Sanders. 'Daddy's an Earl' don't you know. Anyway. There you are. Time to grow-up, settle down and start a family."

Of course Peter didn't settle down. He was having too much fun. Too much everything really; alcohol, uppers and downers, some legal most illegal. But the marriage had survived; they were obviously wildly in love, and each found the other, endlessly entertaining. They'd never managed to have children but that was evidently not due to a lack of trying.

The end came in Rio de Janeiro in 2000, after being forced to leave Miami due to some silly political misunderstanding involving a Cuban rafter. Frustrated in his exile and bored with his enforced idleness, Peter decided he wanted to try some paragliding off the cliffs just north of the city, at Padre Bonita. Leaving Catherine in bed in their hotel room overlooking Copacabana Beach. Peter and Jim

Davis the drummer, took an early morning cab, north to the paragliding site where they rented their equipment. Peter was carrying his cell-phone and his plan was to call Catherine as he approached the hotel and have her come out of bed to watch him gliding high above the beach while he filmed her standing naked on the balcony. "It's going to be so cool" he told Jim.

Unfortunately those were his famous last words. His body was found a couple of days later, deep in a gully in the São Conrado region. Whether it was faulty equipment, an unexpected wind squall or simply Peter's inexperience, nobody ever knew and, after much legal wrangling the lawyers agreed it would remain forever a mystery.

Tom Adams and his wife Laura had provided what comfort they could to the distraught Lady Sanders and slowly her natural resilience had overcome her broken heart. The three of them had remained close friends ever since. It was Tom who had encouraged her to take over the Director's position at the Museum.

"I really don't see any conflict at all" he said. 'All valuable documents and photographs will be safely protected from sticky fingers within the museum's display cabinets and I think Catherine's idea of costumes for kids is a great idea. We could enlarge some of the period photos of people posing, make them life size and then the children could dress-up and be photographed standing in front, as though they were part of the original group. And of course we will contact the local schools to arrange properly supervised tours." He smiled at them both and said, " I think this will prove a wonderful opportunity not only to educate our residents on our history but also to get a new generation enthused."

It still took over half an hour more of diplomatic cajoling on the mayor's part before the two women agreed to a compromise on the format of the exhibit. Finally he was able to escort them from his office to the head of the staircase.

"I'll be in touch later in the week" Jane said. "Then we can discuss the format of the catalogue in more detail."

Descending the staircase to the ground floor Lady Sanders saw Raoul Gomez, also descending.

"It's Mr. Gomez isn't it?" she said. "You're George Attwood's golfing partner aren't you. I'm Catherine Sanders. I work with George at the museum. George was telling me that you've adopted some poor abandoned dog that was tied up outside the Golf Pro Shop. That's very kind of you. I just can't understand how people can be so cruel to dogs."

"Well you've come to the right place if you want to see cruelty" Raoul said. "Those overpaid and overweight public servants in the Zoning Department are the cruelest, most arrogant and heartless people you could ever meet. I'm trying to build a fence to protect my dog and they made me rip it down and apply for a permit. Now they've rejected my application for a permit and say I have to apply to the Board of Architects with site elevations and architectural drawings. Like I'm made of money and have nothing better to do with my time."

"Oh dear" Lady Sanders said. "I'm so sorry."

ooOoo

As he turned to re-enter his office, Adams found Ken Kerman, the City Manager, hovering beside his door. "Do you have a moment Tom? I have great news on the Greenhaven Palace."

Back in the office, Kerman painstakingly walked Adams through his discussion with William J. Park. "It would be a tremendous coup for the city Tom. You have no idea how huge the Park organization is. They have really top-notch prestigious buildings in some of the classiest cities in the world: London, Paris, New York, Dubai - everywhere. Even here in Florida, he has his towers in Sunny Isles, Miami Beach, Key West ... You must have seen them Tom."

"Can hardly miss them" Adams said. "Goddam things are everywhere you look and if you couldn't recognize them by their flashy vulgarity, you'd recognize them by the damned Park name, splashed all over them."

"But think of the money he's got Tom. He's got the funds to do the deal. He's got the funds to save the Palace hotel. Funds which the city just doesn't have."

"Why does it always come down to money with you Ken? For God's sake man. This is Greenhaven. We're talking, history, tradition, we're talking values. It's not always about money."

"I don't disagree Tom. But how do we pay for our history and our values. I know you come from an old and distinguished family and that values are important to you. But values and tradition won't save the Palace hotel. You've read the zoning report. We're going to have to demolish it if we don't restore it. It's a public safety issue. And we don't have the money to restore it." He spread his arms to his sides. "Park does have the money. Only he can afford to save it."

"Where does he get his money though? He might have a lot of it but there's a lot of bad talk about its shady origins."

"Like what Tom? You mean South American drug money? I agree, that's always a possibility here in South Florida, but I had him checked out. I've got a friend in the DEA who ran his name through their data-base. Not a blip. Completely clean.

"No. I didn't mean drug money, I meant East European. From what I hear, he's washing money for the Russian Oligarchs. That's how he's financed all those condos up in Sunny Isles.

Adams got out of his chair and walked over to the window. The distant view of the Alhambra Golf Course in the center of town always calmed him. "What's his proposal then?" he finally asked.

"No specifics yet Tom. But he's bringing his people over next Wednesday to inspect the site. I've got my staff preparing all the ground plans, the zoning specs and original drawings for his inspection. They're all coming at ten in the morning so I thought it would be good for you to meet with him. I checked your calendar, and you're available all day. I thought it would be nice if you took him for lunch. I've booked you a table at La Taberna."

"Have you indeed? Well you can un-book it. I'm not going to meet with some vulgar, upstart oriental. They killed my father unless you've forgotten Ken. I want nothing to do with him!"

"But he's not Vietnamese Tom. He's a Korean. The Koreans were our allies in the Vietnam war. Five thousand of them gave their lives and twice as many were seriously wounded – fighting alongside your father."

"I don't care. He's still a slant-eyed, Johnny-come-lately, a bag man for Vladimir Putin. I don't want to meet him. You take him to lunch if that's what you want but keep me out of it!"

Thirteen. Miami, Florida, 1959

The awful humiliation at the airport was the final straw. The loss of his horses and his precious car had been bad enough but the murder of his men while he stood by helplessly, had at least infused him with a burning anger and a determination to seek revenge. However, watching his wife reduced to tears as strange men tossed aside her clothing and confiscated her most private possessions, while he was unable to protect her, was too much to bear. The once proud and imposing Don Carlos Enriquez no longer existed, and the frail, old man that Oscar Enriquez greeted at Miami International Airport was barely recognizable as his father.

But the humiliations were not over. The house that their friend, Francisco, had rented for them in Greenhaven was obviously no longer within their financial means. Luckily it was only a temporary contract, for a month, already paid for. But Don Carlos was unable to repay his friend.

"Don't worry, amigo," Francisco had assured him. "There is no hurry. Things will work out. This madness will end and you can repay me later. At least young Carlos Jr. is back home, over there managing your affairs. You're a lucky man to have such good boys."

Which of course brought up the subject of Oscar. No way could they afford another term at Groton. Oscar would have to withdraw, and then enroll in Miami Senior High School.

The following month, the three of them were living in a small cramped apartment on Eighth Street with Oscar attending the local high-school and working part-time as a bag boy at the local Publix supermarket. Unlike his parents who were completely broken by this devastating turn of events, Oscar did not mind, in fact he thrived on it. He'd never especially liked Groton school; he'd found the social atmosphere too Anglo and snobbish and he absolutely hated the Massachusetts weather. He had missed the tropics and much preferred going to school and living in Miami. And everywhere he went he took his camera. He quickly became a leading member of the School Photography Society, developing his films in the school darkroom, and soon he began exhibiting and winning prizes for his photographs.

For the parents, adjustment to their new life was more difficult. Although Don Carlos spoke excellent though formal and heavily accented English, his wife did not speak or understand a word. Miami, at the time was a sleepy Southern town where English was the only language and these Cuban newcomers were regarded with a certain suspicion. Unable to communicate, Senora Enriquez remained in the house with her memories and relied on her husband and son to do the shopping.

But gradually the family settled into their new routine. The mother, who had enjoyed maids and cooks all her life, slowly learned enough house skills to manage a small, four-room apartment. She also learned some rudimentary cooking skills, augmented by some surplus, precooked food that Oscar would occasionally bring back from his job at Publix. Don Carlos found a small, hole in the wall Cuban cafe within a few blocks of their apartment and most evenings he would walk there for a shot of Cuban coffee and a cigar. Although he suspected that many of his new friends at the café had been hotel janitors or gas-pump attendants back in Cuba, they all complained about how many herds of cattle they had lost or how many fields of sugar cane those bandits had trampled over or stolen. True or not, it was comforting to share these stories, the sense of outrage and the thirst for revenge that these men evoked, standing on the street outside one of Calle Ocho's many ventanitas. All of them talking Spanish as they leaned against the little open window where the ladies inside prepared the endless tiny shots of café Cubano. With his neatly clipped, white mustache, his crisp white guayabera, light cotton pants and faded Gucci loafers, Don Carlos, among his new friends outside the 8th street Cafe, leaner now and his eyes less piercing, was slowly regaining his dignity and social stature.

And the news from Havana was encouraging. They dared hope at last that there was light at the end of the tunnel. President Urrutia and his cabinet seemed firmly in control and Carlos Jr. was obviously close to the head of the armed forces.

"He's a fine young man that Camilo Cienfuegos" Dan Carlos would tell his friends on Miami's *Calle Ocho* as they shared coffee and cigars. "Friend of my son when they were students. Used to visit my house often. Not a Communist bone in his body. He's head of the army now, waiting for the dust to settle. You mark my words, they will ease out the hotheads. Get rid of the radicals and finally give us the true democracy that Jose Marti sacrificed his life for."

Indeed, thanks to the reporting of Herbert Mathews in the *New York Times*, most Americans had a positive reaction to the new rulers of Cuba. In fact, had it not been for Mathews' interviews and laudatory reports, Castro and his men might have remained skulking in the mountains while the revolution, led by the students of the DRE, passed them by. But it was Mathews' reports that gave him prominence and reassured Washington that he would prove a bulwark against Communism.

As Mathews wrote in one of his regular columns, even before the revolution: "Fidel Castro's program is vague and couched in generalities, but it amounts to a new deal for Cuba, radical, democratic, and therefore anti-Communist. The real core of its strength is that it is fighting against the military dictatorship of President Batista." Years later, Cubans joked that Castro only "got his job through the *New York Times*."

Phone conversations with Carlos Jr. were brief but increasingly regular. Brief, partly because of the expense, partly because of the unreliability of the infrastructure but mainly, on Carlos's side because of the need for discretion.

All Carlos Jr. wanted to do was reassure the family that the house and the various estates were still functioning and under his control. According to all the experts on Miami's Eighth Street, the Agrarian Reform law that was passed in May would strip all the land from experienced landowners and give it to inexperienced, and drunken freeloaders. Carlos reassured his father that, because of Camilo's protection, none of the Enriquez properties were affected.

The need for discretion during the conversations was complex. Don Carlos, if only for reasons of pride, did not want his son to know the reality of their financial and physical status in Miami. This was a temporary situation, there would be plenty of time later to describe the family's privations. Carlos Jr., on the other hand, had a twofold reason for discretion. Not, for a moment did he think that the phone conversations were not being recorded, and so he was discrete for that reason alone. He could not encourage his father in his enthusiasm for some sort of counter-revolution but had to encourage his faith in the American supported Urrutia government. Nor could he be explicit in the amount of help that his friend Camilo was providing for the protection of the family's sugar and tobacco estates. He never referred to Cienfuegos by name, only as 'my friend'.

ooOoo

Another subject Carlos Did not discuss on the phone to his father was the time spent at the Tropicana. Not just because he suspected that his father would disapprove of such extravagant decadence while the family was suffering such privations but also because his father would simply disapprove on moral and religious grounds. The disgrace of Carlos' expulsion from Belén school had not been forgotten. Carlos and Camilo had become, what one wag had described as "the studs of the Tropicana." Both of them were young with movie-star-good looks; one was head of the army and the other was scion of one of the nation's wealthiest families.

During the day they both worked hard. Carlos visited and made his presence felt at all the family holdings around Las Villas province. He represented the family, he conveyed a sense of reassurance to all the estate workers and household servants that life would soon return to normal. Cienfuegos also worked hard. In addition to the usual Public Relations nonsense he had to endure, he also physically participated is suppressing and punishing various anti-Castro revolts. Not only that, he was also involved with the Agrarian Reform law, which is how he was able to make sure the Enriquez family properties were not destroyed by the reforms.

So the nights in the Tropicana were the only opportunity that the two friends had to relax and to exchange confidences. Carlos Jr. never broached the subject of Fidel Castro. Camilo was fanatically loyal to Fidel. It was not so much an ideological thing, it was a human, personal thing. Some even said a dog-like thing. In any event, the important thing was that Fidel was not a Communist.

However, in the privacy of the Tropicana, surrounded by their adoring Flesh Goddesses, Carlos and Camilo were able to discuss their worries about the rest of the MR-7-26. Raul was obviously a Communist and Guevara was increasingly revealing his Communist sympathies. "Our glorious revolution could be betrayed and destroyed from within" Camilo said.

The Agrarian Reform Law was formally introduced on May 17, less than six months after the revolution. In reality, the new law had less to do with improving agricultural efficiency and much more to do with changing the structure of Cuban land-ownership. Under the directives of the INRA, the Agrarian Reform Institute, large estates were to be broken-up and given to 'the people' or reorganized as co-operatives. Other properties, especially those owned by foreigners, were to be confiscated by the State, and estates whose owners had fled the country were to be expropriated.

Thanks to his constant travel, by making his presence known and seen at all the Enriquez's farms and estates, Carlos was able to ensure that the family's holdings were not classified as being abandoned and thus expropriated. At the same time, Camilo used his influence with the INRA to prevent the Enriquez lands being broken up into co-ops. One of his fellow fighters during the Revolution, Manuel Artime, had been appointed second in command of INRA and shared Camilo's genuine desire for agricultural reform as well as his hatred of communism. Camilo introduced Carlos to Manuel as mutual friends and the two of them were able to introduce efficiencies and reforms to the Enriquez landholdings while Carlos still retained ownership. At the same time, Carlos assisted Manuel with the creation of the *Commandos Rurales*, or Rural Commandos, an idealistic movement for young people to volunteer in the countryside with the approval of both the Catholic Church and the Minister of Agriculture.

Already, by July, at the Eighth Street Bodega in Miami's Little Havana where Don Carlos smoked his evening cigar and drank his coffee, horror stories were being told about the destruction of the Cuban economy. One of Don Carlos' new friends learned that his 2,500 acre sugar plantation had been divided into 200 individual holdings and the new owners were digging-up the sugar and replanting the land with vegetables for their own consumption. Another of his friends learned that his large cattle herd had been divided-up and the individual cows had been given to local peasants.

"Can you believe it! The ignorant guajiros; they're killing the cows for meat! They're eating them. The imbeciles will have nothing left."

Phone conversations between Carlos and his father were becoming more agitated and difficult to control. After an evening at his Eighth Street cafe, listening to more and more tales of rampant stupidity and destruction, Don Carlos lost all control and discretion when talking to his son. He ranted and raved about the bandits ravaging his heritage and told Carlitos to arm himself and to fight these communist bastards. Although Carlos Jr. wanted to reassure his father that everything was under control, he did not want to say too much and did not want to arouse any curiosity. He most certainly did not want to mention Camilo Cienfuegos' increasingly important role as his protector nor his friendship with Manuel Artime of the INRA.

The truth of the matter was that Carlos was increasingly comfortable with the post-Batista Cuba. Apart from his relationship with Cienfuegos, which was based on personal friendship, he also had good relationships with the all-powerful INRA and Sorí Martín, the Minister of Agriculture. After decades of Batista's corruption, he approved of the reforms being introduced by INRA and he was excited by the idealism of the Rural Commandos. Carlos felt fairly confident that his parents would soon be able to return to Cuba, if only President Urrutia could exercise more control over the Castro brothers.

So among the soothing noises, Carlos comforted his father that the stories he was hearing were untrue and exaggerated – probably being spread by enemies of the government. He emphasized that Urrutia government was totally opposed to the communists.

"Listen Papi, you know not to listen to gossip. Even the Americans are not worried. Fidel himself has been over in Washington and New York. I heard from my old professors at Harvard that his visit there was a great success. He's even met with Nixon. They love him in the States – they wouldn't do that if he was a communist. Listen, Urrutia's cabinet are sensible men. They're experienced. Things here are calming down. The house is fine, the farms are all fine. I've got everything under control. Let's just let all the dust settle – make sure all the Batista leftovers are dealt with and all the American Mafia have been removed, and then you and Mama will be able to come back home again."

Thus reassured, Don Carlos would comfort his wife and tell her to be patient. Sitting at a rickety plastic table on the cramped balcony overlooking the traffic on Eighth Street he would play dominos with his neighbor and tell him, yet again, what a fine son he had, and how the nightmare would soon be over. Despite the heat and humidity, Don Carlos would always wear, if not a jacket, at least a clean guayabera while his neighbor sat wearing what the gringos inexplicably called a 'wife-beater' vest. Inexplicable maybe, but then so much these days was inexplicable.

The following evening, he would walk slowly along Eighth Street with his stiff leg and his cane; two cigars tucked in the breast pocket of the crisply ironed guayabera, his back straight and a white panama hat firmly on his head. Once more a proud Cuban gentleman of the old school.

"I've spoken with my son," he would announce proudly as he reached his favorite cafe where his friends clustered around the open window, ordering the powerful black coffee. "He assures me that these stories are untrue. It's propaganda being put-out by Batista's thugs. He tells me that Urrutia and his people are in control. There are no communists. It's all lies spread to scare us. He says we will soon all be home again."

Within minutes, somebody would be accusing Don Carlos of spreading communist lies and of being a spy for the Castro brothers and soon they would all be shouting and hurling accusations at each other. Don Carlos would once more return home upset and trembling, slowly climbing the grubby concrete staircase to the noisy, cramped and airless apartment. How had it all come to this?

Fourteen: Ruth's Chris, Greenhaven, 2013

Ken Kerman. Greenhaven's City Manager had booked his usual table in the far corner of the private dining room in Ruth's Chris Steak House. There were few other tables close by and the seating-staff knew to avoid those tables unless the restaurant was especially crowded. This evening was quiet as most of the regulars were attending the big National Parks reception at the Greenhaven Museum.

Dr. Orestes Martinez was a tall, imposing man with a thick mane of leonine silver hair brushed back past his ears. He was dressed in an elegant, grey pin-stripe suit and wore a Harvard Crest striped tie. His handshake was firm and the gaze of his steel blue eyes was direct. Even the blemish of a thin scar on his left cheek enhanced his masculine good looks. "Good of you to take the time to see me Mr. Kerman. I can well imagine the duties of a City Manager must make demands on every moment of your day."

Kerman lowered his eyes modestly and gave a discreet shrug. "The responsibilities are indeed onerous," he said. "But that is all part of Public Service." Ken had indeed sacrificed to accept this dinner invitation; normally he would have preferred to attend the reception at the Museum, but the opportunity to meet one on one with a powerful billionaire like Orestes Martinez was not to be ignored.

After a few more exchanges about the heavy demands and responsibilities of life in the public sector, they also agreed about the rewards. The satisfaction of seeing civic goals achieved and the quiet knowledge that your efforts are improving people's everyday lives are just unique. "It's a blessed opportunity," Kerman concluded, "to be able to give back to the community."

"And that's really why I wanted to meet with you Ken. Understand, this is just an informal meeting – just a 'get to know you' shall we say. But after living in Greenhaven for thirty years, I feel it is time for me to give back to my community."

"Thirty years? I'm sorry. I'd no idea that you'd been a resident for so long. In fact, "Kerman looked slightly embarrassed. "I've only just learned that you actually live here and are one of our residents."

Martinez smiled. "My point exactly. And that is a terrible reflection on me I'm afraid. To think, that I could live in a wonderful community like this, for so long, and have so little effect that I'm not even noticed." He paused to take a sip of water. "I take my morning walk around the beautiful Alhambra Golf Course in the center of town, I eat in many of the town's magnificent restaurants and cafes. I live in a paradise of safe, clean streets, beautiful houses, manicured grounds and gracious public spaces; and yet I contribute nothing."

"But you pay your taxes," Kerman said with a smile.

"That's not enough Ken. I want to do more. I need more meaning to my life than just business. There is more to life than money."

After glancing discreetly around the room, Martinez leaned across the table and spoke quietly. "This is just between you and me, OK, Ken? This is not for public consumption, not for a short while at least."

"Of course. Of course Orestes. Just you and me. You can trust me. In my job, I carry many secrets."

"Quite. I'm sure you do. As I say, it has not yet been publicly announced but in just a few days I am selling my corporation, American Health Care United LLC. I'm retiring."

"My God Orestes. But AHCU is the biggest health-care provider in the nation. That is big news. So. You're stepping down as Chairman."

"No Ken. I'm retiring. I'm selling-up. If all goes as planned, by four-thirty, next Friday afternoon, I will be unemployed. I will be a free man. I will have no further ties or connections with AHCU. I am selling all of my interests; all my shares, all my stocks. Everything."

"But that's been your whole life. It must have taken you years to build a conglomerate as big and successful as that. How can you turn your back on it?"

"For that very reason Ken. It was my whole life and suddenly I realized it was not enough. I'd ignored my family for years. First I lost my mother, then my father without spending any time with them, and then, just last year I lost my brother. I've never married, I have no children. I'm alone in the world Ken. All I've got is this damned company and more money than I can ever spend."

"But you've worked so hard for your success, Orestes. You've given your life for your company."

"You're right. That's really why I've been an invisible man in the community. All my energies went elsewhere, into my business. Greenhaven is where I slept. Otherwise I was always traveling and working."

Taking another sip of water he said "Which is really why we're here today."

"Sorry Orestes, I don't quite follow."

"Next Friday morning Ken, when I wake up, I will have no reason to get out of bed. Without AHCU, I'm afraid I might go crazy." He paused and fixed Kerman with an intense look. "So I've decided that I want to run for mayor of Greenhaven. I want, finally, to get involved with my community. You said it so well earlier, Ken. I want to give back. I want to serve."

"Gracious me!" was all Kerman could say, though his mind was racing. This could be just what he had been praying for.

"So why are you telling me?" he began cautiously. "I mean, meeting like this for lunch. I'm only the City Manager you know. I get appointed by the mayor; unfortunately I don't get to pick the mayor. How exactly do you think I can help you?

"Advice Ken. Advice. You've been around a long time. You have a good reputation. You know how things work. Plus, as City

Manager, you know better than anybody, what the city needs. You tell me what the City needs and I will make sure we get it. I'm a successful businessman; I have lots of energy, I have lots of money. I can get things done and make things happen. Just tell me what the City needs."

This was all music the Kerman's ears. He sat back in his seat and smiled.

"The City really needs just one thing Orestes, and you know ... I think you might be the one person able to deliver it."

"Interesting. What's that Ken"

"Greenhaven needs to enter the twenty-first century Orestes. That's all. It needs to wake up. It needs to blow-off the dust and clear the cob-webs. The city is going broke, it's dying. Everything is old fashioned and fuddy-duddy. Tourists don't come here anymore. They go to Miami Beach, Wynwood, Brickell. They go to places with modern hotels that have Wi-Fi, and cool-hip restaurants that serve exciting food. They go to places with cafes where they can sit outdoors and enjoy the Florida weather. They like to sit in bars and order fashionable cocktails while they check their emails and check-out each other. Do you know you can't order an alcoholic drink in Greenhaven unless you are having a meal in a restaurant or attending a private event? Look at the Greenhaven Palace Hotel. Used to be the most famous and fashionable hotel in South Florida. We had to close it down last year because the building department said it was no longer up to code. Unless I can find a buyer or developer soon, we will have to tear it down. Do you have any idea how many times the commissioners have voted down my request to allow outdoor seating for city cafes?"

He paused to drink some water.

"So with fewer hotel rentals and more failing restaurants, City revenues are declining and we're increasingly unable to provide services that the residents expect. Consequently, property prices are

90

stagnant if not declining which means the City's tax base is shrinking. Need I go on?"

Martinez leaned back in his chair without speaking, wiping his mouth with his crisp linen napkin, he stared at Kerman and smiled. Catching the waiter's eye, he ordered a bottle of Veuve Clicquot, brut. The two men had already started their entrees and till then had just been drinking water. "Please join me in at least a small glass Ken. We don't need to finish the bottle." He glanced up at the waiter. "I'm sure Mike will see that it does not go to waste."

When they were alone again, Martinez raised his glass. "I'm sorry to hear you have so many problems Ken, but you've made me a very happy man. That's why we're drinking Champagne. You've just given me a challenge; a whole new purpose in life." He drained his glass. "We are going to make Greenhaven great again."

For the next two hours the men remained in the restaurant, excitedly discussing ways of revitalizing the City. "I'm one-hundred percent behind you Ken. This is South Florida, we're blessed with year-round sunshine. Of course people want to sit outside at cafes. What's the charm of France and Italy if it isn't the outdoor cafes? And the licensing laws? It's ridiculous; like something out of Prohibition!"

"It goes back further than that" Kerman said. "It was Julia Tuttle who banned alcohol down here, even before Flagler built his railroad."

"You know what we need Ken? Something that will turn things around, put Greenhaven back on the map – but plumb center of the map?" Martinez poured them both another glass of Champagne.

"What's that Orestes?" Kerman asked with the faintest of slurs. Despite his appreciation for the finer, or more expensive things in life. Ken Kerman was not used to drinking Champagne. In fact he was not used to drinking any alcohol, certainly not in public. The fact was he did not enjoy the effects of alcohol, did not like the sense of losing control and he hated the inevitable and messy physical after effects. But today was different. Realizing what a benefit Orestes Martinez could be to the city and the positive effects it could have upon his own career and reputation, Kerman felt exhilarated rather than drunk.

"Tell me what we need Orestes. What's gonna turn us round?"

"The Tropicana Ken. The Tropicana nightclub."

"But that's in New York. In the Bronx."

"No. No. The real Tropicana. The Havana Tropicana. That's what Greenhaven needs if it wants to come alive again. You're probably too young to remember Ken, but before those Castro bandits destroyed my country, Cuba was the entertainment center of the world. It was bigger than Las Vegas, bigger than Nice or Cannes. And you know why? Because of the Tropicana night club." Martinez's eyes appeared to acquire a bright sheen as he remembered the old days of pre-revolutionary Cuba. "You would not believe the show-girls they had Ken; legs that went on forever, slim waists and not slim everywhere else if you follow me. I swear, I fell in love every night with a different goddess. That's what we called them, the 'Flesh Goddesses'. And the performers – all the top names performed, Celia Cruz, Tito Puente, Paul Robeson, Carmen Miranda, Nat King Cole, and Josephine Baker."

He shook his head just remembering it all. "People came from all over the world. Hell! The audiences were even more famous than the performers." Leaning back in his chair, Martinez half closed his eyes as he slowly counted off the names on his fingers. "Let's see, we had Frank Sinatra, Judy Garland, Humphrey Bogart, Lauren Bacall, and Marilyn Monroe. Then we had Edith Piaf, Ernest Hemingway, Jimmy Durante, Rock Hudson, Anthony Quinn, Betty Grable, Ingrid Bergman, Errol Flynn, Maurice Chevalier, Sammy Davis, Jr. and Marlon Brando. I tell you, there's never been anything like it. We even had the Aga Kahn and Princess Margaret."

"It sounds wonderful Orestes, but how does that help us in Greenhaven?"

"Simple. We reopen the Tropicana here in Greenhaven. I know they've tried it in New York and in Atlantic City, but they're not Latin cities. They don't have the vibe. And of course the original Tropicana is still open in Havana – but that's been operated by a bunch of useless, corrupt Fidelistas." He made a face, as though to spit. "No saben su culo de su codo – they don't know their ass from their elbow!"

He raised his glass. "But here in South Florida: you've got the tropical setting, the Cuban population, the local Latin talent. I tell you Ken; we have all the ingredients to make your city come alive again. A smart businessman like you as City Manager, an energetic guy like me, with contacts and unlimited funds as Mayor – I tell you Ken – we'll be unbeatable!"

"You're thinking of the Palace Hotel?"

"Yes, of course. Restore it to its previous glory and give it all the glamor of old Havana."

"Brilliant Orestes. And I might even have a big developer who might want to do the restoration."

"Really? Who's that Ken?"

"Bill Park. William J. Park. The Korean developer. I met with him in his office just last week. He's interested in the Palace Hotel."

Ken Kerman was so excited that he actually held out his glass for more champagne. In less than ten days he had managed to bring together a major, international developer as well as one of the wealthiest men in the state – if not the nation. Greenhaven would never be the same again!

Fifteen. Havana, Cuba, 1959

Whatever he might tell his father, and despite his own good relationships with the authorities, Carlos knew that things in Cuba were far from ideal. The Castro brothers were becoming more dominant and the rift between the MR-26-7 and the government was increasingly open. The revolutionary newspaper *Avance* published a story about President Urrutia buying a luxurious villa and collecting a $40,000 salary while poor Fidel did not even have enough money for a wooden shack in the Zapata Swamp.

By the middle of July, Castro had forced President Urrutia to resign in disgrace and replaced him with Dr. Osvaldo Dorticós who had surreptitiously acted as a lawyer for the MR-26-7 before the revolution. Meantime, from Che Guevara's sinister fortress above the city, la Cabaña, came regular reports of the secret tribunals and summary executions of anyone deemed to be a counter-revolutionary. Carlos was increasingly reminded of the reign of terror in Paris and of Robespierre's Committee of Public Safety.

Although Camilo maintained his cheerful optimism whenever they managed to share an evening relaxing at the Tropicana, Carlos could tell that his friend was feeling the pressure. He could see that the communists were becoming increasingly better organized and influential; he too had heard the stories about Raul Castro's communist sympathies. Most of all Camilo had to be aware of the daily reports from Guevara's la Cabaña about executions and worse. Camilo did not say as much, but protecting the Enriquez properties from the attentions of the INRA was becoming more challenging by the day.

A crisis was narrowly averted in August when some of the Enriquez neighboring cattle ranchers in Las Villas were caught plotting an anti-Castro coup with President Trujillo of the Dominican Republic. It was a widespread and sophisticated conspiracy and the plotters had even planned a provisional government to replace President Dorticós and the Castro brothers.

Alerted to the conspiracy, Castro and Camilo Cienfuegos, with their army hidden nearby, watched the plotters assemble and heard their cries of "Down with Castro" and "Death to Agrarian Reform." As many as two thousand conspirators were arrested that day and all eventually found their way to Guevara's prisons. The assembly point for the plotters and the invading army from the Dominican Republic was at a small airport not far from the Enriquez estate where Guevara had first 'liberated' the horses. The main conspirators were all major landowners and had been friends and neighbors of Don Carlos for decades. If Camilo had not played a significant role in suppressing the revolt, Carlos would probably have been arrested just by association.

In any event, as a result of the foiled conspiracy, the land seizures increased in frequency and the INRA became ever more avaricious and grasping; demanding farm machinery, livestock and even personal possessions – yet without issuing a receipt or even a chit as proof of what had been taken. Owning extensive landholdings in the rich Las Villas province, Carlos felt increasingly vulnerable and wondered how much longer Camilo would be able to protect the family.

Things came to a head in September, when Camilo was forced to accompany both the Castro brothers to Santa Clara and to fire the local administrators, including the head of the INRA for not being aggressive enough. The next time that Camilo and Carlos were able to meet in Havana at the Tropicana, Camilo suggested that Carlos should discreetly remove whatever valuables he had in the Santa Clara estate and store them in the family home in Havana.

"To be quite frank my friend, I am becoming worried about Fidel. He is too trusting. In some ways he is very naive. I've been warning him about the communists for quite a while now. They become stronger day by day. More blatant in their activities. But Fidel just laughs at me. Says I'm paranoid. Calls me a worry wart. He just doesn't see the danger. He's too nice. He just sees the good in everyone. He refuses to see that they are plotting to take over the revolution."

Camilo was leaving by plane the following morning. Castro had ordered him to fly to Camaguey in the center of the island to replace Hubert Matos, the military governor. Camilo was increasingly occupied with suppressing revolts and putting out fires for Fidel. Knowing they would not see each other for several weeks, the two friends made a night of it, and the Flesh Goddesses and the Cuba Libres kept flowing till well past sunrise.

The following week, Carlos drove to the Santa Clara estate and loaded a truck with various paintings in their heavy gilt frames. Most of them had been in the family since colonial times. He also packed some special pieces of furniture, as many books as the truck would hold and a collection of guns. When he returned to the family home on Avenida Quinta he phoned his father in Miami and told him what he had done.

"There's no need to panic Papi. Nothing has changed. But my friend. You know, my old college friend, he just thinks there is no harm in being over cautious."

It was late in October when Carlos heard from Camilo again. It was a brief phone call.

"I'm leaving Camaguey in about an hour, so I should be back in Havana by nine. We need to talk, I have some news. I'll see you at the usual spot around ten-thirty."

It was after midnight when Carlos first got the news. Martin Fox, the owner of the Tropicana came to his table looking worried. "Don't get upset, Carlitos" he said. "But I've just heard a rumor that Camilo's plane has been lost at sea. He took-off from Camaguey more than six hours ago but his plane just vanished from the radar. It's probably just a rumor, you know how things are these days, but I just thought you should know."

In the event, it proved not to be a rumor. Camilo Cienfuegos' plane was never found, his body was never recovered and the fate of the handsome and smiling hero of the revolution remains a mystery to this day. Each year, on October 28, school children throughout the island throw flowers into the sea to honor Camilo Cienfuegos, repeating the spontaneous tribute of the Cuban people who tossed flowers into the ocean when they heard his plane had been lost over the Florida Straits.

Carlos returned home around two in the morning and by three he fell into a fitful sleep. Guevara's soldiers came for him about an hour later, and by the time the sun appeared above the Atlantic horizon, Carlos Jr., bruised and bleeding, was chained in a cell, deep inside the sinister Fortaleza de San Carlos de la Cabaña.

Sixteen, Park Tower, Miami, 2013

Ken Kerman still could not get a good read on William J. Park, partly because Park never seemed to stop talking and his speech was so riddled with non-sequiturs that Kerman's head was spinning within minutes.

Following the inspection of the Greenhaven Palace Hotel, accompanied by the ubiquitous Mr. Qiu, the two of them had lunched at La Taberna restaurant where Park was surprised to learn that Mayor Adams would not be joining them. Kerman explained that the mayor had been called out of town unexpectedly but otherwise was most anxious to welcome Mr. Park to the city.

At the same time he was covering for Adams, Kerman introduced the name of Orestes Martinez as a possible contender for the Mayor's seat. Adam's short-sighted dismissal of Mr. Park and his refusal to meet with him had annoyed the City Manager and, although he was supposed to remain neutral in the mayor's race, he was privately starting to favor Martinez. Hence the visit to Park Tower.

"Mr. Park sir" he said when they emerged from the elevator into Park's penthouse office on the 65th floor. "I'd like to introduce Dr. Orestes Martinez, Chairman and CEO of AHCU, American Health Care United."

"Not any more, I'm happy to say" Martinez smiled as the two men shook hands. "I've sold all my interests, divested myself of every share. I am now a free man, with no further connection to AHCU. Today, as they say, is the first day of the rest of my life."

Park ushered them both over to where some comfortable sofas were arranged around a low coffee table.

"And what do you plan to do with the rest of your life Dr. Martinez, or do you mind if I call you Orestes? Please call me Billy, all my friends do and I have a lot of friends, good friends, great people – lots of them are CEOs like you, celebrities, footballers and reality-show stars, great people and they all call me Billy."

"Well Billy, funny you should ask, as a matter of fact, just yesterday I filed my official papers to run in the next election for mayor of the City of Greenhaven. And my good friend Ken here, mentioned that you and your company might be interested in participating in some development projects in the city. So I thought it would be both prudent and advantageous for us to get to know each other. Obviously I am well aware of your own organization. When I'm in London or Paris, when I'm in New York or San Francisco and certainly when I travel to the Middle East – I always stay in the local Park Tower Hotel."

"Of course. Where else would you want to stay? They're the best hotels. They're tremendous. Believe me, they are truly, truly great hotels. There are no other hotels like them, anywhere in the world. In the whole history of the world there have never been hotels as great as mine; as luxurious, as glamorous or as classy. You know all those Roman Emperors, and Indian Rajas and Arab Sultans, you know like the Kings of England and the Emperors of Russia, and Louis the Fourteenth, you know, the so-called 'Sun King'. You know what? I pity them. I really do. I pity them. Not just because they're all dead, well obviously I'm sorry for them for being dead. That's not a good way to be. Dead, not good. Trust me. Sad. No I mean I pity them because they never, ever knew what luxury living really means. They thought they did. They thought they knew luxury – I bet that Louis went swanking around his palace at Versailles and said 'how cool is this! This is real class'. But none of them, and I mean not a single one of them, had ever stayed at one of my hotels. They never knew real luxury. Sad!"

"Ken tells me that you are possibly interested in renovating the Greenhaven Palace Hotel Billy. Have you met with the current mayor to discuss it with him at all?"

"No Oreo. No I haven't. And you know what - he hasn't come to visit me to discuss it either. I've got to tell you, I appreciate you giving up your time, even though you're retired now and don't have a job so you're not as busy as I am but even so, nonetheless, I appreciate, you making the effort to come and see me today, to pay your respects. I like that. Shows class. And I've got to be truthful now, I feel Mayor Adams has been disrespectful in not coming to see me and thanking me for offering to put my name on one of his city's landmarks. I've got to tell you; having a Park Tower in your city is what puts it on the map. Can you imagine New York City without a Park Tower? No of course not, or London or Paris. That's Paris, France of course, not Paris, Texas. Paris, Texas doesn't have a Park Tower. Never will. Nor will Podunk or any other loser type town. It's only world-class cities that get the Park name on their buildings and that's why Mayor Adams should be more grateful and excited about my offer. Now, you're different Oreo. I can see that. You're a winner. I like winners, I can always spot them. See, it takes one to know one. And winners spot me too, they're drawn to me, attracted to me. It's like magnetism, that's what they say. They say I've got a magnetic personality. Now I don't know about that. Maybe I have and maybe I haven't. I really don't have the time to think about that sort of stuff, I'm too busy spotting winners and making deals. Like you. You're a winner and when you're mayor I think we're going to do some great business together. I like the way you do business. I noticed that scar on your cheek and I immediately felt sorry for the poor bastard who gave it to you."

Martinez half rose from his chair, his eyes flashing with anger till Park, also rising reached out to calm him.

"That's how I am" he said. "I'm direct. I say it like I see it and I see most things. I don't miss much. That's why I'm so successful. I saw your scar and I knew there was a story. A good story that reflects well on you. I know we can do some good deals together. I've been researching your AHCU background. Well Mr. Qiu over there, he's been reading up on it all and telling me about some of the great deals you've made. Definitely a winner."

Snapping his fingers, he signaled to Mr. Qiu who was at his usual position beside the elevator door. "Bring us some Pimm's" he instructed. "Let's toast to our new partnership."

Apart from the initial introduction, Ken Kerman had not said a single word since entering Park's office. In one sense he was delighted the way things were going. He had managed to persuade a big-name, international developer to save the city's landmark hotel and he had also persuaded a billionaire executive to run for mayor. Between them, they would bring in all the financial backing, energy and modern vison that Greenhaven so desperately needed. At the same time, part of him felt like the chicken who'd invited two foxes to guard the hen-house.

Seventeen. Miami, Florida, 1959

News of Cienfuegos' disappearance over the sea reached Miami as quickly as it reached Havana and immediately became fodder for the usual conflicting conspiracy theories of *Calle Ocho* – Miami's Eighth Street.

"He accused Fidel of being a communist and they had him shot before he could demonstrate his proof."

"My cousin saw him, clear as day in Panama. He was in a bank, depositing suitcases of dollar-bills. He'd shaved his beard off and was wearing dark glasses but it was him all right. My cousin's no fool. He recognized him from newspaper photographs, it was that gangster Cienfuegos, no question. He's looted the Treasury."

Don Carlos decided not to say anything to the family. He knew that it would just make his wife worry even more. If nothing else, Cienfuegos represented hope for the future. But Oscar heard the news, next day at school and understood intuitively that his big brother was in trouble.

On October 31, 1959, the whole family gathered, as always at Francisco's home in Greenhaven for Saturday lunch and the regular phone call from Carlos Jr. This had been a routine for the past few months and Carlos was disciplined about calling precisely at noon. At first, they looked for innocent explanations when the phone did not ring.

"Perhaps it's to do with Daylight Savings Time," Oscar suggested. "Maybe he'll call at one-o-clock, our time."

Francisco chuckled knowingly. "Maybe it was a late night at the Tropicana," he said.

But by two-o-clock they knew that he would not be calling that day.

"Perhaps he's been taken ill" Oscar's mother said. "Maybe he's in bed with no-one to look after him."

"Don't worry, mi amor," Don Carlos said. "Maria is still there, and the cook. They will look after him."

"Cook's new" his wife said. "She doesn't know what he likes, like I do. And Maria doesn't care. She's lazy and all she thinks about is boyfriends."

There were no phone calls from Cuba to Francisco's house during the week and when the family gathered for lunch the following Saturday, their expectations were not high. Instead of staying-on, after lunch to smoke a cigar and play dominos, Don Carlos took the family home. "I cannot play while my son suffers" was all he would say.

One of Oscar's new school friends, Raphael, had been a member of the *Agrupacion Catolica Universitaria* (ACU) in Havana

101

before the revolution. The ACU was a sort of Jesuit, non-political lay-group for young men and many of Oscar and Carlos' friends had been members back in Havana. Raphael's father had been a member of Batista's military and so the whole family had fled the island within days of Batista's downfall. Like the Enriquez family, they had arrived in Miami with just the clothes they stood up in and nothing else. According to Raphael, his father was organizing a group of fellow exiles to infiltrate the island and overthrow the revolution. He said that most weekends, his father would take him out to the Everglades, south-west of Miami, where he and his friends would practice target shooting and unarmed combat. Sometimes there would be Americans there as well, and everyone would have to speak English as the Yanquis did not speak Spanish. Raphael claimed the Americans worked for the government.

Oscar knew that his brother was alive. He would have known in his heart if he was dead. But at the same time, he knew his brother was in serious trouble. After several weeks with no news from Havana, Oscar asked Raphael if he could join his father for the weekend training in the Everglades.

Long before sunrise on a Saturday morning in late November, Oscar stood in the parking-lot outside a small Cuban restaurant where Raphael's father and his friends were gulping a quick coffee. Sitting next to his friend in his father's truck and followed by a group of five or six other cars they headed south on US1 to Homestead, where they turned west, into the Everglades. Long after they had seen any sign of human habitation, or indeed, any sign of life, they turned left onto a rutted track which eventually brought them to a grassy clearing in a hardwood hammock surrounded by marshy sloughs.

During the almost two-hour drive from Miami, Oscar learned that Raphael Sr. had fought in the Sierra Maestra for several years, hunting Castro and the MR-26-7 guerillas. He was obviously an experienced jungle fighter. More importantly, though Oscar was not aware of this, Raphael was learning all about the Enriquez family and his questioning finally convinced him that his son's school friend was indeed a genuine believer and not a spy.

"I am sorry about your brother" he said. "I still have my sources on the island. I will make discreet enquiries."

The training was rigorous and, although Oscar was tall and strong, he was fairly exhausted by the time they drove home. The group did not have enough money for a decent supply of bullets. Each man was restricted to a single shot. However, they were trained how to carry a gun, how to keep it dry, how to aim it, how to clean it and how to disassemble and reassemble it. They practiced unarmed combat, some with knives, and most of the time they practiced silently crawling through the long grass, hiding, sitting still for long periods and then springing into action.

When he returned home, Oscar told his parents he had been at baseball practice all day with his school friends. His mother had been barely aware of his absence but his father looked at him thoughtfully. After his third week of training, Oscar returned home with even more cuts and scratches than usual, including a large purple swelling on his forehead and a bloody gash on his cheek. His mother appeared not to notice anything but Don Carlos looked at his son closely.

"Rough game, my boy?" he said. "Come with me. We'll walk to El Centro and get us both a coffee. I need to stretch my legs."

As they slowly made their way along Eighth Street, Don Carlos said. "We had lunch with Don Francisco today, but your brother still did not call. I fear the worst." After a while, he said, "Don Francisco was telling me today about a group called MRR, the *Movimiento de Recuperación Revolucionaria*. Do you know about them?"

Oscar shook his head. "No Señor."

"They sound like an interesting organization. Apparently they still have many contacts and sources of information. Maybe they can get news of Carlos Jr. Check with your baseball friends, maybe one of them has contact with the MRR."

The reason that Oscar was covered with so many cuts and bruises was because he'd been fairly badly beaten by one of the mysterious Americans who had accompanied the training that weekend. Oscar had brought his camera with him for the first time that Saturday. He normally took his camera with him wherever he went and now that he felt comfortable with Raphael's people, he thought he might have some interesting shots, out in the wilderness of the Everglades.

There were two Americans among the group waiting for them when they reached their regular hammock and one of them introduced himself as Frank Bender "But you can call me 'Mr. B'." He was a heavy-set man of medium build, in his mid-fifties, with a very short crew cut. His eyes were hidden behind dark glasses and he spoke with a slightly German accent.

"Let me make one thing very clear" he said. "My friends and I are not members of the United States government. Whatever you might think, I have nothing to do with the United States government. I am only working for a powerful corporation that wants to fight communism. Understand?"

As soon as he saw Oscar's camera he grabbed it from his shoulder and, ripping-out the roll of film, he threw it on the ground. "What the hell is this boy? A fucking camera! You gonna take photos of us all and send them to Fidel? Are you some goddam spy?"

Turning to Raphael Sr. he shouted "What kind of Mickey Mouse operation are you running here Goddam it! Think this is all some kind of game?"

Raphael's father approached the American and took the camera from him. "I'm so sorry Mr. B. He's a good boy. He didn't know. He didn't think. You know how young boys are. Look, I'm going to lock it in my truck. It won't happen again."

Slightly mollified, the American watched them as they spent the morning demonstrating the various skills they had been learning. Gradually Oscar learned that Mr. B. was the group's paymaster and that he had brought a large supply of ammunition so that all of them were able to take several shots at the target.

Later in the afternoon, after watching them perform their unarmed combat exercises, Mr. B. suggested a bit of 'real world experience'. He pointed at Oscar and said "Let's see how tough you really are Mr. Spy-boy. What are you? Six-two? Broad shoulders, pretty-boy face. Bet you get all the little senoritas hot and bothered. Yeah? Let's see. Come on." He spread his arms wide apart and stood facing Oscar, adopting a relaxed stance. "Come at me boy. Give your worst. Hit me. Hurt me. Come on you little spic faggot!"

Embarrassed in front of all his friends that morning when the American had grabbed his camera, he'd been devastated when a whole expensive roll of film was destroyed so casually and brutally. That represented more than a month's worth of savings from the tips he got when he carried customers' grocery bags to their cars. His regular Publix paycheck went straight into the family bank account and he only kept the tips for himself. He reminded himself of his purpose in joining this group. He thought deeply and asked himself, as he often did, what his brother would do in such a situation.

Carlos had always taught him to acknowledge his emotions but to keep them in check. "That's why Papi sent us to Groton and not Belén" he would say. "To learn self-control. You don't want to be one of those hot-headed Latins." Belén was the most fashionable school in Cuba, where the elite sent their sons to be trained by the Jesuits. What Carlos did not mention is that he himself had been expelled from Belén which is why his father first sent him to Groton. Groton was the school that both Enriquez brothers attended in New England. "Look at all the jerks we know from Belén. Always fighting and arguing. Always red in the face from shouting, waving their arms. That's why the Americans make fun of us. Don't lose control brother" Carlos taught him. "Keep your eye on the goal. Don't let them see what you're planning and don't let them know what you're thinking."

And Oscar had kept his thoughts and his anger to himself all day, despite the evil looks and sly jibes that Mr. B seemed to be sending in his direction. But whatever genetic or testosterone mixture of emotions was boiling within him, Oscar kept the fury for this gringo bully under control until he heard the words 'little spic faggot'. That was too much. That's when he exploded and hurled himself, fists flailing towards his tormentor.

Frank Bender, of course knew precisely what he was doing and could have timed the explosion to the millisecond. He barely needed to move. He simply placed his fist where he knew that Oscar's nose was going to be, a split second before it arrived.

With his nose pouring blood, Oscar collapsed to the ground, slightly stunned, but he quickly recovered and sprang back to his feet, only to be knocked back down with a blow to the side of the head. Again he pulled himself up and again he was knocked down. Bender was not using all his strength nor going for the knock-out blow. He was just using his superior, size, experience and skill to keep jabbing and humiliating the little punk into submission. But Oscar refused to submit and kept getting back on his feet until Raphael Sr. pulled Bender aside, saying "Enough Mr. B. That's enough. Leave the kid alone. Let him be."

Bender stood back and just raised his fist at Oscar. "You bring that camera with you next week you little punk and I'll smash your face with it. Verstehst du? Capisci?"

But things became even worse the following Saturday. When Oscar arrived at the clearing with Raphael and his father just as the sun was rising, another group of men were already gathered, including Frank Bender, and all of them were armed with rifles slung over their shoulders. Even though the sun had barely risen, Bender's eyes were still hidden behind dark glasses. "Don't get any ideas punk" he said as he handed an M2 Carbine to Oscar. "You got no rounds in it."

The training that day was much more formal and militaristic than in previous sessions. Much of the morning was spent practicing drills. Standing and marching in formation. Holding, carrying and aiming their weapons. The men were equipped with a wide selection of weapons. From his ROTC training at Groton, Oscar recognized a couple of Springfields and a Winchester. Most of the men had M1s and M2s though Bender himself carried a Thompson M1A1 sub-machine gun.

"I know some of those guys from school in Havana" Raphael whispered to Oscar as they were all sitting on the ground eating their mid-day meal of black beans and rice. "They were in the *Agrupacion Catolica Universitaria* with me, the ACU. I wonder why there are so many of them here today."

"I wonder if they're part of the MRR?" Oscar asked. Turning to Raphael's father, Oscar said "Do we have any members of the MRR here Don Raphael?"

"MRR? What do you know about that?"

"I think it's the *Movimiento de Recuperación Revolucionaria*" Oscar said. "My father mentioned them. Do you know about them?"

Before Raphael Sr. could reply, Oscar was yanked to his feet by Frank Bender who had grabbed his shirt collar. Releasing his hold of his shirt, Bender slapped his hand across Oscar's face, so hard he almost lost his balance.

"I knew it. I knew he was a fucking spy. First sneaking his camera along and now asking questions about the MRR. Goddam it, we got a snake in our camp!"

Using his Thompson as a prod, Bender pushed Oscar towards the new arrivals who'd been sitting on the grass while they ate on the other side of the clearing. "Manuel, come here. We have a spy."

A clean-shaven young man, perhaps a dozen years older than Oscar rose to his feet. Not yet thirty, his eyes were much older than his body and Oscar felt that with his unblinking stare the man could see deep inside him. "What's the problem Mr. B?" he asked.

"Last week I caught this punk trying to photograph us all and now, just a few minutes ago I overheard him asking about the MRR."

The young man turned back to Oscar. "Is this true?" he asked. "Why did you want to know about the MRR?"

"My father wanted to know about them"

"Why?"

"He heard they had good contacts in Cuba. He thought they might be able to find news about my brother. My brother has vanished. We've had no word from him since October."

"Who is your brother?"

"He was a senator. His name is Carlos Enriquez."

At the sound of the name, the man's eyes narrowed and his body became tense. "Tell me about your family" he said.

"There's not much to say" Oscar began hesitantly. "There's just me and my brother. My parents came over after the revolution and my brother stayed behind to look after our property. I was already in the States. At school."

"How did you speak to your brother?"

"By phone. Every Saturday at noon."

"Did he ever mention Camilo Cienfuegos or Manuel Artime?"

"Yes. Camilo was a good friend of his. Carlos knew him before the revolution."

"And Artime"

Oscar shook his head.

"Where are your properties?"

"Well the family house is in Havana and we have some fincas in the country side."

"Where in Havana?"

"In Miramar. On Avenida Quinta."

"And your estates?"

"In Las Villas."

"Where?"

"The Sierra del Escambray near Santa Clara."

The man's body relaxed and moving forward, he hugged Oscar in a tight embrace.

"I am so sorry Oscar. I have very bad news for you. Carlos has been arrested. They are holding him in La Cabaña."

"Are you sure? How do you know?"

"My name is Manuel Artime and I worked closely with Camilo Cienfuegos. We fought together in the Sierra Maestra . We were both in the MR-26-7. We both believed in the revolution until the communists took over. I worked for the Minister of Agriculture and Camilo introduced me to your brother. I liked Carlos a lot. He worked with me on the Rural Commandos project. We'd modelled it a bit on the ACU," he pointed to the group of young men sprawled in the grass. "I don't know if it's true, but the rumor is that Che's people had placed a bomb on Camilo's plane. But what I do know is that just hours after Camilo's plane vanished, Che's G2 soldiers dragged your brother to a cell in La Cabaña."

With his arm around Oscar's shoulder, Manuel lead them over to a large log where they were able to sit comfortably. "To be honest Oscar. Your brother probably saved my life. It was only when I heard about his arrest that I decided to escape. Camilo vanishing at sea could have been an accident. I could live with that. But when I heard about his close friend Carlos' arrest, I knew they were closing in.

Anyone opposed to the communists is now considered a counter-revolutionary."

"Is my brother still alive?"

"Yes. There at least I have some good news for you. I got word just last week from someone who had seen him in the exercise yard. He's still being held at La Cabaña. If they were going to shoot him, Che would have done it right away."

"How did you escape?"

"I'd always been involved with the *Agrupacion Catolica Universitaria* – the ACU, so the Jesuits hid me for a few weeks while I organized the *Movement for Revolutionary Recovery* (MRR). Eventually Guevara's G-2 Secret Police started looking for me, so the Jesuits disguised me as a priest and then slipped me into the US Embassy." He grinned at the memory, "I even carried a hollowed-out Bible, with a pistol hidden inside."

"So how did you get here?" Oscar asked.

"The CIA smuggled me onto a Honduran freighter, still dressed as a priest, and a few days later I was in New York. And that's how I met Gerry Droller here."

Oscar looked puzzled. "You mean Mr. B? Frank Bender?"

Manuel laughed. "OK. Mr. B. then. I swear this man's had more aliases than I've had hot dinners." Lowering his voice, he added. "And he's started more revolutions and brought down more governments than you can imagine. He might be an arrogant jerk and a bully, and he might pretend to be an independent businessman - but he's CIA through and through and he can make things happen. When that old fuddy-duddy Eisenhower finally leaves the White house in January and Kennedy becomes President, Castro's days will be numbered. Mr. B. has assured me that we'll have all the money and guns we'll ever need. They are already setting up some proper training camps for us in Guatemala. When Kennedy replaces

Eisenhower, the Cuban people will finally have a good friend in the White House. You'll see. "

Standing up again, Manuel turned to face Oscar and looked him squarely in the eye. "From what I know of your brother Oscar, I know you are just the type of guy we need. Are you ready to commit? It might need several months of secret work. You won't be able to contact your parents. It will be rough. It will be dangerous. But I would just love to be there with you when we break into La Cabaña and set Carlos free again."

Oscar reached-out and gripped Manuel by the shoulders. His eyes were blinking back the tears. "I'm with you Manuel. Whatever it takes. I'm one-hundred percent with you. I'm totally committed."

The two men embraced again. "When you get home, you can tell your parents the bad news about Carlos. It's better they should know instead of waiting for him to walk in the door every day. Don't give them any details but tell them you will be joining some friends to try and change things. Let them know you will be away for a while. It might be months and they won't hear from you – but that's nothing to worry about. But it is really important that you don't tell them anything you've learned here. I'm not saying you can't trust your father, but Castro has spies at every little coffee and cigar shop along Eighth Street. He has eyes and ears everywhere and he knows we are plotting a comeback."

"Is that what MRR is then?" Oscar asked.

"Yes. It's the Movement to Recover the Revolution" he said. "From the communists."

Don Carlos nodded stoically when Oscar told him the news. "It's what I suspected" he said. "There was no other explanation. At least he's alive." They were walking slowly along Eighth Street towards El Centro for a coffee. "Best not say anything to your mother" Don Carlos said. "Better to let her live in hope." Oscar's mother attended mass everyday now, at the Church where she met a group of fellow exiles who all comforted each other.

"What about if I have to go away Papi."

"Don't worry about it. I'll cover for you. I'll tell some story about you going back to Groton on a special scholarship."

Don Carlos stopped walking and leaning on his cane, faced his son and gripped his hand. "I don't want to know where you're going or what you'll be doing because I don't trust myself not to say the wrong thing to the wrong person. But whatever you're doing, I want you to know I'm proud of you. I know you're doing it for Carlitos and for the family. God be with you my son."

Oscar received the call in May, 1960 and was told to be packed and to be waiting by 8:00AM, in a parking lot outside the White Castle burger joint on West Flagler at 27th Avenue. He was collected by a large open truck with several other men, including Raphael's father, sitting together in the back. Like Oscar, all the men wore stout boots and were dressed in dark, long sleeved shirts. The noise of the diesel engine made conversation difficult as they drove across the Everglades to Fort Meyers on the Gulf Coast, and in any event, the men seemed mostly occupied with their own thoughts. Many of the men were leaving their wives and young children, none of them knew where they were going or even who they were working for. Perhaps the whole thing was a Fidelista conspiracy and they would be shipped back to Cuba, tortured and shot. The truck drove through the center of Fort Meyers along Edwards Drive to the yacht basin on the Caloosahatchee River. Jumping down from the truck they joined a small group of men, including Manuel Artime, waiting on the jetty.

Manuel walked over to shake hands with them all. "You brought your camera?" he asked Oscar who nodded with a grin. "Good man." Turning to Frank Bender, he called out. "We've got our official photographer Mr. B. We need good records, if we're going to make history."

Bender turned his head and spat, before saying "OK. Quit your yapping. Let's move it!"

The ten men picked up their bags and followed Bender towards the quay where they boarded a small motor boat. Within minutes they had cast off and were headed down the Caloosahatchee River, past Cape Coral towards the open waters of the Gulf of Mexico. As they approached the small beach town of Sanibel they veered to the north, passing Captiva on their port side and keeping Pine Island to starboard. Leaving all signs of human habitation far behind them, they motored past pristine beaches covered with the gleam of crushed sea-shells, followed by miles of thick mangroves, their long spindly fingers reaching out into the deep water channels between the islands. Except for the steady, deep thrumping sound of their motor or the occasional splash of a mullet jumping out of the water, they were surrounded by silence, and the men sat quietly, alone in their thoughts. Behind the mangroves, the vegetation was a dark impenetrable forest where no birds sang. After less than an hour, the boat arrived at a long wooden jetty of what appeared to be a deserted island. Bender climbed onto the dock and fastened the boat to one of the pilings.

"Welcome to Useppa Island gentlemen" he said. "Now the real adventure begins."

Eighteen, Greenhaven, 636 Canal Drive, 2013

The Doyle's coral-rock home was set in half an acre of lush, tropical landscaping leading down to a sixty foot wooden dock where their trawler was moored. Built before the days of air conditioning, it was typical of the earlier settler homes, constructed with thick coral walls, a gabled roof and a wide, shaded porch encircling the whole house as protection from the omnipresent Florida sun.

Cars were parked haphazardly all along Canal Drive and a couple of off-duty policemen tried to impose some semblance of order as the guests walked from their cars towards the Doyle's coral house. Lady Sanders had parked her open top, midnight-blue, 1954 Jaguar XK120 in the road in front of 514 Canal Drive, a mock Tudor house which sported a "Tom Adams for Mayor. A name you can trust." sign on the front lawn.

"Oh dear" she said. "I hope they won't get cross that we're going to the Martinez fund-raiser and toss a dead cat or something nasty into the car."

"At the very least" George replied, "they're going to tell Tom that you're fraternizing with the opposition. Your car is hardly anonymous Catherine; they are unlikely to overlook it."

"That's not a problem. Tom already knows I'm going. He wants me to learn all I can." She raised an eyebrow conspiratorially and said, "I'm his Mata Hari."

The sign-in desk was located just outside the front door of the house, in the shade of the wide overhanging porch. It was a six-foot, folding table covered with name badges, lists of guests and a couple of sign-in sheets. There was also a pile of envelopes marked 'Donations'. Posters and signs with "Orestes Martinez for Mayor. A Time for Change" were everywhere and there was a stack of signs for guests to take home and place in their own front yards.

"It's Lady Sanders, isn't it?" said Margaret Doyle, who was sitting behind the table, ticking off names and writing out name tags with a blue, felt-tip marker.

"Yes. And you are Mrs. Doyle if I remember correctly. I think we met at that breakfast thingy at the Country Club last month. What a lovely home you have."

"Thank you, Lady Sanders, and please call me Margaret."

Lady Sanders smiled warmly at her. "Thank you" she said.

"I've only myself to blame" she said to George afterwards, as the two of them moved indoors, clutching their 'Donation Envelopes'. "I should have known that we'd have these annoying, sticky name-tags.

I would have worn something less low-cut if I'd remembered. Now I've nowhere to stick it."

It was a warm and balmy evening and so Lady Sanders had not even brought a wrap for her shoulders which were protected only by the spaghetti straps of her light cotton dress. Dressed with the unassuming simplicity which only the extremely wealthy can afford, her cerulean blue dress showed her slim, lithe body to full advantage. A daily regimen of morning tennis and visits to the gym had given her the looks of a woman in her mid-thirties rather than the mid-fifties which her British Passport claimed. "I'll just stick it on my purse" she said. "Come on George, let's go and find the bar, I'm absolutely parched."

There were at least two-hundred guests at the Martinez fundraiser. Many of them were in the main drawing room, grouped around the bar while others stood in groups outside on the terrace. There was a second bar on the far side of the swimming pool and several small round tables offering a selection of tapas and hors d'oeuvres. The rhythmic sounds of salsa and rumba drifted across the wide sloping lawn from the Doyle's trawler where a quartet of musicians were playing on the foredeck. Other guests, drinks in hand were lounging in the main cabin or leaning over the rails watching the manatees, slowly drifting in the deep water of the canal.

Maurice Mayhew was standing on the wooden-dock with Don Westlake and Harriet Brownmiller where they had been watching the manatees. "Seems a bloody big boat for the canal" he said. "How on earth does Raymond ever get it up here? I mean, there's two bridges between here and the Greenhaven Waterway. Can't imagine how he does it."

"Very, very slowly. No drinks and only at low tide" Don Westlake said. "Dorothy and I've both gone with him a couple of times and I can tell you it's been a close run thing. He can only do it at low tide and Raymond won't have a drink till he's clear out into Biscayne Bay. Same coming back. The rest of us are all slugging it down but Raymond won't touch a drop till he's been through the two bridges. Even in the middle of the canal, where the clearance is greatest, there's still only just a couple of inches to spare."

"Shall we move back up to the house?" Harriet suggested. "This awful Cuban music is getting on my nerves."

"Really?" Don said. "I rather like it. I was just thinking of asking you for a dance."

"You'll do no such thing" Harriet snapped, but secretly pleased by the suggestion. "There's too much Cuban music, Cuban food and Cuban language these days. I swear, they are taking over. And now we have this man Martinez running for mayor. I hope I don't have to talk to him."

"So why on earth did you come this evening Harriet?"

"Herbert said it's our duty. He takes his role as City Commissioner very seriously. He said we have to hear all the candidates and listen to all their positions. But I don't think it's my duty to listen to their vulgar music."

"Anyway, how come the Doyle's are hosting this fundraiser then?" Maurice asked.

"Old friends" Don said. "Raymond said he's known Martinez for years. His law firm did some work for him back in the day and then they became friends; mutual interest in boats I think. Trawlers and such. Said he thought this would be a good way to introduce him to the community."

"He should be running in Hialeah, not Greenhaven" Harriet muttered.

As the group crossed the lawn, towards the swimming pool, Maurice spotted Lady Sanders standing at the outside bar. "Come with me Don" he said. "Time for a refill. Can I get you another drink Harriet?"

"Lady Sanders, how nice to see you again. George, good to see you. What a beautiful evening for a fundraiser."

"We were just admiring the pool" Lady Sanders said. "Checking to see if there were any more dead bodies or alligators." Looking up, she saw Raymond Doyle approaching them at the bar.

"Mr. Doyle" she said. "How lovely to see you again. What a lovely home you have. The garden and the view are delightful. I was just telling my friends here about the exciting history of your swimming pool. Did they ever find out whose body it was, trespassing on your property?"

Doyle shook his head. "Nope. Still a mystery I'm afraid. I always ask Chief Lacroix whenever I see him and he always tells me the case isn't closed and they're still working on it." He shrugged, "But it's been well over a year now, so I'm not holding my breath."

Turning around, he put his hand on the arm of the tall man wearing a light-weight, grey suit, who had accompanied him from the house. Lady Sanders guessed him to be in his mid-sixties but still fit looking with a thick mane of hair, slicked-back over his ears, broad shoulders and piercing blue eyes above a thin white scar across his cheek.

"Lady Sanders, I'd like to introduce you to our guest of honor, Dr. Orestes Martinez. Orestes is an old friend of mine from way back and Margaret and I are delighted to be hosting this fund-raiser for him."

Lady Sanders took Martinez's proffered hand and smiled. "I'm delighted to meet you Dr. Martinez. I'm very much looking forward to hearing your presentation and your plans for our little community."

Martinez made an imperceptible bow before releasing her hand, his steel-blue eyes, holding hers in a smile. "I look forward to presenting my case" he said. "I hope I might even persuade you to vote for me."

She smiled. "Well I have to tell you that I'm an old close friend of Tom Adams, but I will certainly enjoy hearing your case." Turning to Doyle, she said. "It's a very lucky community that has two good and qualified men competing for mayor."

Turning back to Martinez she added "I just hope you have more luck than the last man who stood here wearing a grey suit."

Martinez looked back at her expressionlessly. "I beg your pardon" he said.

"Did Mr. Doyle not tell you about the alligator in the pool?" she asked.

"Oh yes" he said. "The dead body. Wearing a pin-stripe suit if I recall. I'm afraid I had quite forgotten. Well thank you Lady Sanders, indeed I hope I do have better luck than that poor fellow."

About ten minutes later, with the sound of a bell, the guests were all summoned into the living room where Raymond Doyle and Orestes Martinez stood in a far corner facing the room. The guests who could not find space inside, stood on the terrace in groups beside the open French windows.

Following a short introduction from Raymond Doyle, Martinez addressed the room. It was immediately obvious that public speaking was second nature to him and he quickly captivated the whole room. He very quickly but modestly summarized his previous success with his company, AHCU, American Health Care United and then explained how he had sold it just a few weeks previously and was now a man of leisure.

"In the interest of full disclosure, ladies and gentlemen, I have a shameful confession to make. I would rather reveal the truth now, in the early stages of my campaign, rather than have it emerge later." There was a silence in the room as he paused to drink some water.

"I have actually lived here in Greenhaven for twenty-three years but, apart from Raymond and Margaret, I know hardly anybody. I'm not a member of any of the local clubs or associations. I'm not on the board of any homeowners group, I have simply never participated in the life of our community. I have been a parasite. I have been reaping all of the benefits of living in this most beautiful of cities and yet I have contributed nothing. I have been a taker, not a giver."

Pausing for more water, he continued, "In my defense I would argue that I have just been too busy developing my corporation. Although my home is in Greenhaven, most nights I have spent in hotel rooms elsewhere. Most of the past twenty years has been spent on the road, traveling, working. Too preoccupied to live a proper life, to form friendships, to participate in the community." Again he paused and looked slowly around the room. "I never even had time to marry, to have children; to raise a family…. And now of course, it's too late."

Allowing for a moment of quiet reflection around the room, he then shrugged his arms apart "But of course that is a pathetic excuse: too busy making money to actually enjoy life. Ladies and gentlemen, I am not asking for your sympathy, nor even for your understanding. I made the choices and I must accept the consequences. However," and once again he paused to cast his steel-blue eyes around the gathering. "I am asking for your support while I try to make up for lost time. I don't know how many years that I have got left, but I do know I have a tremendous amount of energy, I have far more money than I can ever spend and I have a boundless desire to make up for all the wasted years by becoming a significant and active part of this community. I want to be a full-time mayor, working 24/7. I have no law office to go to, I have no outside interests or distractions. I want to devote myself to making Greenhaven great again."

After outlining a number of proposals, based on the major issues that the City Manager had provided, including the controversial 'Art in Public Spaces' dispute, Martinez opened the floor to questions.

His experience as a public figure was swiftly apparent. He answered questions concerning traffic circles, public parking and open-air café seating with the aplomb of a seasoned politician.

"What would you put as your top priority if you become mayor, Dr. Martinez. What project would you like to leave as your legacy to the city?"

"The Palace Hotel. I would love to restore the Palace Hotel. Each time I drive past it and see the scaffolding and boarded-up windows I feel a deep hurt. I'm told that the city will have to tear it down if we cannot raise the funds to carry-out certain basic repairs. The Palace Hotel is one of the city's architectural gems and to destroy it, I believe, would be a tragedy."

"So how do you envisage a restored Palace sir? We already have hotel vacancies in Greenhaven. We are no longer a tourist destination. The hotel might be beautifully restored, but it would still stand empty."

"No. That's the whole point" Martinez said, becoming animated. "The restored Palace would become the very engine which will drive the tourist revival. The city needs tourists; we need them to fill our hotels and restaurants. We need them to spend their shopping dollars. That's how the city raises revenue to invest in the infrastructure; the infrastructure needed to attract the tourists and to improve the living standards and amenities for our residents."

"But how would the Palace achieve all that – even if restored to its former glory?"

"I plan to rename it The Tropicana."

"Like the Havana nightclub?"

"Exactly. The Tropicana was the most famous and the most successful nightclub in the world. The shows were legendary. All the biggest names in the world wanted to visit: European nobility, middle-eastern sheiks, captains of industry, film stars – they all flocked to The Tropicana."

"But then we'd just be competing with South Beach" somebody objected.

"Not at all. We would be defining ourselves as an adult alternative to South Beach. Let's face it, South Beach is loud and noisy and vulgar. Everything that Greenhaven is not. South Beach is full of that awful hip-hop music. It's all urban-vibe and inner-city chic. It's all celebrity chefs with shaved heads, nose rings and tattoos. That's not who we are. That's not what the Tropicana represents. The Tropicana is for grown-ups. It's for men in smart jackets and women in elegant dresses. It's for people like us; - not wife-beater T-shirts and nipple-piercings."

"So let me understand you, Dr. Martinez," Harriet Brownmiller could restrain herself no longer. "You plan to change Greenhaven, with cafes out on the sidewalks and the old Palace Hotel becoming a Cuban nightclub. And that music that was being played earlier down on the yacht; will that be getting played everywhere, out on the streets?"

Martinez smiled "I'm afraid that's way beyond my purlieu Ma'am. But I'm sure there are all sorts of city ordinances and noise restrictions controlling what music may be played in public spaces. But otherwise, yes, I am in favor of change. We don't need to move in the same direction as Miami Beach, indeed we should not, but we do need to move into the twenty-first century. We need to attract more visitors. We need to change."

Nineteen: Playa Giron, Cuba, April 1961

There was a gentle sound of waves lapping along the length of sand, which reminded Oscar of his childhood dog, Lucy, drinking water from her bowl on lazy afternoons when he was home sick from school, sitting in the kitchen with Marialena the family cook. The lap, lap, lap of the waves was followed by a gentle hiss as the waters receded across the sand, back into the warm Caribbean before returning with yet another gentle assault upon the beach.

"Marialena look. Poor Lucy is hungry. She wants one of your *Torticas de Moron*. Poor Lucy."

Of course Marialena would pretend to be cross but Oscar knew that eventually he would get one of her delicious bon-bons after Lucy had received hers. Those warm, comforting days, sitting in the family kitchen seemed far-off now. Distant memories of an impossible dream; but listening to the lapping of the waves, keeping his eyes closed and picturing Lucy's tongue flicking steadily into her dish while Marialena stood at the kitchen table, stirring her wooden spoon determinedly around the large pale beige china bowl, comforted him. His memories helped dull the crippling pain of the shattered ankle, and the worrisome drip of blood from the bullet in his right shoulder which he could feel slithering slowly down his back.

'Look around you' he told himself. Could there be - anywhere in the world - a more beautiful and peaceful place in which to die?

And indeed, even without dying, Oscar was already in paradise. He lay on a beautiful, deserted beach with his back propped against a solitary palm tree, maybe a dozen feet from the high-tide line of seaweed and broken shells. The sand was soft and almost white, but hard and firm where the tide gently stroked it with a loving caress. The steady lapping sound was almost like children's laughter, as the waves with amorous gaiety, spread smoothly across the sand with knowing intent, covering it with a sensual caress then briefly retreating before returning a moment later, hissing knowingly as the caress inched voluptuously further along the beach. The sound was so restful that Oscar's pains seemed to fade away as his mind drifted and all he wanted was to lie here forever and listen to the laughter of the waves as they caressed the sand in such a slow, curvaceous rhythm, touching it all over, then slipping away and whispering back for yet another soft and lingering kiss.

Lucy had been his brother Carlos' dog, but Oscar was in charge of her when Carlos was away at school in America. When Carlos returned home for vacation, it was hard to tell who was most excited to greet him, Oscar or Lucy. Oscar often wished he had a tail to wag like Lucy, to show how much he loved his older brother while, laughing, Carlos would pretend to lift Oscar into the air by his ears, like he did with Lucy.

Memories of Carlos brought him back to sudden reality; the dull throbbing pain in his shoulder and the agony of the broken bones in his foot reminded him that Lucy was long dead and buried and Carlos was still in prison. Oscar had failed to save his brother. The mission had failed. And now he was waiting to die.

It had been a disaster from the very start. Even the training had been cursed with lack of organization and lack of equipment. No sooner had the men been transported to Useppa Island than Mr. B., aka. Frank Bender vanished for a couple of months leaving behind him no clear chain of command and no documented training program. Luckily many of the men, like Manuel Artime, were experienced fighters and had fought alongside the MR-26-7 in the mountains of the Sierra Maestra. They were thus able, not only to share their own knowledge and skills but they were also able to describe the tactics and strategies of Castro's militias. From time to time there were unannounced visits from various anonymous Americans. Sometimes they would offer a name such as Carl Jenkins or Freddie Goudie but usually they were just identified as 'Jimmy', 'Carl', 'Seabee' 'Big John', 'Bob' or 'Pat'. Like Frank Bender, all the Americans had closely shaved military haircuts and wore extremely dark sunglasses which they never removed, even at night. None of the Americans claimed that they worked for the US Government, in fact they were most emphatic that they did NOT work for the US Government, nor did they ever mention the CIA, other than to deny being members of it. They merely presented themselves as communist-hating friends of the oppressed Cuban people who just happened not to speak any Spanish.

Despite the lack of clear organization from their American paymasters, the Cubans had created their own chain of command. By common assent, Manuel Artime was recognized as the group's political leader. Based on his previous military experience, José Alfredo 'Pepe' Pérez San Román was made military commander and for similar reasons, Erneido Andrés Oliva became his second in command.

It was Jose "Pepe" Andreu Santos who suggested that, in order to establish a legitimate military unit, each man be given a serial number, but it was Manuel Artime who suggested starting with the number 2501 which was the number which Santos took for himself. This way, if word ever got out through informants, or if any of them were captured, the group would appear to be 2,500 men stronger than it really was. Jose Diaz Pou was 2502, Vicente Blanco-Capote was 2503, Carlos Rafael Santana Estevez was 2506 and so on. Manuel Artime was given the number 2550, 'Pepe' San Román was 2538, Erneido Oliva was 2641, and Oscar found himself way down the line in the 3000s.

After a couple of months, despite conflicting messages from the various visiting Americans about their plans and their ultimate goals, the men were developing a routine of tough physical exercises, beginning well before sunrise, as well as undergoing rigorous training with a wide variety of weapons. It was just when the whole group seemed to be coming together as a well-trained and disciplined unit that Mr. B. arrived, unannounced in early July and told everyone to pack-up and ship-out.

Arriving at a deserted section of the Fort Meyers harbor at 3:00AM, the men were packed into the rear of two large military trucks and driven through the night to South Florida's Homestead air force base. No sooner had they arrived, at a remote part of the air field than they were loaded onto a Douglas C-54 Skymaster - a relic of the World War – which immediately, if ponderously, rose into the air. They eventually discovered that their new home for the next two months was Fort Gulick in Panama, a clandestine CIA training center where they received very intense paramilitary training. Oscar, as a boy had been mocked by his brother for being clumsy and soft-hearted like a girl but now, after just a month at Fort Gulick, he could slip silently in the dark of night, through an obstacle course and use his bare hands to kill without a sound.

On August 22, 1960 the group, now numbering more than a hundred, were packed aboard another of the CIA's C-54s and flown to Guatemala where they were housed at Finca Helvetia, a remote, sprawling estate in the mountains, renamed Base Trax. By the end of the month, the group had expanded to include about 1,700 Cubans. It was a strange mixture; some were ex-military from Batista's army and police, some were ex-guerillas, disillusioned with Castro's Revolution while many of the others were university student members of the *Directorio Revolucionario Estudiantil*. Each of the three groups regarded the others with suspicion if not ill-concealed contempt. Rather than relaxing after the move from Panama, the training exercises intensified and each day began on the dot at 5:00am with calisthenics and running. At 8:45, classes in radio and telegram communications were followed by weapons training, then drills and unarmed combat. At noon lunch was held; classes resumed at 2pm and ended at 6pm; dinner at 7pm and then a free evening to listen to the Voice of America with lights-out at 9:45pm. Day after exhausting day.

Weapons training included four-deuce mortars, 75mm recoilless rifles, bazookas, surplus M1 Garands from World War II, machine guns, pistols and five M-4 Sherman tanks. On some days, training included parachute jumping from the C-54 and other days they were shipped to a remote part of Guatemala's Pacific coast where they practiced wading ashore from some rusty LCU landing craft left over from World War II. The most senior training officer was a CIA agent named "Mr. Carl" who walked with a limp and, those few times he removed his sunshades, was noted for his penetrating green eyes. Like all the other trainers, Bill, Bob and Nick, none of the Americans spoke a single word of Spanish, nor did they appear inclined to learn any.

The first tragedy struck soon after their arrival in Guatemala. In early September, a group of about twenty Cubans, led by Roberto San Román , were hiking through the mountains to practice rock-climbing when a sudden rock slide made one of the recruits, Carlos Rafael Santana Estevez, lose his balance and topple over the edge of a cliff. It was a two-thousand foot drop and it required two exhausting days to recover the body. 'Carlyle' as he was affectionately known had been one of the original volunteers back on Useppa Island and he was easily the most popular man in the group. On returning to camp it was Oscar's idea to rename the group *Brigade 2506* in honor of their dead comrade. Carlyle's serial number in the group had been 2506, reflecting his position as one of the founder members. "Excellent idea Oscar" Artime had told him. "This way Carlyle and his sacrifice will be remembered forever." San Román designed an emblem for the brigade with the number 2506 superimposed on a Christian cross.

But despite the rigorous training and the enthusiasm of the men, the long-term objectives and plans of their American paymasters remained as elusive and inconsistent as ever. Some days it would appear that a massive invasion was planned, reminiscent of the D-Day landings in France and supported with overwhelming American air power. On other days the plan appeared to involve the clandestine landings of small groups of well-equipped men at various spots around the island in preparation for a later, well-armed and well-coordinated national uprising. The training fluctuated depending on the current plan; alternating between guerrilla training for clandestine landings and military training in the event of an invasion.

There was serious talk by Mr. Carl of an American bombing run against Havana followed by a parachute attack on the main military centers such as La Cabaña and Campamento Columbia. With the support of Artime, Oscar immediately volunteered for parachute training so that he could be part of the team liberating La Cabaña. The parachute attack was to be combined with a submarine attack on Havana harbor. The sheer audacity of such a large-scale plan temporarily bolstered morale among the volunteers and calmed the simmering rivalries. Each night, Oscar happily dreamed of kicking-in the door of Carlos' cell and liberating him in person.

Two weeks later, Mr. B. arrived at the camp with maps of Santiago de Cuba on the south-eastern corner of Cuba, at the other end of the island from Havana. "This is where we will go in, not Havana" he announced to the leading commanders, a group that now included Oscar. "This is where Teddy Roosevelt and his Rough Riders won the Spanish American War. Hell, this is gonna be our battle of San Juan Hill! Those fucking commie bastards won't even know what hit them."

The lack of any clear direction had a demoralizing effect on the men and accentuated the existing tensions between ex-members of the MR-26-7 and the ex-Batista military. It has been said that if you bring two Cubans together you have an argument, put three together and you have a revolution and bring a whole group together and you have a civil war. The civil war among the members of Brigade 2506 occurred in January 1961 when a whole group of the fighters refused to serve under 'Pepe' San Román, objecting that he had been appointed by the Americans not by the Cubans. The problem was only solved when the twelve ringleaders of the revolt were removed from the camp by the Americans and held at Peten, a secret CIA prison camp in the remote jungles of northern Guatemala.

After the mini-revolt had been suppressed, morale improved as the group's plans and strategy solidified, and by February the invasion campaign was clear and agreed upon by all involved. The date of the invasion was set for early March and would begin with the US air force bombing all the Cuban airfields and destroying all the Cuban planes. This would be followed by the actual invasion with a force of about eighteen-hundred trained Cuban fighters with all their equipment, including tanks. The invading force would be landed on the wide, firm, sandy beaches of the town of Trinidad on the island's southern coast, almost halfway between Havana and Santiago. If all went well, the population of Trinidad would join with the rebels as they marched on Havana, picking-up more supporters along the route. At the very worst, the town of Trinidad was in the foothills of the Escambray Mountains and would provide a refuge where the Brigadistas could regroup. In addition, Trinidad was already home to a large group of American trained, anti-Castro guerrillas.

Oscar was very familiar with the town of Trinidad which was a beautiful old Colonial city not far from the Enriquez family estate near Santa Clara. He had some old school friends and several cousins still living there and he knew they would be sympathetic to the cause. Manuel Artime was also familiar with Trinidad and many of his recruits in the *Commandos Rurales* were based there. Both Oscar and Manuel had become close friends during the months of training and both felt very positive about the Trinidad plan.

It had been almost a year since Oscar had said goodbye to his parents, it had been ten months of non-stop physical challenges and training. Not quite eighteen years old, Oscar was no longer a boy; more than a man, he had become a lean, mean, killing machine. But now the long wait was finally over, all that training was going to be put to use and Oscar was going to rescue his big brother from Castro's Hell on Earth.

In mid-March 1961, the plans were changed again. President Kennedy felt that Trinidad was too 'public'; it would look like a blatant American act of aggression. Despite the bombastic rhetoric of the Presidential election when he criticized Eisenhower for not doing enough to oppose Castro, once in office, Kennedy was far less effectual than Ike. Manipulated by his State Department and protective of his public image, JFK was a disaster.

Kennedy wanted the invasion to take place at night, discreetly; somewhere remote where there were few people and little resistance. Bowing to Kennedy's ambivalence and without telling the members of Brigade 2506, the CIA had selected a place about one hundred miles to the west of Trinidad for the invasion. It was a remote almost uninhabited inlet which was separated from the rest of the country by a vast, impregnable swamp. The name of the inlet was *Bahía de cochinos* – or Bay of Pigs.

Twenty: Greenhaven Museum 2013

George Attwood and Mayor Thomas Adams were sitting in Lady Sanders' office where the three of them were enjoying a late afternoon cup of tea. George was extremely proud of his Royal Doulton, bone china tea set and would never allow any piece of it to be contaminated by a tea bag. George would only brew one carefully measured, loose spoonful of Earl Grey tea-leaves in his tea pot. The water from the kettle was poured into the pot, over the tea leaves only at the very precise moment of boiling while the sound of the kettle's whistle was still ringing in his ears.

"These are rather nice cookies Catherine" Adams said. "They go great with the tea."

Lady Sanders sighed and rolled her eyes at George.

"You know very well Tom" she said. "They are biscuits, not cookies. In fact they are McVitie's chocolate digestives that I have had specially sent over from Fortnum & Mason's in London, along with my supply of Stilton cheese. If you call them cookies again, I won't let you have any more."

"I'm sorry Catherine. I promise I will improve. I can't help being an ignorant American. So anyway, tell me about my rival. What am I up against with the Cuban mafia? Is he going to take over the city?"

"He's not in the least bit Mafia" Lady Sanders said. "He's extremely well-mannered and sophisticated. I'm quite positive that Dr. Martinez would never dream of referring to McVitie's Digestives as 'cookies'."

"What Catherine means" George interrupted, "is that he is tall, broad shouldered with blue eyes, and his accent is more, New

England Brahmin than Cuban. Also that he is unmarried and filthy rich."

"Thank you, George. It is such a comfort to me, knowing that I have somebody who can speak for me, and so sensitively interpret my innermost thoughts. Now bugger-off and make us some more tea."

"Yes, my ladyship. And shall I bring us some more biscuits as well?"

"I don't think that will be necessary - though maybe you should bring a peanut butter and jelly sandwich for our guest."

While George was brewing a fresh pot of tea, Adams again asked about the recent fundraiser at the Doyle's house. "Seriously Catherine, what did you think? Laura doesn't want me to run again but I don't want to step down if the City is going to be taken-over by some vulgar Cuban crook."

"Really Tom. I didn't know you were so racist. Just because the poor man is Cuban, doesn't mean he's a crook."

"No. No. Of course not. The two things are entirely separate, but whatever his nationality, there are some rather unsavory stories circulating which reflect badly on his honesty."

"Such as?"

"They're all connected to his business, the AHCU."

"American Health Care United. But he's no longer connected with it. He's sold all his interest in it."

"Exactly. But, word is that AHCU is under investigation by the Justice Department."

"Really? Why would that be? I thought it was one of the biggest and most successful health-care providers in the country."

"Well there are no formal charges yet, but word is that the corporate success has been built upon Medicare fraud. Word around the courthouse is that AHCU has been falsely billing the Federal

Government for years. That's why Martinez sold-off all his shares and has completely separated himself."

"Hmm. Interesting. And if he was mayor of Greenhaven of course, then he would look entirely respectable." She paused before adding, "Apart from being Cuban of course. Not that he looks Cuban. His hair wasn't greased back, and he wasn't wearing a guayabera or even a 'wife-beater'. He was actually wearing a most respectable suit and tie. Really Tom, you Americans, I love you dearly, but you're all so incredibly racist. Everybody in this country comes from somewhere else. What's wrong with having a mayor who comes from Cuba? I mean I know that you can trace your Adams' family-line back generations – they probably came over on the Mayflower - or possibly even the Ark - but they still came over. Whether you arrive on the Mayflower or on a rubber raft, you're still an immigrant, hoping to achieve the American Dream. I mean, take Phillipe for example, he came over here as a penniless Haitian orphan. Now look at him: he's Greenhaven's Chief of Police. So what's wrong with having a Cuban mayor?"

"I personally don't have a problem with him being Cuban, Catherine. But there is a general sense that the Cubans are taking over South Florida. One by one they are becoming mayors and commissioners of all our communities. I believe that Greenhaven is the only city south of Palm Beach that has not had a Cuban mayor. People are upset when shop assistants and plumbers or gardeners don't speak English; they worry our values are being eroded and we are losing our culture."

"Oh really Tom. You sound like that snobby Harriet Brownmiller. What culture are you losing? Sitting on the couch watching Celebrity Apprentice and The Kardashians? I can assure you that Dr. Martinez speaks perfect English..." she smiled. "Despite having an American accent."

She turned her head as George reappeared in the room with the tea tray, "And notwithstanding George's impertinent teasing; yes, I did find him a most charming man. I don't know about all these criminal rumors, but in terms of how he speaks and presents himself, I found him perfectly acceptable. Obviously, I would prefer to see you as mayor Tom, but if Laura persuades you not to run, then I think Dr. Martinez will be a very fine and dignified alternative."

"What about you George?" Adams asked. "Do you think he'd be OK as mayor?"

"I agree with Catherine. I was impressed with the man. He looks you in the eye, he speaks well and he certainly seemed well informed on all the major issues. I liked him. However," George paused while he considered his wording, "I am concerned about some of the stories I hear about his financial background and the sudden sale of AHCU."

"What are you hearing?"

Once again, George paused thoughtfully to consider his words. "The trouble with rumors is that they take on a life of their own and before long, a piece of idle gossip has become irrefutable fact. Just me repeating such rumors to you only adds to their credibility."

"Good" said Lady Sanders. "Now you've got that off your chest George and eased your conscience, you can give us the skinny. What have you heard?"

"I was talking to Anna Hartman, you know, my golf buddy Sergeant Hartman, and she's been working on Medicare fraud cases for the past year or so. She was saying that a lot of her cases and leads, all seem to point towards AHCU or its subsidiaries. She couldn't tell me much but she says the FBI are looking into it full time. She thinks there's going to be a big court case very soon. She told me she's testified before a Grand Jury in Miami on four separate occasions this past two months alone.

"Well" Adams said. "As you say George. It's all rumor and idle speculation. Until charges are brought, and evidence is presented, it would be wrong for us to judge the man. But what about his plans for the city? Old man Connolly claims that Martinez is going to change everything in the city. According to him, there will be bolita lottery runners in the streets and cock-fighting on the city golf course."

"Actually, he did say Santeria was going to be declared the new religion and that chicken sacrifices would be performed at City Hall." She paused to shake her head. "Honestly Tom. You old WASP families will believe anything about the Hispanics. Of course he didn't say anything of the sort. He offered a list of very sensible suggestions. His emphasis seemed to be on improving the financial health of the City and then reinvesting the increased revenues in basic infrastructure. He's going to reduce the car access in the High Street to one lane in each direction and widen the sidewalks to encourage cafés to spread out like they do in Paris and build benches for people to sit and linger. He wants to encourage tourism. He wants to make Greenhaven a destination for gourmet dining and he plans to restore the Palace Hotel."

"Yes, he wants to make it a nightclub" said George. "He wants to recreate Havana's Tropicana nightclub. You know the sort of thing, dancing girls, sequins, flash and flesh. They even have a popular song they want to play: *y tiene tremeno culo*"

"What does that mean?"

"The girl with a big bum."

"Oh dear. I don't see that going down very well with our voters. That's exactly what old Connolly has been warning us about. Salsa joints and strip bars."

"Oh George is just pulling your leg. Martinez suggested nothing of the sort. He wants to bring back the glamor to Greenhaven. Just as the Tropicana brought all the international sophisticates to Havana in the 1950s, he wants to attract the same free-spending sophisticates to Greenhaven in the twenty-first century. I see nothing wrong with that. I remember my parents used to take the Queen Mary over to New York when I was growing up and they would always include a visit to Havana and the Tropicana. I was so jealous. It always seemed so grown-up and sophisticated."

Raising the teapot to pour both men another cup of tea, she said "After the election Tom, you should hire Martinez as an honorary advisor. I think having The Tropicana in the heart of Greenhaven is a splendid idea."

Twenty-One. Bay of Pigs, April 1961

President Kennedy knew that the invasion would take place at the Bay of Pigs; the CIA command in DC obviously knew also, since it was their decision. Mr. Carl, Mr. B., 'Jimmy', 'Seabee' 'Big John', 'Bob' and 'Pat' – they too, all knew the details. The only people who did not know where the invasion would take place, were the Cubans who were actually going to be there.

Even after the men were taken from the training camp at Base Trax and loaded onto cargo planes, they had no idea of their destination. After they landed, they still didn't know where they were. The Americans would not even tell them what country they were in.

"It's a strictly need-to-know basis situation" Mr. Carl said. The only information he would share was that they were now at their penultimate destination, 'Camp Trampoline'. "Next stop Cuba."

All that the Brigadistas could see, was that they were being held at the harbor of a small town in some Central American country facing onto the Caribbean, while supplies were being loaded onto four or five rusty looking, old cargo ships.

It was Manuel who noticed the uniforms of the soldiers guarding the perimeter of the harbor.

"Nicaraguans" he whispered to Oscar. "We're in Nicaragua."

It was after they had been in Camp Trampoline for twenty-four hours that the ten senior officers of Brigade 2506, including Oscar, were brought together for a briefing on the pier. Already disappointed by the decrepit state of the ships which were to transport them to their destination, the Cubans were horrified when they were shown the landing craft. They were just fourteen-foot, rowing boats with outboard motors. They were open to the elements and, more significantly, open to enemy machine-gun fire.

It was Mr. B. who addressed the men and outlined the plan without actually mentioning the name of the landing place. Even the large map of Cuba that he referred to throughout the briefing, was deliberately hung upside down so that South was at the top and North was at the bottom.

"For security" Mr. B. explained. "Strictly need-to-know."

When 'Pepe' San Román asked about the seaworthiness of the transport ships, Mr. B. quickly dismissed his concerns. "You're going to be escorted by the US Navy" he assured them. "You've got nothing to worry about."

"What about the landing craft?" Manuel asked. "We'll be totally exposed."

"Exposed to what? There will be nobody there. We'll send in frogmen to make sure the landing spots are clear and anyway we'll have aircraft backing you up. You'll be covered all the way."

Mr. B. lowered his voice and beckoned for all the men to get closer. "Listen. I don't want to belittle your efforts or your importance. You know I've been rooting for you guys all the way, since day 'numero uno'. But let's be clear on this. This is going to look like a one-hundred percent Cuban invasion. Officially this is a purely Cuban operation. That's why it's only you guys going ashore. No Americans. That's why we're using old ships, purchased by some Cuban supporters in Miami." He leaned in closer, dropping his voice lower so that Oscar had to strain to hear him. "But this is a full blown American operation. President Kennedy and the armed forces of the United States government are fully committed to making this happen. You are going to be protected by sea, by air and even under the water by US Navy frogmen. You guys have nothing to worry about. Uncle Sam is behind you all the way." Far from being insulted, the Cubans were delighted with the news and their spirits were never higher.

It was only on the following day, just prior to embarkation that the map was turned right-way up and the men were told that Operation Pluto had been given the green light by the White House and that their actual destination was the Bay of Pigs.

There would be three separate landing spots; 'Red Beach' Playa Larga, at the head of the bay; 'Blue Beach' Playa Giron, at the eastern mouth of the bay and 'Green Beach' further east along the coast. The 3rd battalion and the paratroopers would take Green Beach while 'Pepe' San Román would lead the 4th and 6th battalion ashore at Blue Beach. Oscar and Manuel were in the 2nd battalion which was under the command of Erneido Oliva who was to lead the 2nd and 5th battalions ashore at Red Beach.

After the 2nd and 5th battalions had secured command of Red Beach and had unloaded all their ammunition and heavy equipment, they were to advance north to the small village of Palpite where they would be joined by the 1st division of paratroopers. Over four-hundred tons of equipment including Sherman tanks and ammunition were to be landed on Red Beach and another six-hundred tons were to be unloaded on Blue Beach over the next ten days. Everything had been meticulously scheduled; by the ton, by the hour and by the man.

After all the months of indecisiveness and conflicting strategies, Oscar was extremely impressed and reassured by the detailed precision of Operation Pluto. As experienced fighters, San Ramon, Oliva and Manuel Artime were also impressed. Morale among the Brigadistas was at an all-time high as they prepared to board the ships. Lined-up on the pier, they stood to attention as Mr. B. gave his final address. Even Nicaragua's president, Luis Anastasio Somoza, surrounded by his gun wielding bodyguards, had arrived to see them embark.

"You're to hold the beaches for seventy-two hours" Mr. B. said. "Then you'll go straight ahead with us coming in behind you." Sweeping out his arm, his voice rose, as he turned his head to catch each man's eye. "You'll put out your hand, turn left and go straight into Havana."

The men all burst into applause and yelled happy shouts of "Cuba Libre." Even Somoza joined the applause and called out "Bring me a couple of hairs from Castro's beard!"

On Saturday April 15, San Ramon boarded the ship called the *Blaggar* with his two divisions while Oscar and Manuel joined Oliva on board the *Houston* and, along with two other ships and their escorts, they all set sail towards Cuba. All day Sunday as they sailed slowly across the Caribbean, away from the Nicaraguan coast, the Cubans on deck were reassured by the sight of an American naval flotilla escorting them and even a submarine protectively circling their ships. As the sun set behind them on Sunday evening, the men were able to see the coast of Cuba approaching, over the horizon.

By 11:30PM on Sunday night, April 16, the invasion force was ready to leave their rendezvous point just thirty miles off the southern coast. The game was on and the invasion had begun.

While San Ramon aboard the *Blaggar* approached Blue Beach, Oscar and Manuel aboard the *Houston* under the command of Oliva sailed into the Bay towards Red Beach. The plan was that frogmen from the *Blaggar* would place landing lights on Blue Beach in order to guide the landing craft who would then come ashore, secure the beach and start unloading the equipment. Although President Kennedy had insisted that no Americans participate in the landings, a Special Forces veteran named Grayston Lynch, insisted on accompanying the frogmen to the beach and ironically he fired the very first shot in the invasion.

The CIA had already photographed the landing sites from a U-2 spy plane and had noted the dark shadows surrounding the coastline. Unfortunately, what the analysts at Langley mistakenly identified as seaweed were actually sharp coral shoals which protected and surrounded the beach. The frogmen who arrived first, found their wetsuits ripped apart and their hands bloodied as they painfully crawled over the reefs to place their lights on the sand.

In addition to the coral reefs, another thing the CIA planners back in Washington were unaware of was Castro's plans to develop tourism on the island. To that end, and to take advantage of the beautiful beaches, the government was building some vacation cottages along the shore. It just so happened that on the evening of Sunday, April 16, the construction workers were hosting a party with some of the local militia at one of the cottages and so, when they heard sounds and saw lights on the reef, they went to investigate. Driving down to the beach in a jeep, the militia assumed the lights came from local fishermen in trouble and so, to help them, they turned on the headlamps, pointing out to sea and bathing everything on the beach in a harsh light.

Now, on what was supposed to be a deserted strip of coast, still bleeding from the sharp coral, the frogmen were confronted at the stroke of midnight, by the full headlights of a jeep and a crowd of inebriated workers and gun-toting militia.

Taking shelter behind some rocks, Lynch fired off several rounds from his Browning Automatic Rifle, before switching to a Thompson machine gun. Ironically, Lynch's bullets wrecked every part of the jeep except the headlights which continued to blaze across the beach. Meanwhile, the two opposing groups took cover and called for reinforcements. Lynch radioed to the *Blaggar* for an immediate landing of the invasion force, while the frogmen dashed along the beach placing guidance lights for the incoming craft. The militia leader meanwhile, hidden behind what remained of the jeep, radioed the guard house in Giron.

By the time the first of the landing craft scraped over the coral reef to the beach, three trucks from Giron disgorged at least thirty militiamen with guns firing and battle was fully joined. In his haste to summon the landing craft, Lynch had forgotten to warn them about the coral reefs and so, as they approached, the boats were ripped apart and the men had to wade ashore in deep water and under fire. Most of the radios were destroyed by the water when the men tumbled into the sea and so the landing force was left with no form of communication.

President Kennedy's instructions that the invasion should occur discreetly, in total silence only in a deserted part of the country and with not a single American present was drowned out with the sound of heavy gunfire.

Even fifteen miles away, on board the *Houston* which was approaching Red Beach at the head of the Bay, Oscar and Manuel could hear the sound of gunfire erupting. "We're on our way, my friend" said Manuel embracing Oscar. "Very soon we'll be back celebrating with Carlos."

Erneido Oliva called all the men on deck for a final briefing. The 2nd division with Oscar and Manuel would go ashore first to secure Red Beach. This would be followed by the 5th division who would then start unloading all the supplies and ammunition.

But once again, the CIA's information was out of date. Between the small villages of Playa Largo and Buenaventura, the ministry of economic development was building vacation homes for tourists and consequently, just as had previously happened on Blue Beach, there were construction workers everywhere. It being a Sunday evening they had been hosting a number of parties and the whole beach was surrounded by drunken militia men with itchy trigger fingers.

The first shots were fired at the frogmen led by Andres Pruna, Executive Officer of the Underwater Demolition Teams. Pruna was in the process of erecting a sign on the beach which read *"Welcome home: men of the 2506 Brigade"* when the first bullets kicked up the sand around his feet. Pruna himself was a Cuban patriot, but instead of joining the Brigadistas to fight Castro, he had volunteered for the US Navy and eventually joined its most elite unit, the SEALS. However, despite all his tough training, nothing had prepared Pruna for the situation he faced on the beach.

In spite of the bullets flying all around them, Pruna and his companions managed to distribute a dozen lights along the beach as well as wedging the 'welcome sign' prominently into a coral outcrop. Pruna had lovingly hand-painted the metal plaque during the sea voyage from Nicaragua and now, as he heard the pinging sound of bullets ricocheting off his handiwork, he felt all the guilt of a father abandoning his child.

But there was no time for feelings of guilt, the air was thick with bullets and the unarmed frogmen needed to return to the *Houston* and inform the commanders of conditions on-shore. Fully alerted, Castro's militia were already taking-up defensive positions, so that by the time Oscar and Manuel arrived in the first landing craft with Oliva at about 1:30AM, the beach was illuminated with spotlights.

The journey from the *Houston* to Red Beach took about twenty minutes and, because of motor problems, only two of the nine landing craft were operational. It therefore took a long time to transport all the men of the 2nd battalion to the beach and by the time they had all disembarked the ship itself was under attack from Castro's air force.

The Cubans had been assured by the CIA that all Castro's planes had been destroyed in the first bombing raid, but they had not all been destroyed, and Kennedy refused to permit a second raid. Just that one decision by Kennedy alone, guaranteed the failure of the whole operation and doomed the Cubans to their fate.

Castro's deadly fleet of British built Sea Furies which he had inherited from Batista was quickly used to deadly effect. Before the 5th division could join the 2nd division on Red Beach, the *Houston* was hit by a shell close to the waterline and the captain decided to withdraw and head for the open sea. Unfortunately, just five miles away from Red Beach, it was struck again and caught fire. The captain tried to beach the ship on the western shore of the Bay but it started to sink and fuel, spilling into the water, surrounded the sinking vessel with a ring of fire. Two hundred men of the 5th battalion were able to swim ashore where they stumbled around for the next few days, disoriented and with no water, no supplies and no way to communicate. They were the lucky ones. Another thirty of their colleagues were left floundering in the water and those who did not drown or get strafed by Castro's gunships, were eaten by the hordes of sharks that were quickly attracted by the scent of fresh blood. Unfortunately all the supplies, equipment and ammunition was still aboard the *Houston* when it went down.

Although confronted by almost a hundred militiamen on Red Beach, the 2nd battalion were armed with machine guns while the militia were only armed with rifles. The Brigadistas were thus able to hold them off and eventually take control of the village as well as the beach. By the time the sun rose on Monday morning they finally understood why they had not been joined by the men of the 5th division. Oliva had been looking through his binoculars and handed them to Manuel.

"To your right" he said. "One o-clock. See the smoke. That's the Houston, on the rocks."

Artime gave him back his glasses. "That's our ammunition" he said. "That's our hospital supplies. That's everything, on the rocks."

He turned to Oscar. "Any luck my friend?"

In addition to being the official photographer, Oscar was the division's radio man and had been trying without success to make contact with the men on Blue Beach. He shook his head. "Nothing. He said.

Oliva ordered some of the men to rest while they waited for news from the 1st division paratroopers who were scheduled to land just north of them. "Conserve your energy" he told them. "Try to get some rest."

At 9:30AM everyone was awakened by an earth shattering explosion to the south, from the direction of Blue Beach.

"My God!" Oliva said. "Castro must have a nuclear bomb. The Russians must be helping them."

It was several more hours before they discovered the good news that it was not a nuclear bomb. They also learned the bad news, that the explosion was the supply ship *Escondido* which had been attacked by a Lockheed T-33 and that the ferocious sound was caused by ten day's supply of 145 tons of ammunition, 38,000 gallons of vehicle fuel and 3,000 gallons of aircraft fuel all igniting at the same time. All of the invasion force's ammunition, supplies and equipment had been loaded onto two ships. Both ships had now been sunk. The surviving Brigadistas were stranded on two separate beaches about twenty miles apart with no way to communicate.

Twenty-Two: Miami 1961

Oscar had been gone nine months before Don Carlos finally received a letter. The envelope was postmarked Washington D.C. and was brief.

> *Dearest Papi:*
>
> *Just a few words to let you know I am in good health and my studies are going well. My professors are pleased with my progress and tell me that I should graduate soon. Please give many, many kisses to Madre and tell her I miss her.*
>
> *I look forward to seeing you very soon.*
>
> *Love*
>
> *Oscar*

Don Carlos read the letter several times and then replaced it in the envelope. He put the envelope in the inside pocket of his jacket, next to his heart, where it remained. He said nothing about it to his wife who went back to bed most mornings, after rising early to watch the Spanish language news at 6:45AM on WTVJ. Their old family friend, Francisco, would bring copies of ¡Hola! Magazine when his own wife had finished with them and Senora Enriquez would spend much of the afternoon reading about Spanish royalty. By an unspoken, mutual agreement, neither she nor her husband discussed or even mentioned either of their sons.

Ever since Kennedy had been inaugurated President in January 1961, there had been growing excitement at the various cafes and shops along Eighth Street which catered to the growing Cuban community. Unlike the stodgy, elderly and protestant Eisenhower, President Kennedy was young, virile and Catholic. Most important he was anti-Castro and had made a succession of aggressively anti-Fidelista speeches during his election campaign. Everybody agreed that an invasion was imminent but nobody could agree when or where it would happen. That did not dampen the theories and rumors along Eighth Street and, each day, as he sipped at his cafecito on the sidewalk outside El Centro, Don Carlos would listen to the latest version and wonder if it involved Oscar.

Most of the more authoritative stories seemed to originate with the *Frente Revolucionario Democrático* (FRD) and there was talk of a leader called Manuel Artime who Don Carlos learned was also the leader of the MRR. But there were so many different acronyms and conflicting *Movimientos* that it was impossible to keep abreast of them all; so Don Carlos learned to say nothing but just puff on his cigar and listen to the gossip. In addition to stories from the FRD and the MRR, there were constant counter-stories and disinformation from Castro's many local agents, and Don Carlos had learned to be extra-vigilant when discussing anything personal. He had noticed the growing interest and questions asked about Oscar's whereabouts. Don Carlos had finally explained that in return for free tuition at his old school in New England, Oscar was obliged to stay-on during the vacation and perform menial work on the school grounds. Don Carlos' eyes would mist over and his hands would tremble as he spoke.

"It is very shameful for me to say this" he would murmur quietly. "The humiliation for my poor boy. To work like a *guajira*, a peasant, because his father cannot afford his school fees!" He would wipe his eyes and shake his head. "¡*Suficiente! No quiero hablar de ello*. I don't want to talk about it anymore."

Before long, the talk of an invasion was not limited to the Cuban cafes of Miami's Eighth Street. There was daily speculation in the press, and not just the Miami Herald and the Miami News. The *New York Times* and the Washington Post were all reporting stories about secret CIA armies training out in the Everglades and in various Central American jungle camps.

And the war hysteria was not just limited to the Cuban exiles, it was infecting the whole country. President Eisenhower had warned about the coming Cold War but, with the arrival of a young and untested Kennedy, the communist threat to the American way of life had become an existential reality. The communist leader of the Soviet Union, Nikita Khrushchev, had already threatened 'to bury' the West, and the threat of nuclear war was never far from anyone's mind.

Living in Greenhaven, a South Florida City that his grandfather had founded, Alfred Connolly II was acutely aware of the threat that a neighboring, communist Cuba posed to his own heritage. Alfred had just graduated from Harvard in October 1960 and was wondering what to do with his life when Soviet Russia's leader, Nikita Khrushchev provided the answer. After pounding with his fists at the podium at the United Nations in New York, Khrushchev removed his shoe and started banging with it while calling the previous speaker "a jerk, a stooge, a lackey and a toady of American imperialism." The communist threat was no longer just an abstract concept and America needed to defend itself. Having just turned 24, Alfred knew that he had no choice but to follow his family tradition and, on the day following Khrushchev's outburst, he enlisted in the US Marines.

Defending their country was an honorable Connolly tradition. Alfred's father had sacrificed his life in World War II, fighting alongside Patton on the beaches of North Africa, and his grandfather, Ray Connolly, had ridden with Teddy Roosevelt and the Rough Riders up San Juan Hill to liberate Cuba during the Spanish American

War. For the rest of his life, Ray Connolly's face carried a savage sabre wound as a souvenir of that battle. In signing-up for the marines, Alfred fully expected that he would participate in the upcoming invasion of Cuba. He was determined to complete officer training before the actual invasion occurred and he prayed that the invasion would take place in Santiago de Cuba so that he could follow in his grandfather's footsteps and charge up San Juan Hill.

In the event, Alfred Connolly II never went to Cuba, even as a tourist; he was sent to Vietnam instead where he earned a purple heart at Khe Sanh and received a scar across the face during the Tet Offensive. When he returned home after the war, the resulting purple slash across his cheek reminded people of his grandfather, which should have pleased him, but didn't.

He was working as a USMC Military Police officer in the city of Hué during the Tet Offensive, and had been summoned to break-up a bar-room fight between a group of enlisted men from Alabama and a group of army rangers who appeared to all be Cuban-American volunteers. The battle to reclaim the city from the Viet-Cong had been intense and tensions were already high, so the combination of alcohol and racial insults proved an explosive mix. Having lost his helmet during the scuffle, Alfred was mistaken for one of the Alabama soldiers and, while one Cuban grasped him firmly from behind, another one carved his face with a broken bottle of Mekong whisky. After tossing away the broken bottle, the man spat contemptuously into Alfred's bleeding face.

"Don't ever fuck with a Cuban again you ignorant, red-neck cracker" he said. "*Me cago en el maldito coño de la requeteputa podrida que te parió.*"

Alfred's wound required fifteen stitches but during all the chaos and carnage that was Hué during the Tet, medical resources were stretched beyond their limit and he received no attention till long after the wound had turned septic. The scar remained with him for the rest of his life and, in honor of his grandfather, was often referred to as

'The Connolly Scar'. But to Alfred it was always a source of shame, and he never forgave the Cubans who had inflicted it. His grandfather, Ray Connolly had earned his scar honorably, with a sword, fighting for Cuban freedom on the battle field. How ashamed he would be, to know that his grandson had got his scar from a drunken Cuban, wielding a broken bottle in a barroom brawl. The shame, like the scar and his visceral hatred of Cubans, never left him.

While Alfred Connolly II was still in Virginia, undergoing Marine Officer training at Quantico Camp, excitement on Eighth Street was reaching fever pitch. Many of the regulars at El Centro had access to Radio Swan, a clandestine CIA asset which broadcast into Cuba. For days, there had been a plethora of strange messages. "The fish is red" or "Alert! Look well at the rainbow." Men would excitedly spend hours arguing over the hidden meaning. "Place notice in the tree. The letters arrived well."

"Obviously they are calling to the Brigadistas to come down from the hills. The invasion must have started. Soon we will have Fidel swinging from a lamp post."

Then there were news reports of bomb attacks on Castro's air force. All his planes had been destroyed on the ground. Guerrillas were blowing-up bridges, there was serious fighting on the south side of the island, all military leave has been cancelled. The invasion has started and the uprising has begun. Soon the bandit dictator will be gone and we can all go home once more.

Finally Don Carlos allowed himself to believe again, and that evening, for the first time in many years, he accompanied his wife to church. Kneeling beside her in the pew he prayed for the souls of Carlos and Oscar, his two precious sons.

Twenty-Three: Greenhaven, 2013

Jane Mayhew was not happy. Against all her arguments, Mayor Adams and the commissioners had unanimously voted in favor of

Alfred Connolly II's design for his grandfather's statue and rejected hers. As part of Greenhaven's centennial celebrations, the City had finally earmarked the funds to erect a ten foot bronze statue of the city's founder, Col. Ray Connolly.

After eighteen months of various proposals, the city had to choose between the two final designs. The first design, based on contemporary photographs portrayed an energetic looking man in his early forties, shirt sleeves rolled up, tie loosed, with one arm holding his jacket and the free hand clutching a roll of architectural drawings.

"That's the man we know" Jane had argued. "We have photographs showing exactly how he dressed. The family have even preserved that very jacket – it's a linen seersucker. And the symbolism is perfect; he was a hard worker, he did roll-up his sleeves. He was not a trained architect himself but every plan and every architectural drawing for the city required his personal approval. He's the father of this city; he was the visionary and the builder. That's what this statue demonstrates. It's taken a hundred years, but finally he will get his public recognition."

The alternative design, the one promoted by Connolly's grandson and finally approved by the City, portrayed Connolly not as a builder but as a warrior. Dressed in the uniform of an army Colonel, with the USV and crossed swords insignia clearly visible on the collar, he wore a wide brim, slouch hat and glared defiantly at some distant enemy. One hand, encased in a large leather gauntlet pointed in the same direction as his glaring eyes, while the other hand held a cutlass or saber, unsheathed and ready for action.

"That's exactly the essence of the man he was" Connolly told the commissioners during the presentation. "He was always a man of action, dedicated to the defense of his country. He was a proud member of the 1st U.S. Volunteer Cavalry Regiment and he rode with Roosevelt up San Juan Hill, defending us against the Spanish threat."

The mayor's own father had been a U.S. Marine, killed during some secret mission during the Vietnam War, and so he was sympathetic to the idea of the City Father dressed in military uniform. The all-male members of the City Commission also preferred the image of a warrior representing the city rather than the politically incorrect image of a mere developer. Commissioner Brownmiller had even suggested placing him on a horse, but the additional costs had proved prohibitive. Once Connolly offered to pay fifty-percent of the costs, the decision had been unanimous and now, a year later, the unveiling of the statue was going to mark the highlight of the planned Greenhaven Centennial Celebrations.

ooOoo

"Jane, it's too late now to complain. The statue is already complete. It's back from the foundry and will be lifted into place sometime next week."

"Next week?" Lady Sanders said. "I thought it was set for next month. I'll be out of town next week."

"No, don't worry. It's the unveiling which takes place next month. Next week is just the erection. The statue will be covered with canvas until then."

"In my opinion it should remain covered" Jane Mayhew snapped. "It's a complete fantasy. An old man's dream of family grandeur. It's got as much historical validity as some plastic monument out of Disneyworld."

"That's rather unfair Jane. I know you would prefer to see him portrayed as the architect and builder of the city, but there was another side to him also. He was one of the Rough Riders and that deserves to be commemorated too."

"I'm not so sure" Jane persisted. "The uniform for a start. As far as I can tell, it was based on photographs of Teddy Roosevelt. I've not seen any photographs of Connolly himself in uniform."

"But maybe that's because he wasn't famous back then." Lady Sanders said. "He hadn't even started work on Greenhaven. He was

148

just an army volunteer in '98. Roosevelt was already a national figure, that's why there are so many photos of him in uniform."

"So why is Connolly dressed in the uniform of a Colonel? I know the army records of that period are pretty unreliable, especially with all the sickness and desertion, but even so, I can't find any record of Connolly anywhere. We have a ton of records and photographs of him after he marries Nordmeyer's daughter and starts developing Greenhaven, but nothing from further back. We've got a whole host of material to create a statue based on historical fact. But using taxpayer money to erect a public monument based on conjecture and speculation just strikes me as wrong and unethical."

"I'm sorry Jane. As you know, I have the highest respect for your historic scholarship; I have read every single one of your books and I understand and respect your concerns – but the fact of the matter is that the commissioners' votes were cast in a public forum, and now the statue itself has been cast – in bronze. It's a done deed. I had hoped that you would perform the unveiling at the ceremony. But I quite understand your refusal. As Director of the City Museum, Catherine has kindly agreed to take your place if you remain adamant."

"Don't worry about me" Lady Sanders said. "I'm quite used to being second choice. My father always admitted he'd have preferred a boy and I always suspected that Peter would have preferred his wife to be a Californian girl rather than an English one."

"Nonsense! He was always insanely in love with you."

"I know. I was just teasing. Don't worry, I'll be happy to unveil your statue – however, historically incorrect, as long as there is free champagne."

"And just so that you know Tom" Jane sniffed. "I'm not giving up my research. I'm going to dig further into Connolly's background. I'm not so sure he even went to Cuba. There's always been something mysterious about that Cuban connection in his history."

ooOoo

The juke-box at the Tenth-Hole Diner was playing *"Bésame Mucho"* by Consuelo Velázquez when Karl Lewis slid his chair over to join Sgt. Anna Hartman and George Attwood where they were eating their breakfast.

"Well I guess we're going to have to get used to all this Cuban music when the new mayor gets elected" he said, nodding his head towards the juke box.

"It's not Cuban music" George said. "It's Mexican."

"Same shit. It's all Hispanic." Karl removed the toothpick from his mouth. "Mind you, I don't mind a bit of salsa now and again." Lowering his head over the table and lowering his voice, he added. "If a new mayor can get Chuck to change his music selection in here, I'll vote for Martinez myself. I've been listening to Vera Lynn and the goddam Andrews Sisters on that jukebox ever since the Korean War."

"What makes you so sure Martinez will win?" Anna asked.

"Cause he might run unopposed. Tom was having lunch here the other day and he was saying he might not run again. Laura wants him to retire so they can travel more. I wouldn't blame him. He's been a good mayor, but maybe time for a change."

"So what do you think of this Martinez guy?"

"Well he's obviously smart" Karl said, toothpick jauntily back between his teeth.

"Why do you say that?"

"Stands to reason. He's a billionaire. He's made hundreds of millions Got to be smart."

"Or crooked" said Raoul Gomez, joining them from another table. "According to this week's *New Times*, his health care company, the AHCU, has been ripping-off the Medicare program for decades."

"They're just saying that because he's Cuban" George said. "I've met the guy and he seems very straight. I liked him."

"Yes. Just because he's Cuban don't mean he's a crook" Karl said with a grin towards Raoul. "I'm sure there must be some Cubans who aren't criminals."

"Right" said Raoul, who was Cuban by birth. "Just like I'm sure that somewhere there's a gringo who's not an ignorant, bigoted, douchebag."

"Have you still got the *New Times* article Raoul?" Anna asked. "I'd like to read it when you've finished. Sounds interesting."

"So what's got you in such a cynical mood Raoul?" George asked. "Still fighting City Hall?"

"Bureaucratic bastards!" Raoul said. "They've rejected my fence application again. Say they want a floor plan of the house and elevation drawings. I mean, what the Hell! It's just a goddamned fence around the front yard. What do they want floor plans for? Architect wants eight-hundred just to do the drawings. Already cost me two-grand for the first fence, then another five-hundred to tear it down. Then there's at least another fifteen hundred for fees and drawings, and all the time poor Jose-Marti is stuck in the house because I haven't got a fence!"

Twenty-Four: Playa Larga, Cuba, April 17, 1961

Oscar felt a terrible sense of failure; he was the official radio operator for the second battalion but was unable to provide any information to his commanders. There was no response from San Román's forces on Blue Beach and no news at all from the men of the fifth division who were supposed to have joined Oliva's forces on Red Beach.

"Just keep switching channels" Manuel advised him. "Keep listening, don't give up."

It was only later that Oscar learned that all the brigade's mobile radios had been rendered useless by the sea-water when the

Brigadistas had to wade ashore on Blue Beach and the men of the fifth battalion had to swim ashore from the sinking *Houston*. Even worse, the dedicated communication truck which would have linked the Brigadistas with each other and the outside world had been onboard the *Escondido* when it exploded.

"Commander! Look. Look up there" Oscar called to Oliva, pointing north to where a couple of the Brigade's lumbering C-46s were circling slowly and the sky was filling with opening parachutes. "It's the first-battalion of paratroops."

"Excellent! At last" Oliva said. "We'll leave the beach to join them at Palpite and then we'll be able to control the road from the north. Call them in and let's coordinate."

But again, with an overwhelming sense of failure, Oscar was unable to raise any response from the radio. He knew what radio channels the first-brigade would be using and he knew they were equipped with a powerful transmitter so he could not understand the lack of communication. What Oscar did not know was that the paratrooper's radio transmitter and much of the heavy equipment had been dropped further north than planned and was now lost in the vast Zapata Swamp.

The CIA had selected the Bay of Pigs precisely because it was separated from the rest of the country by the impregnable Zapata Swamp and therefore would be deserted and uninhabited. They were not to know that Fidel Castro was very familiar with the area and had visited it often as a boy on fishing trips. He was aware of the beautiful beaches which is why he had started developing it as a tourist destination and which is why the invading forces were confronted with so many construction workers and armed militia.

But the swamp remained a reality. The Zapata is a vast, million acre wilderness of impassable wetlands. Equipment or even paratroopers landing in the swamp would be swallowed-up, not just by the swamp itself but also by the ferociously aggressive, ten-foot Cuban Crocodiles which live there.

The second brigade had spent the morning fighting off the lightly armed militia from the village of Playa Larga and those militiamen who had not been killed, had fled north on the single road across the swamp to where Castro was already consolidating his troops. Under Oliva's command, the second battalion cautiously moved north towards the village of Palpite where they were joined by the remnants of the first battalion of paratroopers. The original plan was to march north along the road crossing the swamp to join the Autopista Nacional on the other side – the main road to Havana. Lacking the men of the fifth battalion, who had gone down with the *Houston*, and missing many of the paratroopers and their equipment which had been dropped in the swamp, Oliva gathered his forces in Palpite while Oscar tried to get word from Blue Beach.

"God help us!" Manuel suddenly said, pointing north along the road across the swamp. "It's Castro's goddam army!"

With a force of nine-hundred soldiers loaded into sixty buses and trucks and preceded by a fleet of T-33 soviet tanks, Castro's army swiftly advanced south, along the road crossing the swamp, towards the village of Palpite. Oliva's men were totally outnumbered.

"I've got them" Oscar suddenly called. "Pepe San Román is calling in. He wants to talk to you, commander."

Quickly Oliva and San Román exchanged news. None of it was good. Oliva was however able to call in some air support and less than an hour later two of the Brigade's B-26Bs strafed and bombed Castro's soldiers as they approached Palpite. This gave Oliva's men time to dig-in defensive positions just south of the village from which they could defend the road from the north. For the rest of the day and well into the night, the fighting was continuous as Castro sent more and more troops down the road across the swamp. In less than four hours Castro's tanks fired more than two-thousand shells on the Brigadistas.

Of Oliva's original 370 men, 20 had been killed and another 50 wounded by the time the bombardment calmed around midnight.

Ammunition was dangerously low and there certainly wasn't enough to last them through another day. They would have to take advantage of the darkness and pull back to rejoin San Román

"We're going to have to withdraw" he told Manuel. "Tell everyone we're heading south to Blue Beach."

Oscar hated the idea of retreating but understood the impossibility of surviving much longer on Red Beach. Marching beside his comrades along the shore line, he maintained radio contact with San Román and updated him on their position. The remnants of Oliva's two battalions limped into Camp Giron on Blue Beach just before 9:00AM on Tuesday, April 18.

While Oscar and Manuel had been holding back Castro's forces at Red Beach, San Román's two battalions had managed finally to assemble ammunition and some equipment, including tanks from the remaining supply ships. After getting some food and much needed rest, Oliva's men of the second battalion were able to rearm themselves and load up with ammunition before setting off, back towards Red Beach.

A couple of miles north-west of Blue Beach, Oliva's forces were confronted by the Fidelistas and quickly dug-in, ready to defend their position. Even though Castro's forces outnumbered them more than five to one, the government troops, still recovering from the previous day's losses, did not seem anxious to do battle. For the rest of the afternoon, the two sides just exchanged insults and the occasional gunshot. Meantime, back on Blue Beach, San Román's forces tried to get more supplies dropped to the beach from the lumbering C-54s, but the first set of parachutes were caught by the wind and drifted away to land in the swamp. The second drop was caught by another gust of wind and landed in the sea.

Things remained fairly quiet until early evening by which time Castro had moved all his heavy artillery within easy range of the Brigadistas and all through the night he pounded away at their positions.

Oliva's men of the second battalion, well dug-in and armed with mortars, were able to hold their position guarding the western end of the beach even when attacked by tanks. In an effort to get better reception on the radio, Oscar had climbed a tree on the edge of the swamp when he was hit by sniper fire, and a bullet tore through the back of his foot. He dropped to the ground and started to crawl back to join the others where Manuel somehow lifted him and carried him to safety. For the next few hours they were under heavy attack, and loading, firing and reloading his machine gun filled Oscar with so much testosterone fueled energy that he never felt the pain in his foot. The fighting continued until two in the afternoon when ammunition was again running low. Oliva ordered his men to fall back once more and rejoin San Román's forces on Blue Beach.

Oscar had his radio strapped to his back and his arms draped over the shoulder of Manuel Artime and another soldier as they slowly retreated along the beach. A single shot rang out behind them and Oscar got a second bullet in his shoulder.

"They're aiming for the radio" he gasped as Manuel laid him on the ground. Manuel and the other soldier were both armed with Thompsons and they sprayed a storm of bullets into the vegetation behind them.

"We got the bastard for you" Manuel said as they lifted Oscar once more between them. "You saved my life buddy. If your shoulder had not been in the way, that bullet would have gone through my heart."

Eventually Oliva's men made it back to Camp Giron on Blue Beach but found it deserted. San Román had already destroyed all the camp's equipment and had instructed his men to retreat individually into the swamp with plans to regroup in the woods on the far side. He himself was waiting for Oscar in order to transmit his final radio message to Grayston Lynch and the other CIA controllers on board the *Blaggar*, anchored some twenty miles offshore. Following San Román's instructions, Oscar transmitted the following message.

155

"Am destroying all my equipment and communications. Tanks are in sight. I have nothing left to fight with. Am taking to the woods. I cannot wait for you."

While many of Oliva's men moved north with San Román towards the town of San Blas and a possible road across the Zapata Swamp, Oliva and Artime with a dozen other men elected to follow the coast eastwards, and thus to skirt the southern edge of the swamp. Eventually, they reasoned, they might even reach the city of Trinidad or the Escambray Mountains. Manuel had managed to locate a stretcher from the remains of the hospital supplies and, after wrapping Oscar's ankle in bandages and treating his shoulder wound with alcohol, they placed him on the stretcher and set off along the beach.

After about a hundred yards, the sharp agony from bouncing around on the stretcher was proving too much to bear and Oscar called them to stop.

"This is crazy" he said. "Your chance of out-running them is already slim and carrying me will just make it impossible. Leave me here. Put me against that palm tree over there." He looked up at his friend Manuel and smiled. "Even if I bleed to death, I'll be looking at a beautiful, peaceful view."

"And if the Fidelistas come?" Manuel asked.

"They will either shoot me or they will take me to a hospital." He squeezed Manuel's hand and grinned. "Either way it's better than bouncing around on that goddam stretcher."

Gently they placed Oscar with his back to the tree, facing the Ocean. They took his radio and topped-up his water bottle. A few, brief words, a quick embrace and then they were gone and Oscar was finally alone, listening to the gentle caress of the waves along the sand.

Grayston Lynch on board the *Blaggar* was overcome with a bitter despair. More than any of the other Americans he knew what the Brigadistas had been through, the lies they had been told and the way they had been betrayed. Having been on the beach himself he could imagine what they were going through, and when he received San Román's final message he took it very, very personally and never forgave the American President for his act of betrayal. He turned to Andres Pruna, the leader of the underwater demolition team.

"We need volunteers Andy. There's men out there, alone and frightened. We put them there and we let them down. I can't order you to go. It's insanely dangerous. Castro's men will be everywhere, but those survivors need us."

Pruna just grinned. "We're already on our way."

For the next three days the frogmen combed the shores and inlets of the Bay of Pigs, looking for survivors. They focused on the western shore where the *Houston* was beached and where the men of the fifth battalion were still wandering around lost and often delirious with thirst. Although the fifth battalion had seen no action, most of them were cut and bleeding from the sharp, needle-like vegetation and their feet were wounded so badly by the sharp coral that many could not even walk. One by one the frogmen brought them back to the boats.

The eastern side of the Bay was far more dangerous than the west, as Castro's soldiers were everywhere. Additionally, any survivors would probably have already melted away into the swamp, but Pruna decided he owed them at least one quick search. Coming ashore from the east and carefully navigating the coral reef, he raised his head above water and saw a deserted beach. There was no sign of life and he was about to turn back when he noticed a slight movement in the distance. There was a huddled shape at the foot of a palm tree and as Pruna approached, he realized it was human.

Oscar was feeling very peaceful. He still had some water left in his bottle, and he was enjoying the soothing sound of the waves. He tried not to think about his brother Carlos and he tried hard not to think about the pain in his leg. He knew he was drifting in and out of consciousness and he wondered if he was possibly losing his mind. The bright sunlight on the water made everything indistinct and hazy. At first he thought he was imagining things when the large black shape emerged from the water and approached him across the sand. It was a tall man dressed entirely in black rubber with flippers on his feet and his face obscured by a mask.

Oscar felt strangely calm and detached. Perhaps this was Death, come for him at last. Perhaps he was dying.

"Who are you?" he asked.

"My name is Andy" the man said. "I've come to take you home."

Twenty-Five, Greenhaven Country Club, 2013

"It's Lady Sanders, isn't it?" A tall man in tennis whites approached her, carrying his racket. "We met a few days ago at the Doyle's." He removed his dark glasses and she recognized those piercing blue eyes. "Orestes Martinez" he said.

"Yes, of course Mr. Martinez. How nice to see you again, I had been meaning to compliment you on your speech the other evening. I was most impressed with some of your suggestions." Shaking hands, she said "I'm afraid my hand's a little sweaty, I've just finished a doubles-match with some friends." Indicating his racket she asked. "Have you just played? I didn't see you out there on the courts. In fact I don't think I've seen you at the club before. Do you play often?"

He shook his head. "After living around the corner for over twenty years, I finally joined the club only last week. Now that I'm retired I need some new interests. But I don't know that I'm ready to play yet. I've just been hitting a ball against the wall for the past couple of hours. I've signed-up with the club-pro to start lessons next week."

She looked at her watch. "Why don't we have a quick game now? Look, there's a court free."

"I don't think you understand. I haven't played since I was a
student in Havana.' He paused and looked at her awkwardly. "Before
the Revolution. That's half a century ago!"

"Yes. But you're a big strong man and I'm just a frail little girl."

Martinez raised his eyebrows and looked at her. He saw the
toned muscles of her tanned arms, the long legs beneath the short,
pleated tennis skirt, the trim body and the energy which glowed from
her golden skin. "If I'm going to run for mayor and become a
professional politician" he finally said with a smile. "I guess I need to
get used to public humiliation. Getting wopped by a frail little girl
will be the least of it."

"Three-zero" he said half an hour later. "I believe that gives you
the set. What do you say we head to the bar instead and have a
drink?"

"I thought you'd never ask."

After a quick shower, Lady Sanders joined him at the club bar,
wearing a simple cotton dress which matched the blue of her eyes.
Martinez, dressed in a blue blazer and an open-necked white shirt had
already started on a rum-and-coke while the barman brought Lady
Sanders her regular gin-and-tonic.

"I'm afraid I started without you" he said. "Being so thoroughly
and publically beaten by a woman – especially a frail little girl – was
so humiliating that I'm afraid I've turned to drink."

"The Cuban national drink I see" she said, nodding to his glass.
"The Cuba Libre."

"I'm impressed. For a European, you seem to know a lot about
the Cubans."

"I've lived in South Florida for almost thirty years, Mr.
Martinez. There's no way you can live here and not know everything
about Cuba. In fact, after so many years in Miami, most of us even
think of ourselves as half Cuban."

"But you still speak with an English accent. I barely see you as American even, let alone Cuban. I see you as part of London society – not South Florida."

"Well, you see me wrong. I moved here just after the Mariel boatlift. I was here all through the Cocaine Cowboy era. And I vividly remember the Dadeland Mall shootout.

"There's more to Cuban culture than drug-gang shootouts, Lady Sanders. Anyway, they were Colombians, not Cubans. Not all us Latins are the same you know and not all of us are gangsters."

"Yes of course. I'm so sorry. I do apologize, that did sound terribly insulting didn't it. I really didn't mean it that way. I love Cuban culture. One of the reasons I didn't return to England after my husband died was the *cafecitos* – I can't live without my daily dose of café Cubano, my Cuban coffee. And salsa of course. My husband and I took salsa dancing lessons you know." She pointed to her phone. "That's all I have on my playlist; salsa and meringue music. Celia Cruz, Willie Colon, Mark Anthony, Tito Puente – oh don't get me going. I love it. I was always so jealous of my parents when I was a little girl. They always used to visit the Tropicana when they were on this side of the Atlantic. I so wanted to go with them on those trips."

"The Tropicana? In Havana?"

"Yes. That's why I was so excited to hear your plans for reviving it here in Greenhaven."

"I see" Martinez said, nodding to the barman for two more drinks. "I obviously misjudged you. You really do know your Cuban culture."

"Listen. Whenever I return from a trip to London or Paris, the first thing I always do is go for lunch or dinner at *Versailles* or *La Carreta*. I've got to have my black beans and rice and I'm addicted to ropa vieja & picadillo."

"What about your husband?"

"Peter? How do you mean?"

"Was he Cuban?"

"Good Lord no. Red neck, good-old Southern boy."

"But he liked Cuban music?"

"It was he who introduced me to salsa. He was crazy for it."
Sipping thoughtfully at her drink she added. "In a way, it was his love
of Cuban culture that, indirectly, led to his death."

"In what way?"

"Well he was killed because he was bored and decided to go
hang-gliding off the cliffs when we were staying down in Rio de
Janeiro – so I can't blame the Cubans for that. But the reason he was
bored and the reason we were down in Rio was because the Miami
Cuban community had run him out of town."

"Really? Why."

"Do you remember the Elian Gonzalez story?"

"The little boy who was found floating in the sea, after his
mother drowned, trying to cross the Florida Straits? I sort of
remember it. It was around the turn of the century, I think. I was out
of town through most of it."

"You remember the Miami fisherman, Donato I think his name
was, he found the boy and brought him ashore and then his relatives
who live in Miami wanted to adopt him but the father, back in
Havana wanted him returned to Cuba. So all the local Cuban
community united behind the uncle, Lazaro, who was on TV every
night, and in the papers denouncing the bandits in Havana who
wanted the boy back. And then there was his teenage cousin,
Marisleysis, who quickly became a substitute mother for the little
boy. Her teeth were in braces and she was still training to be a
hairdresser, but she too was on TV every night – and she had this, I
don't know – a quirky, innocence – that we all fell in love with. And
of course it was all over the international news, featuring the Clinton-
Gore administration in Washington and the Castro brothers and

Elian's dad in Havana – and it finally came to a dramatic, front-page climax when the US Attorney General, Janet Reno – who just happened to live in Miami herself – sent in a SWAT team to seize the boy and send him back to Cuba."

"Yes. I remember it all now: that photograph on the front page with the armed soldier in black armour and the terrified little boy. Tensions were really high. I remember there were semi-riots on Eighth Street. So how did that affect your husband?"

"Peter found the whole thing fascinating and amusing and, being a professional musician, he wrote a song about it. You've got to understand, Peter found absolutely everything amusing. What ever happened, he always found a funny side. He wasn't cruel. Far from it, he was a gentle, gentle man. That's why I married him. And he always made me laugh. That's why I love him." She finished her drink and nodded to the barman.

"And?"

"Sadly, the Miami Cuban community did not find the song funny. We were living in a condo down in Coconut Grove at the time and the condo-association forced us to leave because all the Cuban protestors were preventing anybody from entering the building. There were death threats and people saying bad things about him on the radio and TV. So we flew to Spain and then eventually on to Brazil."

"What was the song about?"

"It was just a little ballad. It was never anything big – not until all the protesters made a big thing out of it. It was just a little bit of whimsical fun."

"Did Peter write it?

"Some of it. He wrote the music but his friend Chuck wrote most of the lyrics. Chuck was Peter's attorney who'd always wanted to be a rock musician but his dad made him go to law school instead."

"So what was the song? Can you sing me the words?"

"If you'd ever heard me sing you'd never ask that question."

162

It took two more gin and tonics before Lady Sanders started to quietly sing.

"It's a most amazing tale —— the way you walked in my heart's door:
Six dolphins, and a boy, and a faithful pescador
You showed a watching world the meaning of amor
And you even made a jackass out of Mr. Albert Gore

Ah, ... Marisleysis, Marisleysis,
I look for you alone among all the other faces
Be my INS commando and put me through my paces
My jewel of the Straits —— Marisleysis.

We can't forget the day that we first saw you on TV
You captured all our hearts —— our Calle Ocho fantasy
But you'll never mean to all of them just what you mean to me
To Donato, you are just another fish in the sea.

Marisleysis, Marisleysis,
I look for you alone among all the other faces
With your mouth the size of Gitmo Bay and shiny metal braces
You're my Caribbean queen, Marisleysis"

"Are you sure you want to hear more? It was all so long ago. Elian's probably married with kids by now and Marisleysis is probably a grandmother. Janet Reno is dead ... and so is Peter." She finished her drink. "It was his last song, you know. Before he died."

"Please finish it" he said. "I want to hear it all."

"We're meant to be together —— I know that it's our fate
But when Lazaro's around, I'm scared to ask you for a date

163

Is there something I can to do to help him channel all that
hate?
Would it help to give him Janet Reno's head upon a plate?

Marisleysis, Marisleysis,
I want to take you far away from where the tear gas and the
mace is
You're the daughter of the mother of all immigration cases,
Mi cafecito de la Calle ....
Marisleysis"

She nodded to the barman for a refill, her eyes glistening
with emotion from the memories. "It's been years since I've
even thought of that song" she said. "I'm amazed that I still
remember the words."

"That was beautiful" he said. "I loved the humor. But I
can't believe they drove you out of town just for that. I mean I
can see that the tone of detached irony might strike some as
being a bit condescending. But I doubt that many of the Cubans
along Eighth Street would even have understood the words. Are
you serious – there were death threats?"

"Oh believe me, the threats were real. We even had to leave
town in a hurry. We had to drive up to Atlanta to get a flight. It
wasn't safe to go to Miami airport."

"But why? I don't understand."

"It was the final verse that really caused the problem. I
substituted 'cafecito' for 'papaya' when I sang it just now. Peter
was trying to end up with a Spanish version of 'you're the apple
of my eye,' so the original version, the one they played on the
radio, actually ended with

You're the daughter of the mother of all immigration cases,

Mi papaya de la Calle ....
Marisleysis"

"Ah" he said, nodding his head in understanding.

"Now you follow me" she smiled at him. "Now you understand. You see, we had no idea. We thought papaya was just an exotic, tropical fruit. We had no idea it's the Cuban slang for a lady's naughty bits. Polite Cubans never even say the word 'papaya'."

"Absolutely. We say 'fruta bomba'. The word 'papaya' is extremely vulgar."

"Worse than that; really offensive. Basically we had just insulted Elian's sacred, innocent and virginal cousin and publicly called her a whore." Picking up her glass and chuckling at the memory, she said. " That's why we had to leave town in such a hurry. And of course, poor Peter never came back."

ooOoo

"You quite sure now Mr. George, you don't want none?" Darlene asked. "If you decide later-on you want grits with your breakfast, it'll be too late."

"I quite understand Darlene" George replied. "I accept full responsibility. If I suddenly develop a craving for grits when I'm half way through eating my bacon and eggs – I will have only myself to blame."

"Just so as you understand" Darlene huffed as she went to the kitchen to place their order.

"You should surprise her one morning by asking for grits" Anna suggested, having changed into her police uniform after their game of golf.

"You don't understand Anna. Darlene and I have been sparring over grits since she first started working here. That's been twenty years now. It's what keeps us both going. If she stopped persuading me to order grits, or I suddenly started eating them, why, the whole earth would shift on its axis and there would be no further point in living."

"Can't have that then" Anna said. "Then I'd have no one to play golf with."

"You can always play with me" Raoul Gomez said as he joined them at their table.

"It's not the same. You always beat me Raoul, but George is a gentleman and always allows me to win."

"I'm President of the Alhambra Golf Association" Raoul said. "I have to win. I can't be beaten by a woman. Besides; I'm Cuban. It's a macho thing."

The gentle harmony of the Andrews Sisters was suddenly replaced by the syncopated rhythms of Pérez Prado's orchestra playing *Mucho Mambo*.

"I should have known you were here Raoul" said Karl Lewis, sliding his chair across the floor to join the other three and nodding with his head towards the jukebox. "Soon as I heard the music, I knew it was you."

"Better get used to it Karl. When we get our new, Cuban mayor, all that cracker crap you and Chuck like so much will be gone. Out the door and good riddance. We're going to get some good salsa and rumba." Raoul had come over from Cuba as part of Operation Pedro Pan which brought over fourteen thousand unaccompanied Cuban children to the United States during the early sixties. The only accent that Raoul had was from New Jersey, where he'd spent most of his life working for the US Postal Service before retiring to South Florida. However, his friend Karl still treated him as somebody just "off the banana boat" whose Spanish accent was unintelligible.

"You can go back to Hialeah if you want to listen to all this Hispanic crap."

"Oh don't be so stuffy Karl" Anna said. "I like this music. Makes you want to move and shake your booty!"

"That's as maybe" Karl said, removing the ever-present toothpick from his mouth. "But Tom Adams is running again so I don't think your Martinez feller is going to be playing bongos and sacrificing chickens in City Hall anytime soon."

"When did you hear about Tom running again?" George asked.

"Yesterday. He was in here for lunch. So I said to him, 'what's this I hear about the old Palace hotel being turned into a strip club?' "What do you mean?' he says. 'Well' I says. 'Martinez says he wants to turn it into a Tropical night-club. You know, with topless girls in thongs and sequins and shit. 'Where do you hear that?' he says. 'It's in his speeches' I say. "I've heard him with my own two ears. That's what he's going to do if he's elected. So what do you think about that Mr. Mayor?' I says. 'Well' he says. 'We can't have that then can we? Not with the Palace. Not if I'm mayor of Greenhaven' he says.

"But he didn't actually say he will officially run?" George asked.

"Not in so many words" Karl replied. "But it stands to reason, doesn't it. He ain't going to let that Cuban crook turn our city into some Las Vegas knock-off - so that means he's going to run again, in order to stop him."

"Come on Karl" George said. "You can't keep calling the man a crook. You've got no proof and it's insulting. I know you do it just to tease Raoul here, but I've got a lot of Cuban friends in Miami. Lots of the professors who were my colleagues at the University are Cubans. Lots of my students were Cubans. There is something about this election which is getting very racist and ugly. There's an anti-Hispanic tone which is getting increasingly nasty. Let's face it, Florida has only been part of the USA for less than two-hundred years but it was part of the Spanish Empire for three-hundred years. Until the Cubans arrived, Greenhaven and Miami were just sleepy little Southern towns on the edge of the map."

"Nothing wrong with that" Karl said. "I liked it when we were a sleepy little Southern town. Anyway, the man is a crook. Not because he's a Cuban but because he's a criminal. You ask Sergeant Hartman here. You read that *New Times* article didn't you Anna? Says he's been ripping off Medicare for years. Years. Am I right or am I right, Anna?"

"It certainly suggests some suspicious patterns. But it doesn't offer any definitive proof" Anna said. "And it doesn't come out and call him a crook. Let's put it this way, even if everything the *New Times* says is true, there's still not enough there for me or my boss to go and arrest Orestes Martinez. So until there is …" she turned to look at Karl, "I suggest we stop calling our mayoral candidate a crook."

Following their breakfast, Anna gave George a lift to the Museum in downtown Greenhaven in her squad car.

"So what did you really think of that *New Times* article?" George asked. "Does it match your own Medicare research?"

"Let's put it this way" Anna said. "I didn't throw it away. I made a copy for Chief Phillipe and I've filed it away with the rest of my evidence."

"So is Karl right? Is he a crook?"

"He's a very clever man George. Even if there was Medicare fraud going on it could be very hard to prove. Anyway, I'm sure he made sure he kept his own hands clean. AHCU is a big complex organization with lots of different layers. It's like one of those Russian dolls, you know, with everything hidden inside something else. It's driving me crazy."

"A riddle, wrapped in a mystery, inside an enigma" George said.

"What's that?"

"Just something Churchill once said. Describing Russian foreign policy."

"Sounds like a pretty fair description of Martinez's corporate structure as well."

"Ex" George said. "Ex corporate structure. Don't forget he sold all interest in it. He's totally divested himself from it. He's got a good precedent for getting away with it. Don't you remember that other big health care company that was busted for Medicare fraud back in the late nineties."

"Colombia?"

"Yes Colombia. Well their CEO got out just before they were busted and went on to become Governor of Florida."

"Weren't they found guilty?"

"The company was, yes. They were fined $1.7 Billion. Biggest fraud case in history I think."

"And the CEO?"

"Ex. Ex-CEO you mean." George smiled. "He's still Governor of Florida."

"I don't know why you can't arrive at work on your bicycle like any normal janitor George" Lady Sanders greeted him as he arrived in the Museum. "Arriving with a police escort like this is going to give you ideas way above your station. You'll be asking for a raise next."

"Oh no your ladyship. Just serving you is honor and reward enough. Honest. A handful of rice and a kick-up the bum is more than sufficient."

"Well that's good because we have lots of work to do today. I've offered Orestes Martinez the use of our Community Meeting Room for a Town Hall meeting tomorrow night, so we have lots of chairs to set-up, and of course when I say 'we' I mean you."

"I didn't know you were in contact with him."

"I bumped into him at the Country Club yesterday. We played a game of tennis together and then had a few drinks at the bar."

George said nothing but raised an eyebrow.

"Well after a few drinks, it was getting quite late, so we decided to stay-on at the club for dinner."

"Is he a good player?"

"His technique isn't so good. He says he hasn't played since college. But he's very fit and still in good shape. I'm sure it will all come back quite soon."

"Especially with a little personal coaching."

"All right Aunty George. That's enough of your prurient innuendos. Get working on those chairs."

"How many your Ladyship?"

"let's do a hundred-twenty."

"Big turn-out then?"

"I think so. Everyone is certainly very curious about our possible new mayor."

"And are you still curious?"

"I'm afraid I chickened-out. I didn't get drunk enough to ask, or maybe felt that he wasn't drunk enough for me to ask him the big question that's been bugging me for weeks."

"What's the big question Catherine?"

"His name of course. My God! Am I the only person who's had a classical education around here?"

"How do you mean? What's wrong with his name?"

"Don't you remember your Aeschylus? The Greek playwright. He wrote the *Oresteia Trilogy*."

"Oh right. Orestes, son of Agamemnon. Killed his mother, Clytemnestra. Butchered her if I recall."

"Exactly! So what kind of mother would call her son Orestes?" She paused to think. "Of course I never had children so what do I know? Oedipus I can understand. He'll always love his mother. But Orestes. I mean that's like calling a boy Cain so he can kill his brother." She shrugged her shoulders in bewilderment.

"I tell you George. It's become an obsession. How can a mother possibly call her son after a figure in Ancient Greek Tragedy, famous for murdering his mother? I've checked it out. Poor Dr. Martinez is not an aberration. Apparently Orestes is quite a popular boy's name in Cuba. I just could not pull up the courage to ask such an intimate question. But I'm determined to find out."

George gave her a hug. "OK Catherine, you go and worry about the Ancient Greek tragedies and how the Furies from the Fifth Century BC can come and wreck vengeance in the twenty-first century. Meanwhile, I'll go and move chairs."

"You're the chairman George. You're the chairman."

Twenty-Six: Havana, Cuba, 1979

Ramon Fernandez had been in jail before, many times, and so when they arrested him yet again for pimping, he was not too concerned. He knew how the system worked, he knew how to do time. In the six years since his first arrest at the age of fourteen, he had visited several of Havana's Correctional Camps and Youth Re-education Centers and he felt comfortable in all of them. Since he first pimped his younger sister to some Soviet sailors, Ramon had always maintained a stable of young girls desperate for money. There were always Russians looking for some exotic Latina pussy and plenty of Czechs, Poles and Bulgarians looking for tropical fun in the sun. But the real payoff came from the tourists of Western Europe; the French and the Spanish. They had real money to spend. The Eastern Bloc customers provided Ramon with his bread and butter but the European tourists supplied the jam. Unfortunately, such tourists were few and far between but there were enough to keep Ramon comfortable. He had his own Vyatka motor scooter, he had an apartment not far from the Avenida de Maceo, the Malecón, where most of his business was conducted and he was never short of cigarettes or alcohol. Not yet twenty-one, Ramon was proud that he had made something of his life.

Born in the year of Castro's revolution, Ramon had never known his father. His mother had always been vague about what happened. Sometimes she said he was a hero of the Revolution but killed by Batista, other times he was a counter-revolutionary, jailed by Castro. In any event, his mother had abandoned him at the age of twelve when she went-off with a soldier from Bulgaria, leaving Ramon to look after his kid sister, Carmen.

Carmen had been the first girl he had pimped-out but there was never a shortage of young girls, and boys, anxious for his guidance in the trade. At six-foot-two, with broad shoulders, Ramon exercised daily and knew how to look after himself. Nobody messed with him, or his stable; even the *guardia* from the PNR when they arrested him from time to time, took care not to provoke him.

171

But this time was different.

Instead of taking him to the usual jail in the center of the city, he was shackled and placed on a bus to the *Combinado del Este*, a maximum security prison a few miles south east of Havana. The vast prison compound was ringed with white painted guard towers and spiraled coils of razor wire which glinted between two, twenty-foot high, chain-linked fences. Despite the grim surroundings Ramon felt fairly confident about his future. From what he understood, most of the prisoners here were politicos not real criminals. To Ramon, this meant lots of middle-aged softies that he would be able to manipulate.

After the usual bureaucratic, processing bullshit, Ramon was shown to his bunk in a massive holding cell with beds for at least a hundred men. After that, he was led-out to the prison compound, a vast open space surrounded by high walls and regularly spaced watch towers. Ramon had heard enough stories to feel a slight nervousness when he saw all the armed guards looking down on the men below; it would be like shooting fish in a barrel, he thought. The yard itself was teeming with men, most of them bare chested, many of them sporting tattoos and all of them looking tougher and nastier than Ramon had imagined.

Pulling off his shirt, partly to blend-in and partly to display his muscles, Ramon started to circle the yard, hoping to see a face he might recognize. It was on his third circuit that he met his protector.

"You're new here aren't you?"

The man looked to be in his late thirties. He was the same height as Ramon and, though he was wearing a shirt, appeared to be in good shape. He had steel blue eyes and he regarded Ramon with an amused smile.

Ramon nodded warily.

"You just arrived today?"

Ramon nodded again.

"Never been here before?"

Ramon shook his head.

"Good. Well you can be my bitch."

Ramon was not sure that he had heard correctly or understood.

"What?" he said. "What the Hell are you talking about?"

"You'll be my bitch" the man repeated, calmly. "You run errands for me, you let me fuck you and I look after you. Make sure nobody messes with you."

"You've got to be crazy old man. Why would I do that?"

The man hardly seemed to move before Ramon found himself pinioned from behind with the point of a knife nicking at his Adam's apple.

"This is one reason" the man said. "Do you need another?"

Twisting Ramon's arm, he turned his body so that he was facing the compound. "See that guard over there on the left?" he said. "See the other one over there by the door? They're looking at us. Notice what they're doing? No? I'll tell you what they're doing. Nothing. That's what they're doing. Nothing."

Releasing Ramon's arm, he turned his body so that they were facing each other again. The knife had vanished. The man smiled again.

"Now do you understand? You're going to be nice to me, and I will look after you. Trust me, there's no shortage of young guys in here who'd like to be my bitch. You should consider yourself lucky. So tell me, what's your name?"

There was a pause while Ramon dropped his eyes to the ground.

"Ramon" he finally said.

"Good. Well welcome Ramon, welcome to *Combinado del Este*. My name is Carlos Enriquez and I run this place."

It had been a long and brutal journey that had taken Carlos to the *Combinado del Este*. During the nineteen years since the death of his friend Cienfuegos and his own arrest, Carlos had visited probably all the major prisons in Cuba. After his first night, held in a cell in Che Guevara's *La Cabaña*, Carlos had been moved back to the center of Old Havana where he spent several weeks in a cold and damp dungeon in a disused old Colonial Fortress, *Castillo de Santo Domingo de Atarés* overlooking the harbor. His cell was deep underground and was crawling with rats which eventually he just ignored, except when they bit him. He was so deep under the earth that there was no light at all and though he tried to orient himself when he defecated, and make sure it was at the far end of the cell, eventually he would slip or fall into his own mess. The only way he could measure time was by the visits of his jailors. They never spoke to him, or each other, but would lead him in silence, up long flights of slimy, stone stairs to a large room on the ground floor where they tied him to a post and beat him with belts and their fists. They never told him why they were beating him and they never asked questions. Sometimes the beatings would happen in daylight, sometimes at night by the light of flaming torches fixed to the wall by the original Spanish Colonial iron clamps.

Occasionally he would hear screams of pain echoing in the darkness, and so he knew he was not alone. But most of the time he was surrounded by silence, except for the dripping of water and the scurrying sounds of the rats.

Eventually, after he had been softened-up, he was brought back to Guevara's headquarters, *San Carlos de la Cabaña*, overlooking the city. They stripped him naked in one of the outer courtyards and hosed him down, cleaning off the accumulated filth and blood from his stay in the prison of *Atarés*. Then he was tossed in a cell, still naked with nothing to cover himself, but at least there was daylight and the beatings stopped.

On the third day, he was taken to a large room and given a chair to sit on beside a small table. After maybe an hour, Che Guevara arrived and, sitting across from the table, offered Carlos a cigar, leaning over to light it for him.

"I met your father, you know" Guevara said. "A couple of times. A fine man. I'm sorry he decided to leave. He could have been an asset to the Revolution."

Carlos did not talk much, still disoriented from the weeks of silence and the pain of the beatings he had received. Guevara, did not seem to mind. He asked a few innocuous questions and waited patiently as Carlos slowly formed the words of his reply.

Suddenly, stubbing out his cigar, Guevara rose to his feet. "We'll talk again" he said. Turning to a guard on his way out he added, "get this man some clothes to wear."

Carlos remained in his cell at *La Cabaña* for more than a year, not that he had any sense of time. He had several meeting with Guevara, always cordial, always accompanied with a cigar. Guevara would ask him about his relationship with Camilo Cienfuegos; how they knew each other, what they talked about. He also asked about Manuel Artime and about the *Commandos Rurales*. He asked about both men's political views and how they viewed communism. His questioning was never overtly threatening, more like academic curiosity.

But from time to time, Carlos would be questioned by other people, and then the routine would be different. For a start there would be no cigars. He was always taken to the same room and would sit on the same chair and wait for about an hour before the door opened. But he would never know if it was Guevara with a couple of cigars or the other men. The other men carried thin canes and, after they had removed his shirt, they would beat his back until the skin broke. In between the beatings they would ask him questions; detailed questions about his family's possessions and where they could locate certain documents or keys. Carlos would tell them everything he

175

knew; he had gradually lost all sense of pride and his resistance was long drained and beaten out of him. Besides, he didn't care – his possessions were long lost to him. The only problem was that he could not even remember things, and so many of his answers were too vague or contradictory. This would result in yet more beatings as they slowly flayed the skin off his back.

When Guevara was the person entering the room, Carlos was so relieved and grateful that he never mentioned the other men. He was so appreciative of the cigar and the civilized discussion with his friend Che, that he did not want to spoil things or break the magic moment. His back was covered by his shirt and he would sit up straight so as not to lean back and touch the chair. But there came a point when the questions focused more on Manuel Artime and Carlos' kid brother. Where exactly was Oscar? What were Artime's plans, who were his contacts. Why was Oscar not living with his parents in Miami. Gradually the visits from Guevara became less often, they were shorter and finally they ceased. But the other men came more often and Carlos' back had no skin left and was simply raw flesh, sticking to his shirt till he could no longer take it off at night.

The final visit from Guevara was in June, 1961, not that Carlos had any idea what year it was, let alone which month. He had not seen Guevara for several weeks and was sitting on his chair, waiting for the other men to arrive when Guevara opened the door. Sitting down he gave Carlos a cigar and lit it for him, as though it was just one of their regular visits.

"I've got an old friend of yours" Guevara said after both of them had got their cigars going. He nodded to the guard at the door who went outside and then returned with another man. It took Carlos a while to identify his old friend but finally, beneath the unkempt hair and the long matted beard, he recognized Manuel Artime. Manuel was in handcuffs and stood beside his guard, staring expressionlessly at Carlos.

"Manuel" Guevara said. "You remember Carlos don't you? He certainly remembers you. He told us all about you. That's why we were waiting for you on the beach. He told us everything. Amazing what a man will do for a cheap cigar."

Before Carlos could digest the meaning of the words or even think about reacting, Guevara gave a curt nod to the guard and Artime was led out of the room.

Carlos never saw Guevara again and was moved from *La Cabaña* the following morning. For the next several years Carlos traveled all over Cuba, as he became a tourist in Castro's prison gulag. He spent the first five years in the horribly overcrowded Presidio Modelo, on the Isla de la Juventud. That's where he first learned to survive. With four or five thousand prisoners crammed in a prison built for two thousand and with food for maybe one thousand, Carlos was forced to make ruthless use of his superior height, his strength, his education and every possible advantage he could summon to fuel his will to survive. As his back healed and his strength returned, he rose to a position of power among the other prisoners. It was he that organized the food riots and encouraged some of the others in their hunger strikes. By the time he was moved to Boniato prison at the other end of the island, in Santiago de Cuba, his reputation preceded him and he allied himself with only the toughest of the criminals. Most of Cuba's political prisoners, of whom there were thousands, fought hard to retain their 'political' status. Known as '*plantados*' the stubborn ones, they refused to be associated with criminals and insisted on their dignity as political dissidents. Carlos did not. He had lost all his ideological beliefs and retained in his memory, only the look of sheer contempt on Artime's face as he was led out of his cell door. Over the years Carlos received indirect news about his family, living the good life in Miami and about his brother Oscar, wealthy and successful. He was happy for them but felt ever more forgotten and abandoned.

Gradually, the will and the ability to survive in such horrendous conditions hardened and atrophied all Carlos' finer feelings. Any sign of softness, however deep and well-hidden would betray a man and destroy him in the *gulag*. Wherever he was sent, whether Nieves Morejon Prison in Santi Spiritus, Reloj Club Boinas Rojas military camp in West Havana, or Kilo 7 Prison in Camaguey, Carlos immediately asserted himself and was quickly running the rackets. As the years passed and other prisoners were released, he built a network of criminal associates throughout the island and, because they were purely apolitical, interested solely in crime, they flew below the radar. They were merely criminals in a criminal society; they represented no threat to the State. It was during his stay at the Reloj Club military camp outside Havana that Carlos made many useful contacts with the military commanders in the *Grupo de Administracion Empresarial S.A.* (GAESA), the military monopoly that runs Cuba's economy.

In Castro's Cuba, all economic activity is controlled by the military's GAESA, which is why the military elite remains loyal to the Revolution. In such a criminal society, the only seriously recognized crime is to engage in opposition to the regime. All other activities, legal or otherwise, are simply different ways of earning money and surviving.

It was an ugly and brutal life, but at least Carlos had learned to survive. If young men were his only option for sexual gratification, then so be it. Ramon Fernandez was just one of many such boys. But lying awake, in his bunk at night, Carlos never forgot the Flesh Goddesses of the Tropicana.

Twenty-Seven: Greenhaven, 2013

The statue of Colonel Ray Connolly had been erected on its stone plinth in front of City Hall in mid-June but the unveiling ceremony was not scheduled till Monday, July 1st, the one hundred and fifteenth anniversary of the Battle of San Juan Hill in Santiago de Cuba. This was the famous battle when Connolly had ridden with

Teddy Roosevelt and his Rough Riders to liberate Cuba from the Spanish. His grandson, Alfred Connolly II had decided that this would be an auspicious date to honor the founder of the city.

In honor of the occasion, all the schools in Greenhaven had been closed for the day so that the children could attend the ceremony and all city employees had also been given time off to attend. Connolly Way which ran beside City Hall had been cordoned off and, since 8:00AM, workers from Parks & Recreation had been erecting rows of benches for the public to view the ceremony as well as rows of white plastic chairs for the VIPs.

For the three weeks since its erection, the statue had been covered with a heavy, green canvas tarpaulin, shielding it from public view. No photographs had been released and so there was a genuine curiosity and an air of excitement before the public unveiling. The VIP section was directly in front of the statue and facing City Hall while the general public section was directly behind and again fully facing the shrouded statue and City Hall. The side section, with only a oblique view of the statue was reserved for the schoolchildren who had been assembling on their allotted benches in noisy, excited groups since 10:30AM.

The unveiling was scheduled for noon and even though 'Miami Time' was a concept with which everybody was familiar, Greenhaven and its denizens prided itself on a strict adherence to an Anglo-Saxon concept of 'proper' time. George even referred to it as GMT, Greenhaven Mean Time. Noon in Greenhaven meant 12:00PM, not 12:40 or 12:57 PM which was more normal in Miami. Consequently most of the seats and benches were filled by 11:45AM despite the heat of the mid-day sun, as people knew the ceremony would start on time. Being locals, most people were dressed in loose fitting cotton clothes and of course everybody wore some variant of a lightweight straw hat with a broad brim to shield them from the worst of the sun's rays.

George and Karl were sitting with Charles Wilson, the owner of the Tenth Hole Diner as they watched all the seats on the benches around them filling up with the excited citizens of Greenhaven. "Where the Hell is that Cuban reprobate?" Karl muttered. "I can't keep his space for much longer." Meanwhile, the white seats of the VIP section were also filling up and Sergeant Anna Hartman and a couple of her colleagues from the Greenhaven Police Force were checking the IDs as well as the VIP passes. Ken Kerman was sitting in the center of the VIP section with his guest, William J. Park, the well-known international developer. Maurice Mayhew's wife Jane was unfortunately doing research at the State Capital in Tallahassee and therefore unable to attend the ceremony and so he was accompanied by an attractive young lady whom he introduced to everyone as an intern research-assistant from his law firm.

"Where the Hell were you?" Karl said as Raoul finally appeared. "It's been a goddam fight just keeping you a seat. Look how crowded it is. Don't you have any goddam clocks in Cuba?"

"They don't need clocks in Cuba. All they do is sit around in Government offices waiting for some fat dick-head to stamp some goddamned papers" Raoul said. "Cuba's nearly as bad as Greenhaven. That's where I've been all morning. Waiting for some broad with a big saggy ass to stamp my paper so I can appear before the Board of Architects and waste some more time next week."

"Still got the old fence problem?" George asked sympathetically. "How's Jose-Marti doing?"

"Poor bastard's locked up in the house all day without a fence, while I'm sitting around at City Hall."

Raoul sat down in the space next to Karl. "If you must know. I'm also late because I got caught-up with old Maurice Mayhew over there with his new bimbo that's he's introducing to everyone as an assistant law clerk." He leaned in towards Karl "but I happen to know she's a hat-girl at the Hard Rock Casino up in Broward County. Very friendly girl, if you know what I mean."

"I guess his wife's out of town then."

By tapping his finger on the microphone, Mayor Adams alerted the crowd that the ceremony was about to begin. He began by thanking everybody for attending and apologized for making them all sit in the July sun. "Had Teddy Roosevelt and the Rough Riders been more considerate, they would have fought the battle of San Juan Hill in early December when the weather is more suited for sitting outside. However, July 1st was the date they chose and so here we are today, to commemorate the anniversary of that battle and honoring one of its soldiers. The soldier we are honoring today is the founder of our city, Colonel Ray Connolly and here, to tell us more, is his grandson, Alfred Connolly II."

There was a polite round of applause as Connolly replaced Adams at the rostrum. For a man in his late seventies, Alfred Connolly II still had a commanding presence and, looking around the crowd before speaking, he held his audience with the fierceness of his stare. He began by discussing the relationship between his family and Cuba. He explained how, after graduating from college he had joined the marines to go fight in Cuba. "Most people here are too young to remember how it was in the sixties. Castro had just had his communist revolution and was imposing his anti-American dictatorship just ninety miles off our coast. Khrushchev, the Soviet leader was supporting the Castro dictatorship and threatening to crush us. War with communist Cuba and their Soviet masters seemed inevitable." He paused and surveyed the crowd with a fierce scowl. "In any event, I never did go to Cuba; I was sent to Vietnam instead, and instead of war with Cuba, we continue to co-exist while Castro's totalitarian regime still controls the island that my grandfather risked his life to liberate." After reminding his audience of the many sacrifices that the Anglo-Saxons had made in support of Cuba he emphasized that Greenhaven had never had a Cuban mayor. "But we are here today to celebrate the life of a man who not only helped liberate Cuba from the yoke of a foreign power, but also by sheer determination and vision, created this beautiful city where we all live today."

With an obvious sense of family pride, Connolly described how his grandfather had first come to Miami with Henry Flagler at the end of the nineteenth century and how he had volunteered to join the Rough Riders, an all-volunteer force lead by the future US President, Theodore Roosevelt, to fight in the Spanish American war. He described the celebrated battle of San Juan Hill, where his grandfather had received the famous saber slash which disfigured his face for the rest of his life, and which had led to the liberation of Cuba from the tyranny of the Spanish Empire.

Finally, he described how his grandfather's vision had created the City of Greenhaven.

"With the construction of a new road at the start of the century, linking Tampa with Miami, where others saw only the swamps and the rocky sloughs of the Everglades, my grandfather saw a paradise. With the same determination and courage that he displayed on the battlefields of Cuba, he now attacked the challenges of transforming the barren wilderness of South Florida into the glorious metropolis that we know today."

Eventually, having described his grandfather's various accomplishments in greater detail, he introduced Lady Catherine Sanders, Executive Director of the Greenhaven Museum.

"That's all?" Lady Sanders said when Connolly showed her the golden tasseled cord. "I just pull it and the shroud comes off? I don't have to break a bottle of bubbly or anything?"

When Connolly shook his head she said "Oh good. I've always thought what a horrid waste of perfectly good champagne that is. OK then, here goes."

As Lady Sanders pulled the cord, two Parks & Rec. employees, hidden behind the statue pulled the tarpaulin backwards so that it slid to the ground and Ray Connolly was revealed in all his glory.

There was a gasp of admiration from the crowd which rose spontaneously to its feet with a burst of applause. It certainly was an impressive statue; standing maybe ten feet high, Connolly stared grimly forwards in the direction that his extended arm was pointing, seemingly straight down the middle of the City High Street towards a Starbucks Coffee shop, while the other arm, bent at the elbow, held his unsheathed cutlass, ready for action. Despite the shadow cast by the broad brim of his slouched hat, the vicious scar across his cheek was clearly visible. The bright sun, shining off the newly polished bronze dazzled the onlookers' eyes and made the image of Connolly even more impressive.

"Nice job Catherine" Tom Adams said. "You appeared to do that unveiling with grace and a practiced ease."

"I hope you're not suggesting that I am experienced in the habit of undressing strange men Tom" she smiled.

"Congratulations Lady Sanders, that was most impressive." Ken Kerman, the City Manager had wanted to introduce his guest, William J. Park to the mayor but just as he approached Tom Adams, the mayor was pulled away by Alfred Connolly. "We need to talk" Connolly said. "Let's go to your office."

As Adams walked away with Connolly towards his City Hall office, Kerman decided to introduce Park to Lady Sanders instead. Kerman had long had an obsession with the English aristocracy and had recorded every episode of Downton Abbey. Although they had met only a few times, Lady Sanders, played an active though fairly decorous role in many of Kerman's more fervid nocturnal fantasies. But no sooner had he addressed her than she turned her head away, distracted by some disturbance in the crowd.

"What's going on over there?" she said, turning to ask George.

"The schoolkids seem to be up to some mischief" he said. "They're all pointing and laughing at something."

"Beastly little tykes" Lady Sanders said. "I'd better go and see what's the matter."

Lady Sanders left the VIP section to join the crowd of noisy, sniggering school children who were looking up at the statue. "Now what seems to be the matter here?" she asked. "You know, this is a formal public occasion and there are a lot of journalists around as well as at least two TV crews. So you're supposed to all be on your best behavior. Now you wouldn't like your parents to watch the six-o-clock news this evening and to see their child horsing around and being silly, now would you?"

"Please miss" one of the boys managed to stop laughing long enough to address her. "It's the statue. Look!"

Because the schoolkids had been placed at the far side of the viewing area, they were looking at the statue from a side elevation rather than seeing it face-on, and because the angle of the sun cast that side in shadow, the statue appeared in dark silhouette form. Lady Sanders turned her head to where the boy was pointing. "Oh my goodness!" she said. "My goodness me!"

"Billy" Maurice Mayhew called out. "I didn't know you were coming today. Ken, you should have told me." Shaking William J. Park enthusiastically by the hand he introduced him to his legal assistant. "Milly, I'd like you to meet Mr. William J. Park. Mr. Park is one of the biggest and most successful developers on the planet. He has buildings in every major city in the world."

Grasping her hand, Park said "Maurice nearly got it right but I'm not just one of the biggest and most successful developers. I am the world's biggest and most successful developer of all time. Nobody has their name on as many buildings as I do. Nobody else has the tallest skyscrapers in London, Paris, New York and Tokyo. And they're not just any old buildings; they are quality buildings. First class, top drawer buildings. Classy. And big. Everything I build is big. Huge! Like this statue see. If it was me building this statue, I wouldn't stop at ten feet. I would have made it twenty feet tall, thirty feet, so you can see it from the other side of town. And I wouldn't have left it natural bronze like that. I would have painted it. Gold. That's what I'd have painted it, gold. So it stands out and you can't miss it. Anyway Miss Milly, are you and Maurice joining us for lunch? Ken tells me you've got some great restaurants here in Greenhaven, so why don't you join us and I can tell you more about my buildings."

The Parks & Rec. people had already started stacking up the chairs and moving the benches by the time Lady Sanders rejoined George in front of the statue. "Well at least it's clear why Connolly is portrayed as the father of the city" she said. "At least we won't have to mark it on the plinth."

"How do you mean?" George asked.

"He has a woody"

"What do you mean? Who? Who has a woody?"

"Ray Connolly. That's what the kids are laughing about."

"What do you mean?"

"It's his sword. He's holding it at waist level, pointing forwards and slightly elevated. Well, viewed from the side, the silhouette looks as though he is sporting a massive erection. I mean massive. Most impressive!"

Twenty-Eight: Kaieteur Falls, Guyana, 1979

One of the historian, Jane Mayhew's favorite maxims was, 'you cannot trust history, it is full of lies and deceits.' This is why she took nothing at face value and continued digging into her research-papers until she was able to personally verify each one of her primary sources. According to Jane, even something as widely accepted as the foundation of the City of Greenhaven by Raymond Connolly was open to question,. Connolly was a well-known veteran of the Spanish American war and a close friend of Henry Flagler and Teddy Roosevelt, but nonetheless, Jane meticulously examined the original land-deeds, contemporary photographs and signed architectural drawings before she accepted Connolly's role in the creation of the city.

Jane Mayhew was probably not aware of the origin of the name of the Kaieteur Falls in the remote jungles of central Guyana. Indeed, it's unlikely that she would have heard of the waterfall, even though it boasts the highest single drop in the world. However, had she researched the origin of the name she would have been pleased to see it vindicate her maxim, that official history can never be trusted.

For more than a hundred years, since its discovery by British surveyors in 1870, it was popularly accepted that the Kaieteur Falls had been named for Kai, a local Indian chief, who acted to save his people by paddling over the falls in an act of self-sacrifice to Makonaima, the great spirit. It was only later, when linguists had studied details of the local culture that they discovered that Kaieteur has been named after an unpleasant old man who was placed in a boat and shoved over the fall by his relatives. Thus the fall was named "Kaieteur" which means - "old-man-fall" in the local dialect.

Four times higher than the Niagara Falls and twice the height of the Victoria Falls, the roar of the Potaro River, falling at 23,400 cubic feet per second in a single drop to the rocks below, makes it impossible to hear any other sound; makes it almost impossible to even think. This is why Oscar Enriquez had been wearing industrial grade ear-muffs for the two days it had taken him to climb to a thin ledge of rock behind the fall of water and then to attach himself to the cliff wall with nylon climbing rope and several pitons.

It was late afternoon by the time Oscar felt himself securely attached to the rock and he was worried about falling asleep while he waited. He had been climbing upwards through the jungle for two days without sleep and it was only the dull pain in his still-damaged foot that sometimes kept him awake. Once again he made sure the pitons were firmly attached in case he nodded-off while waiting.

He found it surprisingly dry behind the vast curtain of falling water and the powerful smell of guano added to the cave like sense of enclosed snugness. Oscar needed to stay awake. The birds would not arrive till dusk, but when they did, it would be fast, without warning and he would need to be fully alert.

The first one arrived just as the afternoon light began to fade. Here in the Tropics, just five degrees north of the Equator, dusk arrives abruptly, almost like switching off the light. Suddenly there was an explosion of activity, almost audible above the pounding roar of the falling water, as hundreds and then thousands of white collared swifts, or Makonaima birds, burst through the wall of water at speeds in excess of a hundred miles per hour yet managed to somehow stop themselves within the space of a few feet without smashing into the rock face. Armed with his battered Leica camera, Oscar was capturing the extraordinary moment as these legendary birds literally came home to roost. Among the fastest living creatures on the planet, this particular species of Swift, unique for its white chin and white collar feathers, roosts by the thousand, every night beneath the vast shelf of rock hidden behind the powerful Kaieteur Falls. As dusk falls and all the swarms of insects emerge from the jungle, the birds indulge in a high-speed orgy of eating above the canopy and then, using their maximum burst of speed to pass through the immense weight of falling water, they shoot into the cave.

Oscar had been commissioned by *National Geographic Magazine* to capture the previously undocumented moment when the swifts returned to their nests and he felt pleased with all the images he had captured on three rolls of film while the light lasted. Once more, checking the pitons in the rock face while munching on yet another energy bar, Oscar prepared for a nervous night perched precariously on a ledge behind the falls. It was too dangerous to climb-out in the dark and in any event, he hoped to get some bonus shots when the birds took off again at dawn's first light.

Thanks to the pressure from Andres Pruna and his team of US Navy frogmen, Oscar had been treated at the Navy's Walter Reed facility in Bethesda, MD for over three months after his return from the Bay of Pigs. The first month was touch and go as the bullet in his shoulder had become dangerously inflamed and septic. It took another month to reconstruct all the bones in his foot and a third month for him to learn to walk again. After four months he was able to return to Miami where he and his father, Don Carlos, both walked with pronounced limps to share a cigar and coffee at El Centro on Eighth Street. Don Carlos wanted to show-off his son, the 'war-hero', to all his guayabera-wearing friends but the attention just made Oscar uncomfortable. As far as Oscar was concerned, the whole operation had been a disaster. He had failed to release or even locate his brother; all his comrades had been killed or captured and he himself would spend the rest of his life walking with a limp – to Oscar, a mark of shame. Above all, Oscar blamed President Kennedy and the CIA for what he saw as a betrayal and he never forgave them for their lies and incompetence.

Oscar had won a few local photography prizes as a schoolboy and that helped him make some contacts at the *Miami Herald*. After showing some of his photographs taken in Central America, and at the landing site in Cuba, he was able to get some freelance photography work. After the Herald teamed him-up with Miguel Brodsky, a young sailor based on Biscayne Bay, the two of them filmed and photographed all over Florida's southern coast and soon built a national reputation for nature photography in the Everglades.

Having lived in crowded camps, surrounded by the smell of other men for over a year, and filled with a lingering sense of bitterness and failure, Oscar relished the solitude that his work as a wild-life photographer gave him. His images of Big Cyprus Swamp landscapes filled with wild egrets, crocodiles and alligators as well as Florida panthers provided enough income for him to help support his parents while maintaining his own independence. He spent as little time in Miami as possible and soon his only friends, apart from

Miguel, were the Park Rangers and Coast Guard patrols that he encountered on his explorations around the wild places of South Florida.

Oscar had been home for more than a year when he learned that negotiations between Kennedy's US government and Castro's Cuban government had resulted in the release of 1,113 captured prisoners from the Bay of Pigs in return for sixty million dollars' worth of food and supplies. Oscar immediately rushed to Donner Key in Miami where the released prisoners were arriving. Anxiously he read the lists of names which were published in the *Herald* and was delighted to see that 'Pepe' San Román, Erneido Oliva and Manuel Artime were all included in those who'd been released. He didn't entertain any hope but nevertheless he looked for the name of Carlos Enriquez, but his brother was not on the list.

It was almost a week before Oscar heard from any of the returned prisoners and then Manuel sent a message, via Don Carlos, for Oscar to meet him at the Church of the Little Flower in Coral Gables. Manuel Artime was sitting alone, on a bench outside the front door of the church when Oscar arrived. The two men embraced but Oscar was immediately aware of a certain reserve in his old friend. His embrace had been perfunctory and his manner was detached.

"I saw your brother Carlos" he said.

Oscar's heart skipped a beat and he just stared at Manuel.

"Where?" he finally said. "How was he?"

"It was just a brief meeting. I saw him at *La Cabaña* - where they kept some of us for a few weeks of special attention."

"Carlos was there? You got to talk to him?"

There was a long silence while Manuel sat expressionless, looking at Oscar, before he responded.

"He was sitting in a room with Che Guevara, the two of them were smoking cigars."

Again, there was a long silence while Manuel watched Oscar's face.

"According to Guevara, it was Carlos who had informed them of our plans. He was so well informed that they were all in place, ready to meet us on the beach."

The two men sat in silence, staring at each other.

Finally Oscar said "And you think I was the source? You think I betrayed us to my brother?"

"I don't know Oscar. I don't know. I mean, none of us knew what the plans were. None of us knew where we were going to land – so how could you have told him? And how could you communicate? And why would you let yourself get shot?"

Manuel pulled out a pack of Lucky Strikes and lit one. "I don't know Oscar. I don't know. I go round and round in circles and it's driving me crazy. But I can't get rid of the memory of his face, just sitting there with Guevara, the two of them lounging in their chairs comfortably, puffing away on cigars while we were being beaten on the floor below."

He paused to spit on the floor. "And let's face it: we were betrayed. They were there waiting for us. Maybe it was the Americans who betrayed us, maybe it was Carlos, maybe it was you. You did escape after all. You weren't captured like the rest of us."

Manuel dropped his cigarette to the floor and ground it to death with the heel of his boot. "I don't know what to think anymore. I don't know who to believe. But anyway, I needed to come and see you and look into your eyes and ask you. Did you betray us Oscar?"

Oscar stared back. "No. I did not ever betray you Manuel; or the cause. And I don't believe Carlos did either. I don't understand. I'm as confused as you are."

Manuel rose to his feet and put out his hand. "I believe you Oscar. But you understand, things can never be the same again. I'm sorry. Maybe it's unfair but the doubt is out; it can't be put back in

190

the basket. One last thing. Watch-out for Mr. B. He's always had it in for you. Be careful."

The two men shook hands and then Manuel turned and walked away while Oscar entered the church to calm his troubled thoughts.

It was a few weeks after this meeting that Oscar received a very generous commission from the *National Geographic* to take some photographs of the giant anaconda in its native habitat, deep in the Amazon Jungle. Already an introverted soul; following his meeting with Manuel, Oscar relished these solitary assignments deep in the South American jungles. The bitterness against both the American and the Cuban governments continued to deepen. The conspiracy theories about betrayal and his own overwhelming sense of guilt concerning Carlos, all culminated in a desire to avoid human contact and to hide himself away in the world's most remote and private places.

Over the next few years Oscar became a world expert on the Amazon river basin and spent more time in the jungles of Colombia, Venezuela, Peru and Brazil than he ever did in Miami. He had become a star photographer for the *National Geographic* and participated in many documentaries with David Attenborough and the BBC. In the world of nature photography and filmmaking, Oscar was becoming a well-known name, but for the rest of the world, Oscar had slipped from sight and fallen off the map.

On his brief visits home, Oscar was increasingly depressed by his mother's near total dementia and his father's failing health. It took a long while before Oscar discovered that the main reason for their physical decline was Medicare fraud. Partly out of pride, and partly due to his lack of understanding of the US bureaucracy, Don Carlos did not let Oscar know their Medicare accounts had been corrupted. Somebody had used their Medicare cards to defraud the government and, as a result, his mother was denied the medication she so desperately needed. Unable to even get a walker to help her move around, she fell several times, breaking her fragile bones, not to mention her spirit.

Luckily, with the commissions he was now earning, Oscar was able to pay for his mother to be placed in a Miami nursing home and to purchase a small apartment on Eighth Street within walking distance of both the nursing home and El Centro so that his father could still get to both, albeit with a wheelchair that Oscar had also bought him. Because their Medicare accounts had been corrupted, without Oscar's financial support, his parents would have been completely destitute. In any event, within two weeks of entering the nursing home, his mother was dead, a random victim of Medicare fraud. Collateral damage.

It was in April 1980, when Oscar was filming whales off the coast of Patagonia in southern Argentina, that he learned that his father had fallen seriously ill and had been taken to hospital. Immediately abandoning the film crew, Oscar chartered a small plane to Buenos Aires and took the first flight to Miami. For the next four days Oscar sat at his father's bedside, holding his hand while the old man slipped in and out of consciousness. Sometimes Don Carlos knew where he was but other times he thought he was still home in Havana and anxiously asked Oscar for updates on the state of the horses in the Santa Clara estate or the tobacco harvest in their Pinar del Rio fincas. Most of the time the old man slept and Oscar would watch the news on the television.

That is how Oscar learned about Castro's decision to open the port of Mariel and allow any Cuban who wanted to leave the island to do so. Once again, Oscar hoped that his brother might have been included in the list of refugees, but from the US news reports it soon became obvious that the only people crossing over from Mariel were blue-collar, working class people who had been occupying embassies in Havana.

Sitting beside his dying father and holding his pale, frail hand while he listened to his labored breathing was probably the lowest point in Oscar's life. Watching the TV news throughout the day and seeing the hundreds of rejoicing Cubans being reunited with their relatives in different processing centers around Miami, just reminded him and emphasized how he had failed his adored older brother. Carlos would not be coming to Miami, he would remain in Castro's gulag forever.

It was early May when Oscar buried his father. He placed his father next to his mother in a plot in Caballero Rivero Woodlawn North cemetery on Eighth Street, again within walking distance of El Centro. It was a dark, rainy afternoon when they buried Don Carlos beside his wife, but it was a good turn-out from El Centro and Oscar invited them all back to the apartment for cigars and Bacardi rum. One by one, the old men with their trimmed white mustaches and their crisp guayaberas clasped Oscar's hand and offered their respects –both to him as a Bay of Pigs veteran and to Don Carlos, as a gentleman of the old school.

Manuel Artime also attended the funeral. He waited till Oscar had tended to all his guests and toasted the memory of his father. Manuel raised his glass of rum and clinked Oscar's glass in a sign of friendship.

"Word is that Castro is messing with President Carter" Manuel said quietly.

"What do you mean?"

"It appears that Castro is emptying all the jails and mental hospitals. He's sending them all over here."

"What are you saying?"

"There is a chance that Carlos was released. He could be here in Miami."

Twenty-Nine: Greenhaven 2013

Leaving the rest of the city's dignitaries admiring the new statue of Ray Connolly on its plinth in front of City Hall, Alfred Connolly and Thomas Adams climbed the ornate stone staircase leading to the

Mayor's office. "One of my grandfather's greatest joys" Connolly said, stroking the smooth surface of the well-worn stone balustrade. "He would be delighted to see how well this staircase has survived."

"Jane Mayhew calls it the 'Jewel in Greenhaven's crown'" Adams said. "Meaning that City Hall itself is the crown. And I've got to say that I'm very proud to be mayor on the day when your grandfather's statue was finally erected in front of his 'crown'."

"That's what we need to discuss" Connolly said as they entered the mayor's office and closed the door. "You have to run again Thomas. I'm hearing terrible things about this Cuban crook. You have a civic duty to protect this city from the danger he represents."

"Alfred my friend. You have to stop calling him a crook and you have to stop referring to him as a Cuban. I will not participate and will not be associated with any racist campaigns. Each time you make these statements you make me less and less willing to run. Now I will fight him on the issues, if you persuade me that his plans are harmful but I will not fight him on personal or tribal issues."

"Too late for that Tom. You missed that boat."

"What do you mean?"

"His people are already putting the word out that you're anti-Cuban."

"How? That's ridiculous!"

"That's what they're doing. Gone through the electoral role and picked everybody with an Hispanic surname and sending his people round to say that you're running an anti-Cuban campaign. Nothing in writing of course. All verbal. In Spanish. Hell. They're even saying it on Spanish talk-radio."

"How do you know all this?"

"My pool man. My yard man. Even my cook's been telling me about it. You may not realize it but there's a hell of a lot of Cubans live in Greenhaven and they aren't all yardmen and auto-mechanics. I had no idea until I started researching property records and electoral roles in City Hall last week. They've been sneaking-in under the radar."

"Enough Alfred! Enough. Nobody's sneaking. I know the demographics of this city. It's my job for God's sake. And calling me anti-Cuban is just going to backfire. Jesus! My daughter's married to a Cuban. My grandkids are half-Cuban.

"All right. All right, Mr. politically-correct. I guess you don't know Cubans like I know Cubans. I had to fight with them, back in the sixties, in Vietnam. Nasty, vicious bunch." Unconsciously, Connolly brushed his fingers along the scar on his cheek. "OK. Forget about the Cuban aspect then, but there's plenty of other stuff. For a start, he's quite openly talking about turning the Palace Hotel into some sort of Latin strip club. Says it will bring in the tourists."

"The Tropicana you mean?"

"Yes. That's what he wants to call it. Goddam man isn't even mayor yet and already he's changing names and planning to change everything my grandfather created."

"I don't think it's a strip club he's planning. I think it's more like a night club he has in mind."

"Same difference. Half-naked girls with feathers and sequins, showing their tits and encouraging vice. That might be all right for Hialeah or even Miami Beach, but it's not right for Greenhaven. And that's just the thin edge of the wedge. If he's boasting about turning one of our finest civic buildings into a girly-bar before he's even elected; God knows what he'll be suggesting once he's in office. Can you imagine what sort of dress code he'll enforce in City Hall – tight spandex dresses and long finger-nails.

"Alfred. Alfred. I mean it. I won't listen to this racist nonsense. If that's your only objection to the man, then our conversation is over. I want no part of this exaggerated racist nonsense."

"All right. All right. But I do have more serious objections. The man is a criminal and he is going to be indicted by the Federal

Government on charges of fraud. I agree that there have been plenty of South Florida mayors arrested and jailed for corruption; Hialeah, Miami Beach, North Miami, Homestead, Sweetwater – the list is endless – but never Greenhaven. There has never been a hint of corruption in this city and that's why we have to keep this man Martinez out of City Hall."

"Alfred. These are very serious allegations. You've got to be careful. You've no proof. Where are you hearing these rumors?"

"My son, Alfred III. You know he runs a hedge fund on Wall Street and he's also Chairman of the Nordmeyer Family Trust in D.C. His people know people. They know what's going on, and what's what. It's their business to know stuff. They've been getting signs to avoid the health-care industry for a while, specifically to divest any holdings in AHCU, Martinez's corporation. Word on the street is that the Feds are preparing an indictment. Could be even bigger than the Colombia scandal back in the nineties."

"What sort of indictment?"

"Fraud. Systematic Medicare and Medicaid fraud – going back years."

"Are they charging Martinez or just his company?"

"Just his company, as far as I know."

"So he could be in the clear. He's divested himself of all interest in the company. He's made himself very clear on that point."

"Exactly. He's taking all the right steps to avoid going to jail. Becoming mayor of Greenhaven will make him even more untouchable and it will make any criminal charges seem more like dirty politics. You've got to run Tom. This man could taint the whole city."

"I'll need money Alfred. This won't be like our normal elections. He's got unlimited funds to spend."

"Three hundred grand already, just on the Spanish language talk shows and I'm told he's planning a whole campaign in *El Nuevo*

Herald. Just tell me you'll run Tom and I'll talk to some of my contacts about funding. But I need your assurance first."

"OK. Meet me here tomorrow at noon and I'll have my answer. I need to talk to Laura and I need to make my own enquiries about this indictment. Tomorrow, Alfred."

The subject of their conversation, Orestes Martinez, was actually having lunch nearby at La Taberna restaurant with Lady Sanders when Ken Kerman came over from an adjoining table. "Your ladyship" he said. "Dr. Martinez. How lovely to see you both. I'm just over there with Mr. William Park and Maurice Mayhew."

"Who's the young lady with Maurice?" Lady Sanders asked. "Is that his daughter?"

"No. Maurice and Jane don't have any children. I believe she's a legal assistant from his law office."

"How generous and thoughtful of him to take her to lunch. By the way, here's a suggestion for all of you. After lunch you should take the young lady to look at the new statue of our City Father. Not from the front where you were all sitting earlier, but from the side where all the schoolkids were placed. I think she will be very impressed."

"Thank you, your ladyship. We shall certainly do that. I believe the addition of this statue will add greatly to our civic pride. Thank you."

"I hope you will all be coming to my Town Hall meeting tomorrow at the Museum Ken" Martinez said. "As City Manager, I know you have to remain neutral, but you should still come and hear my proposals. And please encourage Mr. Park to attend, I really want to talk to him some time about my plans for the Tropicana."

While Martinez and Lady Sanders continued making plans for the following evening's Town Hall meeting, Ken Kerman rejoined his guests. "You never know" he said. "Dr. Martinez could be our next mayor very soon. He asked me to remind you that he's having a Town Hall meeting tomorrow at the Museum and he wants us all to attend."

"Sorry. No can do" Maurice said. 'I've got to go to the Hard Rock Casino up in Broward. They've become one of our major clients." He turned smiling and placed a hand on William Park's arm. "But obviously not as important as the Park Corporation."

"What about you, Miss Milly?" Park asked. "Will you be coming to the Town Hall meeting?"

"No. She'll be assisting me I'm afraid" Maurice said. "Lots of work to do" he said, squeezing her knee under the table.

"I'll certainly be there" Park said. "For a start, I want to show my support for Martinez. It's time for new mayor. Time for a change. Greenhaven is too old and stuffy, it needs new life in it and a new mayor is a good place to start, especially with a smart business man like Orestes. I've been looking at his business background. Very impressive. Lots of smart deals – and I know all about smart deals. I've been making smart deals all my life, that's how I can recognize somebody like Martinez. He's a winner. Takes a winner to spot a winner and I can always spot them. You mark my words. Martinez will be the new mayor and that stuffy old fuddy-duddy will be out."

"You don't like Tom Adams?" Maurice asked.

"He's a loser. He's pathetic. Low energy. No respect. He's never come to visit me at my office. Never offered to meet with me when I'm here in his city. He offers me no respect. He's a loser. Now Orestes over there; he's come to pay his respects. He's a go-getter. He's a winner. With him in City Hall and me redeveloping the Palace Hotel, Greenhaven will never be the same again."

"I hear he wants to develop the Palace Hotel as some sort of nightclub." Maurice said.

"Yes." Kerman confirmed. "He wants to recreate the glories and glamour of the Tropicana nightclub they used to have in Havana in the fifties."

"It's going to be terrific, amazing, it'll be huge, better than Havana in the fifties because it will be in one of my Park Towers." Turning to Milly, Park said. "See, Greenhaven doesn't have one of my buildings in it yet. That's why they're not really on the map yet, like Paris or New York. But after I've converted the Palace hotel into a Park tower and installed Orestes' nightclub – then we really will be on the map!"

"And hopefully that will attract outside investors" Kerman said.

"Don't worry about that Ken" Park reassured him. "With all my Russian contacts, they'll pump so much money into Greenhaven it will make your head spin."

Thirty: Miami 1987

"I don't know, Carlos" Oscar said. "I think even for international drug-kingpins this might be considered somewhat excessive."

The two brothers were standing on the main deck of a one-hundred and twenty foot super-yacht that Carlos had just purchased at the Miami Boat Show. It was not the size of the yacht itself which caused Oscar's reservation, but rather the twin staircases leading down from the private quarters on the upper deck.

"Imagine the girls, little brother. Dressed in feathers and little else as they slowly sashay down the stairs. Can't you picture it? Let me tell you, I have pictured little else for the past twenty years." Carlos dragged on his cigar and threw his arm around Oscar's shoulder.

"Listen, I have meetings set-up in Cadiz, in Palermo and in Monte Carlo. Can you imagine what effect this baby is going to have on those guys? I'm picking up some dancers in Havana on the way over and those girls are going to make those European guys pee their pants. They'll all want to work with us."

"I'm just worried a boat like this will draw too much attention" Oscar said. "There's a record of you buying it here in the US and paying cash. If you'd bought it in France or Rio the trail would be colder."

"All in feathers" Carlos said, squeezing his brother closer and ignoring his words. "Tits bouncing between the plumes. Some of them shaved, some of them flashing a black bush between the white feathers. Shimmying down the twin staircases, arm in arm like one of the Busby movies – you remember, those black and white movies we used to jerk-off to. Ah Oscar! You were too young. If only you'd been there with me and Camilo at the Tropicana in the old days. It would have blown your mind. Gorgeous girls, you can't imagine. Not like these skinny, uptight broads you see here in America.

"Don't forget" Carlos said a few days later as he embraced his brother in a farewell. "You're in charge now bro. I'll try and let you know where you can contact me once I 've got settled in France, but it could take a while. Don't worry bro. I'll be back by mid-September. We've got big plans for the fall."

As Oscar reflected later, they had 'big plans' most of the time. Carlos had no concept of anything that was not a 'big plan'.

Though slightly nervous of the responsibility, Oscar was actually pleased to have sole charge of the operation. He saw Carlos' plan to open new markets in Europe, as representing a positive reinforcement of his plan to bring everything back under control. Oscar had no desire to wrest power from Carlos. He had no wish to be boss. But he did want to 'tidy things up a bit'. Perhaps it was a result of the organization suddenly expanding at an accelerated rate with too few control mechanisms, perhaps it was due to Carlos' increasing consumption of cocaine, perhaps it was no more than a worry about being in charge of one of the biggest drug importing organizations in the country.

It had all developed so quickly that Oscar could still not believe the reality of his new life. In the space of less than five years he had been transformed from a reclusive and scruffy, nature photographer into an elegant, jet-setting, millionaire-boss of a vast criminal cartel. The two bothers owned art-galleries on Miami Beach, elegant mansions in Greenhaven and Palm Beach. They maintained apartments in New York and San Francisco not to mention fleets of cars, planes and offshore power boats.

No sooner had Oscar signed Carlos out of the downtown Miami processing center for Marielitos in 1980 than Carlos had started making plans. He dismissed the story that Oscar told him about Che Guevara and the cigars as old news and irrelevant.

"Yes, I was sitting there with that monster and yes I was smoking a cigar, but I was not lounging." His eyes flashed with anger as he remembered the meeting. "The reason I was not lounging was that my back was a piece of raw flesh from all the beatings, and I could not lean back against anything." Pulling up his shirt, Carlos showed Oscar his back; almost twenty years later the scars were still visible, the skin a shiny pink, crisscrossed with hatch marks from the whippings." Oscar's stomach knotted with shame and guilt at the sight.

"If that's what Artime and all those pricks in Alpha 66 want to think - fuck them! I'm not wasting my time worrying about him. I've already wasted too much time. That's nearly twenty years of my life I've wasted." He clasped Oscar around the shoulder in a big hug. "No more my brother. From now-on, you and I are going to make-up for all that wasted time."

Carlos had all his plans already made even before arriving in Miami. Although he'd been locked away in the Cuban gulag, he knew what was going on in the outside world and he had all his criminal contacts already in place. Initially Carlos did not intend to involve Oscar in his activities. Carlos was well aware that prison had changed and hardened him and was aware that all his current associates were as brutal as they were ruthless. Not only did he still feel protective about his kid brother but he could also see that dreamy, artistic Oscar, with no criminal experience, would be eaten alive by the sort of people with whom Carlos now associated. Oscar would be more of a drag on his plans than an asset.

But things changed dramatically when Carlos learned more about Oscar's activities down in the Everglades.

"You're kidding me! You know the shoreline like the back of your hand? You know every little hidden creek and slough all over the Everglades?"

"Yes, and don't forget I know most of the Park Rangers and the local Coast Guard. Half of them smoke pot while we're sitting out there watching for wildlife and my friend Miguel Brodsky has been sailing this coast all his life, he knows it even better than me. His father used to run booze over from Bimini during Prohibition. He knows the ocean currents and every possible landing site between here and the Texas border."

But it was Oscar's contacts and detailed knowledge of the jungles of South America that finally settled things and altered Carlos' plans.

"This is just amazing bro! You know, I never take on equal partners. I'm always the boss. That's just the way it works for me. But now bro. You're my partner. It's going to be fifty-fifty all the way."

Oscar didn't care. He was just so overjoyed to have his brother back and to be able to make up for all the years that he felt he'd failed him. He would have done anything for his brother. Even so, consciously switching overnight to a life of crime would normally have been more of a struggle, if Oscar did not already feel so bitter against the American government for its betrayal at the Bay of Pigs. Additionally, having watched the suffering of his parents when their Medicare account was abused and the system seemed not to care, had only hardened Oscar's heart against American society.

Oscar was already familiar with many of the jungle labs in Colombia where the cocoa paste was processed into cocaine and Carlos, who accompanied him, was quickly negotiating with the cartel leaders to purchase the final product. Carlos had his own contacts who could fly small aircraft, and Oscar knew remote landing strips not just in Colombia but throughout Central America. Almost twenty years of filming wildlife in the more secluded parts of the Southern States had given Oscar a detailed knowledge of hidden landing sites stretching from the Everglades in Florida to the Bayous of Louisiana.

Carlos' network of underworld contacts were able to provide the ships and sailors to transport the drugs from Colombia to the Caribbean and he soon had a fleet of go-fast power boats able to make the final run to the hidden creeks and inlets along the Southern Florida seaboard. It was not only Oscar and Miguel's detailed knowledge of the coastline that was so invaluable but so too was his network of friendly Park Rangers, local coastguards and rural Sheriffs all of whom helped guarantee the smooth, uninterrupted running of the operation. The final factor which persuaded Carlos to allow Oscar's friend Miguel to join the organization as a junior partner was his mob connections. Miguel's father had smuggled booze for the mob during the 1920s and as a result his godfather was Meyer Lansky, the Mafia's financial boss. Miguel was thus able to introduce the two Enriquez brothers to 'Fat Tony' Salerno and the Genovese family as their New York distributors.

Above all, what made the Enriquez brother's operation so successful was the Cuban factor. During the two decades in prison, Carlos had developed a sophisticated network of hardened Cuban criminals, both inside and outside the island. Many of his contacts on the island worked closely with GAESA, Cuba's military monopoly which had its fingers in every activity on the island. One of Carlos's contacts was General Arnaldo Ochoa whom he had met in the early seventies, during his brief imprisonment in the Reloj Club military camp. Carlos learned that Ochoa had been a friend and colleague of Camilo Cienfuegos before his death and the two men had exchanged pleasant memories of their old mutual friend. By the mid-eighties, after Carlos' release, General Ochoa had become one of the most powerful men in Cuba and a close friend of Raul Castro. Carlos and Oscar's boats and planes were thus able to land and refuel in Cuba with the full protection of the regime's military establishment. It was this Cuban connection that gave the brother's smuggling organization such a unique advantage over all the other Colombian and American cartels.

The same planes and boats that brought the drugs into the country were also used to transport the vast amounts of cash out again. Some of the cash was discreetly deposited in banks located in Bal Harbour, just north of Miami Beach, where the local police force had developed a sophisticated money laundering operation, but most of the cash was shipped-out by sea and by air. From their primary bank account in Panama which received the cash, funds were wired to various other banks in Switzerland, Austria and Liechtenstein. Carlos' knowledge of international finance and the breadth of his criminal contacts throughout Latin America was phenomenal. He even had contacts in Cuban intelligence and within the Cuban military. After twenty years in prison, Carlos was like a coiled spring and the enthusiastic energy he brought to the enterprise was unstoppable.

The two brothers complemented each other perfectly. While both were cerebral, Oscar remained detached and discreetly in the background, whereas Carlos was more openly involved. Oscar focused on the logistics of their enterprise, planning the routes and locations, masterminding the transport. Carlos put together the deals, negotiated with the suppliers and oversaw the distribution.

Carlos' decision to expand the business into Europe meant that Oscar would have to emerge from his private shell and meet with some of their more unsavory partners, specifically the New York Mafia distributors. If the brothers were to collect their money, Oscar would finally have to get his hands dirty.

Thirty-One: Greenhaven 2013

As usual, Harriet Brownmiller was having great difficulty trying to decide which wine she preferred. "You say that Lady Sanders selected all these wines herself?"

"Yes" George replied. "Lady Sanders devotes a lot of her time researching what libations will prove most suitable for the Museum's guests."

"Let me have a taste of that Pinot Noir again. Fresh glass please."

Eventually she settled for the Cabernet Sauvignon and reminded George that she was a member of the Museum.

"I know, Mrs. Brownmiller. A most esteemed and distinguished member of the Museum if I might say so. But nonetheless, I still need to charge you five–dollars for the wine."

Finally, after Harriet went off in search of free food, grimly clutching her glass of wine, George was able to serve Karl and Raoul with their beers.

"I still don't feel right being here" Karl said. "Feel I'm being disloyal to Tom."

"That's stupid" George said. "You need to educate yourself on what the issues are and what each candidate proposes. Anyway, Tom hasn't even committed yet. He's still not sure if he wants to run, so that's why we need to hear from Martinez."

"Well, I don't even need to hear what he's got to say" Raoul said. "I'm voting for Martinez anyway."

"Why is that?" George asked.

"Don't even ask him" Karl said, pointing his toothpick at his friend.

"He's a fellow Cuban" Raoul said. "So he must be good. Stands to reason."

"See what I mean" Karl said. "These spics and dagos all stick together."

"Not only that" Raoul said. "They say he's going to change things around. Bring Greenhaven into the twenty-first century. Maybe get rid of that goddamned Historic Preservation shit. Maybe a Cuban mayor will help me finally get a fence for my yard and set Jose-Marti free at last."

"Ladies and gentlemen" Lady Sanders was standing at the podium and holding the museum's brand new cordless microphone. "Thank you all for coming here this evening and I'd be grateful if you would now take your seats. Can you hear me at the back of the room?" Looking directly at George she said. "George, if you would kindly close the bar for a while and persuade your unruly looking friends to sit down, then we can start the proceedings on time for once."

With a few late arrivals sneaking in, all the seats were quickly filled and many people were soon standing at the back of the room, leaning against the bar, or lined-up down the side. Lady Sanders explained that this evening's presentation would be given by Mr. Orestes Martinez and the following week, the museum would host a presentation by Mayor Adams.

"My understanding is that he submitted his papers at the Town Hall this morning and so, following Mayor Adams' own Town Hall presentation, the Museum will host a debate between the two candidates, two weeks from this evening. And now, please give a big hand to our first mayoral candidate, Dr. Orestes Martinez."

For the evening's performance, Martinez made use of the museum's overhead projector to offer a PowerPoint presentation. It was obviously a very professional and expensive production and, with Martinez's own experienced and eloquent talents, he soon had the whole room in his hand. His talk was similar to the one he had previously given at the Doyle's fundraiser but the dramatic visuals made everything come alive. He talked about sidewalk cafes, easing traffic flow and building a trolley system throughout the city. "We have to get cars out of the downtown area and make Greenhaven pedestrian friendly" he said. "Residents like leaving the car at home and walking to the shops and restaurants, but so too do tourists. When you're on vacation you like to feel relaxed; you like to stroll. Think of some of the world's greatest tourist destinations: Paris, New York, San Francisco, London – what do they all have in common? They are all great cities for walking, so that's what we must do for Greenhaven. He quoted New Urbanist studies done in Copenhagen and elsewhere, illustrating his talk with photographs and visual animations of pedestrian and bike-friendly cities.

"He's certainly done his work" Lady Sanders said to George whom she had joined at the back of the room and where he had prepared her a gin-and-tonic. "I've got to say, I'm very impressed."

"I know what you mean" George said. "Tom's a good friend but this guy's got a vision. Maybe we do need a bit of shaking-up. This is all exciting stuff."

At the end of the presentation, Lady Sanders returned to the podium, shook hands while thanking Martinez and then invited questions from the floor. Once more, displaying the relaxed skills of an experienced public speaker, Martinez fielded all the questions with charm and direct answers. "I think you've won them all over Orestes" Lady Sanders murmured to him as she prepared to take the final round of questions.

"Yes Harriet. Mrs. Brownmiller, wife of Commissioner Herbert Brownmiller, you have a question?"

"Yes, I do have a question. Dr. Martinez you did not mention during your presentation this evening, your project for turning the Palace Hotel into some sort of Latin Dance Club. Is that no longer part of your plan for the city?"

"Well I don't know that a Latin Dance Club was ever part of my plan for Greenhaven, but yes, I do plan to be restoring the currently shuttered Palace Hotel to its former glory, and that will indeed include developing a very glamorous and sophisticated nightclub called the Tropicana. In fact, I'm delighted to see we have Mr. William J. Park – the world renowned developer who will be working with the city to restore the Palace Hotel and develop the Tropicana – sitting right here in the audience."

"Nightclub! What's that mean? Half naked girls in feathers and sequins?" Alfred Connolly II had risen to his feet. "I've kept quiet all evening. I've not said anything while you go on about changing my grandfather's street plans and all your talk about traffic flows and foreign cafés but I knew underneath it all was the hidden agenda, the Cuban nightclub. I'm seventy-five you know. I've been around and I know you Cubans. There's always a hidden agenda. Like Mrs. Brownmiller said, the bottom line here under all this fancy talk is a Latin Dance Parlor – and we all know what that means, Well not in my town Jose, we won't stand for it. You can take it back to Cuba!" Pushing angrily to the end of the row, Connolly, followed by Harriet Brownmiller and a few other residents pushed through the crowded aisles to the exit at the back of the room.

"I am so sorry Dr. Martinez. That was absolutely unacceptable." Turning to address the room, Lady Sanders said. "Unless we can maintain a civilized tone of mutual respect, there will be no more questions and I will thank Dr. Martinez for a most interesting and stimulating presentation."

"I would like to say something to Dr. Martinez" William Park had risen to his feet. "Dr. Martinez, earlier this evening you asked a question but I do not think you gave the correct answer. You asked 'Paris, New York, San Francisco, London – what do all these cities have in common?' You said something about walking in them, but you did not mention the most important thing these great cities really have in common." Park paused dramatically as he looked slowly around the room. "They all have a Park Tower. That's what they all have in common. That's what puts them on the map. New York has

208

Park Tower on Park Avenue, London has Park Tower on Park Lane, that's what makes these cities great, so when we transform the Palace Hotel into a Park Tower, Greenhaven will be welcomed into the select club of the world's greatest cities with its own Park Tower."

"Well it won't actually be called Park Tower, Mr. Park. It's going to be called The Tropicana. That's the whole point of the project. We are recalling the glamour and the sophisticated nightlife of the original Tropicana. It would not work in a Park Tower. I thought we had agreed on that."

"Never! I would never agree to such a thing. I'm the greatest developer in the world. My name is gold. Pure gold. Why would I ever build something and not put my name on it? That's a horrible idea. It's bad and disgusting."

"Well I'm sorry for any misunderstanding Mr. Park. Quite unintentional I assure you. But if that building gets restored and I am mayor of this city, it will be called The Tropicana."

"Then you won't be mayor! You're a loser. I can always spot a loser and you're a loser. A winner would understand that Greenhaven can never be great again without a Park Tower and that's what I'm going to build here, and it will be great. It will be amazing. It will be huge!"

As Park's voice rose in pitch, other angry voices were raised as well and throughout the hall, people all appeared to be arguing with each other. Grabbing the microphone, Lady Sanders announced. "Thank you ladies and gentlemen but the meeting is now closed. There will be no more questions" and leaving George to close down the bar and close-up the museum, she hustled Martinez out the side door and into the street.

Park was still fuming, even though Martinez had left. "I can't believe it" he said. "I have never been wrong before. I thought Martinez was a winner. He's a rich businessman; he's successful, he makes lots and lots of money. Why is he so obsessed with a stupid name? Some horrible, cheap Cuban nightclub's name!"

209

Ken Kerman looked at him anxiously. "I don't know Mr. Park. Maybe I can meet with him tomorrow and explain your perspective."

"All right. I'm not a proud man. I can admit when I've made a mistake" Park said, ignoring Kerman. "It's not often, in fact I can't think of any other time I've made a mistake. But here's what we're going to do."

They both moved to the bar where George was sorting the clean and the used glasses onto separate trays and pouring the half emptied wine bottles together (by varietal) and then re-corking them for the Art Show scheduled for the following evening.

Leaning on the counter, Park pulled out a corporate check-book and wrote on it with a pen that George loaned him from behind the bar. "There" he said. This is made out to Mayor Adam's Political Action Committee. I don't want him being outspent by that lousy, grandstanding, Cuban showboat. You can let your Mayor know that I've got his back. We're going to make Greenhaven great again and we're going to build a Park Tower to prove it."

Kerman looked at the check when Park handed it to him. "But Mr. Park. That's a million dollars!"

"Listen Ken. We are keeping that Tropicana bastard out of Greenhaven whatever the cost. Get that check into the PAC bank account and let the battle begin."

"A brisk walk, some cool night air and then a couple of good stiff drinks. That's what we need" Lady Sanders said as she escorted Martinez a couple of blocks to The Globe which served food and alcohol till the early hours.

"Who is that ugly old cracker?" Martinez finally asked after his second rum and coke. They had sat in silence for almost fifteen minutes after arriving at the bar; he was obviously wound tight with fury and for the first time Lady Sanders was aware of ruthless brutality beneath his otherwise elegant demeanor. Feeling thoroughly embarrassed and somehow responsible for the evening's debacle she sat quietly, waiting for the alcohol to work its magic.

"That's Alfred Connolly II" she said. "The grandson of the city's founder." She was tempted to lighten the mood by telling Martinez about the statue's unfortunate side-profile but decided the moment was not right. "Unfortunately he's obsessed with lionizing his grandad and making sure that nothing changes in the city."

"Treats me like I just got off the boat like Al Pacino in Scarface. What's with these ignorant crackers? I'm a Harvard graduate for Christ sake. I've got a law degree. I'm a licensed doctor and they treat me like I'm some wife-beater from the barrio. I don't have an accent, I don't cuss, I don't do drugs. What the hell do they want? What does it take to be accepted in this town?"

Lady Sanders was tempted to tell him that as far as she was concerned, being English herself, they were all a bunch of Colonial hicks anyway, but again, she judged the moment to be inappropriate.

"I don't think you should judge the others by Connolly. He is a bit extreme about Cubans but, from what I've been told, it's because he got his face, bottle-smashed in some bar-room brawl by a group of Cubans. I don't know if the story's true but it certainly explains his attitude. I imagine that seeing such an ugly scar across his face each time he looks in the mirror just increases his anger."

Gently placing her hand on his arm and smiling coquettishly, she said. "Your scar is so much more discreet and elegant. He's probably just jealous." When Martinez did not respond she added, "And again Orestes, I cannot apologize enough for this evening."

"And then that goddam Korean." They were on their fourth round by now and Martinez was slightly slurring his words. "What a fucking egotistical lunatic! Sorry Catherine, I didn't't mean to swear, I guess I'm still rather upset. But I tell you. That Park guy is out of it. I can't understand why the City Manager persuaded me to work with him. Park Tower! What a joke."

Sensing that it was time to change the conversation and move onto less contentious and upsetting subjects, Lady Sanders ordered another round of rum and coke for Martinez and a gin and tonic for herself.

"Tell me Orestes, how did you get your name? It's very unusual. I've never met anybody called Orestes before."

"Really? It's very common in Cuba. It means, 'he who controls the mountain'."

"It doesn't have any other meanings? Or implications?"

"No. Not that I know of. Like what?"

Thinking about it afterwards, Lady Sanders blamed the fifth gin-and-tonic. Had she not drunk her fifth then she probably would not have pursued the conversation and the evening could have ended differently.

"What about Greek tragedy? Did you ever read any Aeschylus?"

Martinez shook his head. "Nope. Don't think so. Might have done but you know, school was many years ago. Too many."

"I was thinking of a trilogy of plays that Aeschylus wrote, called the Oresteia. Ring a bell?"

He shook his head and drank from his glass.

"In the play, Orestes is the son of Clytemnestra and Agamemnon."

Martinez looked blank and taking a deep breath, Lady Sanders plunged ahead. "Well Orestes killed his mother. Clytemnestra. He slaughtered her actually. So I've always been curious why any mother would name her son Orestes."

There was a long silence while Martinez just stared at her, obviously fighting to control himself. Finally he smashed his glass down on the bar and stood down from his stool. "I thought dealing with those racist crackers was bad enough and then that crazy kook. But just when I think the night cannot get any worse, you accuse me of murdering my mother. Murdering my own mother. Well fuck you lady. Fuck all of you!" Tossing a hundred dollar bill onto the counter, Martinez staggered to the door and lurched-out into the night."

"Oh dear" said Lady Sanders.

Thirty-Two: New York 1989

Two black Lincoln stretch limousines with tinted windows glided north along Park Avenue to a screened-off construction site in mid-town Manhattan a few blocks south of Central Park. A large gate in the chain-link fence was opened by a couple of construction workers in bright yellow hard-hats, and the limos quietly passed inside before the screened gate was closed again and padlocked shut.

The construction site covered half a city block, and large billboards facing the street, proclaimed it the site of the future Park Tower. An artist's rendering showed a towering skyscraper with the name 'Park' in large gold letters affixed above an imposing three-story entrance way. Inside the site, construction work was still below ground, digging down to Manhattan's granite core, preparing the foundations strong enough to bear the immense weight of the projected monument to a developer's ego. The spot where the limos had parked was surrounded by vast piles of various materials needed for the construction. There was a line of giant cement trucks, their vast drums slowly turning as they waited to disgorge their loads into the rebar-enforced molds below.

In all directions there were signs of activity as hundreds of men with hard hats climbed ladders, carried planks and communicated with each other, often in Polish, on hand-held walkie-talkies. At ground level, above the work area, there were several temporary buildings. Porta potties were scattered throughout the site as were various large trailers and shipping containers being used as offices and canteens for the workers. In the far corner of the site, close to where the limo was parked, stood a large pre-fabricated warehouse. Moving as a group, the men from the limos, all dressed in long dark overcoats and pin-stripe suits, wearing identical orange hard-hats, entered the warehouse and closed the door.

The interior of the warehouse was brightly lit with fluorescent lights, powered by a noisy generator. The five men from the limo gathered in a semi-circle around a pile of about twenty concrete beams. Each beam had a rough textured finish and measured eighteen feet in length and eighteen inches in diameter. An unshaven worker in blue overalls and carrying a large sledge hammer looked at the five men expectantly. Oscar gave the man a nod and, swinging the hammer over his head, he brought it down on the edge of one of the beams in a powerful blow.

The end of the beam cracked open and another lighter blow knocked away the lose concrete, showing the beam to be hollow. Oscar reached inside and pulled-out a heavy plastic bag and carried it over to a trestle table. "Each bag is twenty-five kilos" he said. "There's ten bags in each concrete post. There are twenty posts for a total of five thousand kilos – or five and a half tons of pure product."

Oscar gestured towards the bag and one of the men, pulling out a switchblade, cut a small slit in the plastic. After sniffing the white powder on the blade into his nostril he nodded his approval to the others. "It's good" he said, licking his knife before returning it to his pocket. While the man with the hammer started smashing open all the other concrete posts, the man with the knife cut a long strip of black Gorilla Tape from a large roll and taped it over the slit he had made in the bag. Another man was already directing a large panel truck which was reversing to the warehouse entrance where it could be discretely loaded with the two hundred plastic bags.

Although it was William Park's construction site which was being used for the drug exchange, Park was in no way involved and had no idea of the transaction. It was simply that a real construction site was needed for delivering the concrete beams and his was the largest in Manhattan. Under guise of doing a business deal, Oscar's friend Miguel Brodsky had met with Park on-site and had taken photographs of the site's interior layout.

Leaving an assistant to witness the loading and to confirm the bag count, Oscar returned to one of the limousines accompanied by Vincent 'Blue Eyes' Lucchese and his driver. Vincent Lucchese was an underboss for the Genovese crime family run by Anthony 'Fat Tony' Salerno. The Genovese family controlled all the concrete needed for construction in New York and so replacing the broken concrete beams would be a "no brainer". Lucchese was also the national distributor for Carlos and Oscar's cocaine. Normally he dealt directly with Carlos but had met with Oscar several times over the previous five years.

"Clever idea, using that concrete" he said as they headed downtown towards Wall Street. "Was that your idea or Carlos?"

"I spent seven months in Venezuela a few years ago" Oscar said. "I was filming a documentary on the Orinoco River. One of the friends I made owns a construction company outside Caracas and it was his idea. We brought the product over the border, trucked it to his factory and manufactured the posts. Carlos knows one of the sub-contractors working on Park Tower and so we were able to order the concrete posts from Venezuela to be shipped to the New York construction site." Oscar grinned, "I'm pleased the way it worked. All legitimate looking, out in the open. Quite elegant really. I think we might try it again."

Just south of Wall Street, near Hanover Square, the limo approached an old Victorian warehouse. The driver had called ahead and the doors swung open as they approached, closing again as soon as the limo had entered the building.

Leaving the driver in the car, Oscar and Lucchese entered a small office with a large glass window overlooking the warehouse. Lucchese poured them both a glass of single-malt whiskey.

"That's good" Oscar said appreciatively. "What brand?"

"Yamazaki" Lucchese said.

"What?"

"Yamazaki. It's Japanese whisky."

"My God. But it's so good. Is there anything those people can't make?"

"Cocaine?"

Both men laughed. Simultaneously both their phones rang. The two of them listened for a few moments, smiled and put the phones back in their pockets. Shaking hands, Lucchese said "I assume you got the same confirmation. All bags weighed, counted and loaded. We're good to go." He raised his glass. "Now you just need to be paid."

They clinked glasses.

"Twelve million" Oscar said. "A nice round figure."

The two men returned to the warehouse where the driver had prepared seven, identical large suitcases.

"This one is empty" he said and placed it on a large industrial scale. "As you can see, it weighs fourteen pounds."

He then placed another suitcase on the scale and showed that it weighed fifty-eight pounds.

"That's forty-four pounds in hundred-dollar bills" Lucchese said. "Two million dollars."

Each bag weighed the same and, after Oscar opened one of the bags at random, to check the contents, Oscar told the driver to load the six filled suitcases into a Dodge Ram Cargo Van which was also parked in the warehouse. Oscar planned to drive to Teterboro Private Airport, just across the Hudson River in New Jersey where one of his pilots was waiting for him with a plane and a scheduled flight-plan to Panama.

The two men had returned to the office for a final drink while Lucchese's driver loaded the van.

"Remember the old days when we used those money-counting machines?"

"Do I! Can you imagine how many hours it would take us to count twelve mill!"

"That's assuming it didn't burn out first. Those Braun machines used to get so hot after just a couple of million you had to take a break just to let them cool down."

"Weighing it just makes life so much easier."

"Listen man, I can remember back in the day when we used to count it all by hand!"

"Right. And it wasn't crisp hundred dollar bills. We had grubby fives and tens. Shit man, it took forever to count."

"True" Oscar said. "But back then we weren't counting in the millions."

The two men laughed and clinked glasses.

Thinking about it later, which he did quite often, Oscar realized that it was pure coincidence. Obviously, much of the rest had been planned and controlled, down to the second, but the business with the glasses was pure coincidence. The very moment their two glasses touched in the toast, there was the most almighty explosion and the large, heavy, double-doors to the warehouse burst apart, shattered into shards and splinters of thick wood. With a blinding flash of light and a deafening roar, it was as though the simple contact of their glasses had ignited some nuclear device and brought about the end of the world.

In some way it had.

By the time that Oscar and Lucchese had regained their sight and the hearing, they were both lying face down on the floor with their arms cuffed behind their backs. At least forty, armed Federal agents, all dressed in black body armor and balaclava masks had swarmed throughout the building and a large, armored Humvee blocked the shattered exit. The agents had a wide selection of acronyms in white lettering on their backs including the FBI, DEA and IRS along with a NYPD SWAT team.

While the two men were read their Miranda rights, Lucchese's driver emerged from the back of the truck where he had protected himself just prior to the forced entry. He swung the truck doors open and pointed to the suitcases. "Twelve million" he said. "We just weighed it."

Pulling one of the suitcases towards him he said "This is the one Enriquez checked. You should find his prints and DNA on some of the notes."

Pulling Oscar roughly to his feet, two of the agents each grabbed an arm and led him out into the street where they pushed him into the back of a police cruiser.

"Where are you taking me?"

"Not far" an agent said. "Just a couple of blocks. We're going to the New York Metropolitan Correctional Center. It will be your new home."

Thirty-Three: Greenhaven 2013

Bobby Darin had just finished singing "Mac the Knife" and the Platters were starting "Smoke gets in your Eyes" when Sergeant Anna Hartman sat down next to George at his table in the Tenth Hole.

"So, where were you?" George asked. "I had to play all nine holes by myself. And what the hell happened to your face?"

"Sorry George" she said. "I was involved in a late night altercation."

"What with? A fire truck? My God. I've never seen such a black eye!"

Leaning across the table he examined her face more closely. Anna's left eye was swollen, tight-shut behind a large, angry purple bruise and her lower lip was also swollen.

"And the other fellow?"

"Behind bars."

"Anyone I know?"

Leaning forward, Anna lowered her voice. "Keep it under your hat, though it will be all over the news soon enough. It was the mayor's opponent, Orestes Martinez."

"You're kidding me!"

Anna shook her head.

"Orestes Martinez? Not a look-alike? Not a body double?"

"Nope. Not even an evil twin brother."

"But I saw him last night. I heard him speaking. In fact, I was so impressed, I think he's got my vote. I can't believe it."

"You'd better believe it George and I think you'd better hang onto your vote. Mr. Martinez is in deep doo-doo! DUI is the least of his problems."

"Oh God - of course! After his Town Hall presentation. Lady Sanders took him off for a drink. Not too many men can survive a drinking session with Catherine. So tell me, what happened?"

"It was ten fifty-four and I was just finishing my shift with officer Murphy, going down Connolly Way, back to the station when this black Lincoln Town Car comes screeching past me, must have been doing at least sixty in a thirty zone. So I flick on the lights to pull him over but he just accelerates faster. Then we get to the intersection with Nordmeyer Avenue and as he's turning left he's going too fast and spins out of control, smashes into a fire-hydrant and comes to rest against one of those giant Banyan trees. So we've got smoke coming out of the engine and water shooting into the air from the hydrant and Martinez trying to open his door which is wedged against one of the Banyan roots, plus he's making a mess of it because he's so drunk. So Murphy smashes the driver's window with his baton and somehow the two of us get the door open. I mean, we were expecting that engine to blow, any minute. So the next thing, Martinez comes bursting out at me like a mad man. "You stinking bitch" he's screaming at me. "Look what you've done!" And then he sucker-punches me in the mouth. I tell you George. I've seen the guy lots of time and heard him speak and he always seemed so civilized. But I was shocked. He's an animal and very powerful. I mean, you know me. I'm no shrinking violet. I know how to handle myself. But he was all over me. If Murphy hadn't been there, he'd have killed me. He was absolutely manic. Even Murphy couldn't hold him and you know Murph, he's three-hundred pounds of pure muscle. Luckily, we'd radioed-in and so we had four-more back-ups pretty fast and they tasered him. Murphy looks even worse than I do and one of the other officers was kept in hospital overnight."

"Well I'll be ..."

"It was so bizarre. And all the time he was yelling that we're all racists and picking on him because he's Cuban. Screaming that he's not a mother killer. He never killed his mother - or his brother and we should remember Harvard Yard, and all the time he's yelling he's also punching and kicking until they finally hit him a couple of times with a taser."

"Drugs do you think? Like that guy near Key Biscayne who chewed somebody's face off?"

Anna shrugged.

"I'll tell you something else very strange George. After we'd booked him in, they stripped him so the medics could check him out. I swear to God. He was covered in tattoos. The only place I've seen tats like that is in prison, or on serious South American gang-bangers"

"Good God!"

"Gets even stranger. The Chief's feeling a little sensitive about having the potential new mayor locked up in his jail, especially since we had to rough him up a bit to take him in and he's badly bloodied. So he calls around for a bit of political advice, you know, to make sure his ass is covered, and the State Attorney advises him to hold Martinez as long as possible. Word is that the Feds might want him for all this Medicare stuff I've told you about. Also even though we didn't get any fingerprint matches, we're waiting for DNA results. I tell you, those tats gave me the chills. We pulled-in a Russian mobster a couple of years back. A real brutal killer. He was covered in tats like that. I don't know what's with Martinez, but there's more than meets the eye."

"So Catherine" George asked when he arrived at the museum. "How did drinks with the new mayor work out."

"Oh George" Lady Sanders said. "I think I might have blown it. He was already a bit upset after those awful attacks by Connolly and Park, but then I just made things so much worse by asking him about his name."

"You mean about Orestes killing his mother, Clytemnestra?"

"Exactly. I don't know why. I was just curious. It's not like I suggested that he'd killed his mother, honestly. I mean it was just an academic question; nothing personal at all. But anyway it really seemed to upset him and he just stormed off. I just don't understand why he reacted so passionately."

"Well that explains that I suppose."

"What do you mean?"

"I'm afraid he's been arrested."

"Oh my God! DUI?"

"Well yes. But driving drunk under the influence is the least of his problems."

"Why? What else?"

"Resisting arrest with violence. Attacking police officers. Several police officers actually, one of whom is still in hospital."

"I can't believe it!"

"And then there's this. All the time this is happening, he's screaming that he did not kill his mother. He's not a mother killer - and he didn't kill his brother either."

"Oh my God! What have I done? Oh the poor man. Where is he?"

"Still behind bars. I'm sorry Catherine but this is serious stuff"

"But it's so hard to believe."

"I know. I know. I feel about him the same as you. His speech last night was fantastic. But it seems there's a whole dark side that we knew nothing about. His body for example is covered with tattoos."

"Well lots of people these days have tattoos George. Look, I have a little butterfly on my ankle."

"These aren't little butterflies Catherine. It's not even 'I Love Mom'. These are gang insignia. Prison tats."

"Well, we can't just leave him there George. We need to bond him out. He's got a campaign to run."

"I'm not so sure about that anymore Catherine. Apparently, he might have other problems with the Feds – in addition to the assault charges. And on top of that, after you left last night, that Korean guy wrote Tom Adams a million dollar check for his campaign."

"Oh dear" Lady Sanders said. "Oh dear."

Thirty-Four: Ray Brook, FCI, NY 2010

The *Loxia curvirostra*, more commonly known as the red crossbill, is a member of the finch family and is commonly found throughout the conifer forests of North America. They tend to migrate randomly in response to changes in food supplies but their nomadic wanderings are usually restricted to a wide swathe of territory roughly following the US/ Canadian border.

These stubby little nomads are unique in a number of ways. From a distance they can be easily distinguished by their piercing call notes and songs, with a harsh repetitive 'kip-kip-kip' sound. Although their calls, at least to the human ear, are uniquely distinctive from other birds, the crossbills themselves can differentiate, within those calls, slight variations which indicate as many as eight different sub-species that may occupy the same conifer grove but which never intermingle socially or, more importantly, sexually.

But by far, the most uniquely distinguishing feature of the bird is the one which gives it its name, its crossed bill. A bird's bill or beak consists of two parts. The upper portion of a bird's bill is called the maxillary rostrum, which consists of the premaxilla bone and the maxillary beak. The lower portion of the bill is known as the mandibular rostrum and is made up of the mandibular bone (or mandible) and the mandibular beak (or gnathotheca). In most bird species, the upper and lower beaks match each other and meet at the end. But the mandibles of the *Loxia curvirostra*, do not match and they cross at the tips, so that the pointed end of the lower beak points upward while the tip of the upper beak points down. Using their crossed mandibles for leverage, crossbills are thus able to efficiently separate the scales of conifer cones and extract the seeds on which they feed.

The particular crossbill perched on the wire was obviously a male, as shown by its brick-red chest and darker red rump. Although far away from its normal habitat range, it could well be a Newfoundland crossbill, attracted by the copses of black spruce which grew thickly on the other side of the fence. Its body was over six inches in length and the upper beak reached almost a full inch to its downward pointing tip. The coiled razor wire which it grasped with its feet still retained some of the snow from the recent storm, and

Oscar was able to capture the snow's pristine whiteness in his charcoal drawing.

The Ray Brook Federal Correctional Institute is located in a relatively isolated and beautiful area in northern New York State, entirely surrounded by forests of maple, beech, birch, red pine and white pine as well as the black spruce which attracted the crossbills. In the morning after a heavy snowfall, Oscar could see the tracks of all sorts of wild life and was able to recognize a multitude of local species from smaller animals like opossums, raccoons, foxes and deer to larger animals like moose and even black bears.

There was the famous occasion about five years earlier when a large, rutting moose, stumbling through a snow drift had found its antlers entangled in the chain link of the outer perimeter fence. Before the prison guards helped set the furious animal free, the warden allowed Oscar, escorted by two armed guards, to go outside the perimeter fence and sketch the large beast as it struggled to free itself. As the warden explained later, the guards were not armed in case Oscar tried to escape; the guns were to shoot the moose in case it broke free.

Oscar's drawings and water colors were famous throughout the Bureau of Prisons, they were all drawn from life and featured the local fauna, but always in a prison setting. Perhaps his most iconic image was a pencil drawing of a squirrel gnawing on an acorn which it held delicately in its paw while sitting on the window-ledge of a prison cell, leaning nonchalantly against the iron bars. From the cheeky glint in its eye and the soft down on its cheeks to the glistening, individual flecks of fur on its back, the animal seemed alive and ready to spring off the page.

While at Miami Federal Correctional Institute awaiting trial, Oscar had produced a watercolor of a flock of parrots perched along a strand of razor wire fencing. The birds were so lifelike and the color of their feathers so vibrant that you could almost hear their noisy, screeching chatter. Again in Florida, at the Federal Penitentiary at

Coleman, Oscar had captured the moment when a brightly colored
iguana, balanced on a set of pull-up bars in the prison exercise yard,
blew out its blazingly-red, throat dewlap in an effort to attract any
nearby lady iguanas. In the center and foreground, Oscar had colored
the iguana green with the bright red dewlap, but the rest of the pencil
drawing was uncolored. The background of the sketch showed two
muscular and tattooed inmates also preening for each other while in
the distance, armed guards leaned over a watch tower rail, observing
all.

Oscar had not always enjoyed such artistic freedom in prison,
indeed the first couple of years had been extremely unpleasant while
they tried to break him. For eighteen months they subjected him to
what was known as Diesel Therapy, which meant moving him
constantly from one Federal Institution to another. No sooner would
he get settled into a new prison and start gathering his thoughts than
he would be woken at 6:00AM and be loaded onto a prison bus to be
moved to yet another institution. Most federal prisoners who were
moved around the country travelled by air. Con Air, as it was called,
wasn't exactly first class but it was much better than the bus and at
least it delivered its passengers to other federal institutions. Not only
did the prison bus have hard metal seats which the inmates slid
around on as the bus lurched through sudden intersections and
unexpected bends in the road, but it mainly traveled to county jails,
not federal prisons.

Within the US penal system, federal prisons are the cream of the
crop and definitely the way to go. In terms of food, accommodation,
recreational facilities and inmates' rights, the rules and standards are
enforced by Washington D.C. In the State prisons and county jails on
the other hand, standards are definitely not the same. Small town and
rural sheriffs, especially in the South, tend to find great humor in the
concept of 'inmates' rights' and so during the ten days that it took to
transport Oscar by bus from Miami MCC to the Atlanta Penitentiary,
he was forced to sleep on the filthy cement floors of various county

jails filled with white meth-addicts, black crack-dealers and various deplorable, red-neck wife beaters.

Apart from the physical punishment, the other reason for this diesel therapy was to keep Oscar incommunicado. By the time his attorneys had discovered his new location he would be transferred again, spending another week on the bus before appearing in yet another State.

None of this was unexpected however. Within hours of his arrest, agent Summers had explained his options quite clearly. They had sat Oscar in a comfortable chair in an office of the US District Courthouse, offered him cigarettes and a coffee after removing his handcuffs.

"Listen Oscar. We know you shouldn't be here. We know your background. Anyway, you're just incidental. We've been after the Genovese family for years now; we put 'Fat Tony' Salerno away for life about five years ago and now we're going after the rest. We've had Lucchese's driver on our payroll for over seven months. But what we really want is your brother, Carlos. He's the one that's been in bed with them for so long and he's the one who's got the goods on the Castro brothers. He's the guy driving the bus. You help us get Carlos and you'll get it easy; one year, two max. And it will be soft time. We'll send you to Danbury, you'll like it there. Good company; politicians, CEOs, people you can talk too. You've got lawyers there and bankers; heck - they might even give you some investment advice – assuming we leave you anything to invest." The three agents in the room all chuckled pleasantly. "Again, that's all up to you."

"Let's face it, you can't fight this thing. I mean, I'm not even talking about the hours of wire taps we've got on you, and the photographs and documentation for the past year since you've been on our radar. Just what we got today's enough to put you away for life. We've got you there, in-person with over five tons of pure coke. We've got you explaining how you brought it in – you realize of course Lucchese's limo was wired and his driver recorded everything.

And finally we've got your prints on twelve mill, in cash. Sorry Oscar, it's a slam dunk. You're well and truly up shit creek I'm afraid." He gestured to his colleagues, "We are your only paddles"

They paused to pour him more coffee while he had an opportunity to digest the information, and then they continued.

"We can do it the easy way or the hard way. The easy way is you plead guilty to a couple of charges and you give us Carlos and agree to testify against him. That way we don't need to have a trial – judges always like that – you can spend a couple of years improving your tennis game at Danbury." The agent turned his head and addressed his colleagues. "Do they have a golf course at Danbury Tom? I think they used to."

"Anyway" he turned back to Oscar. "The other way is you make it hard for yourself, you don't cooperate, you don't give us Carlos and you go to trial. You do that and we'll have no choice but to throw the darned book at you. You won't go to Danbury. You'll go to bad places where you'll wish you've never been born. We will bury you. What we've got on you … you'll get life. Easy. That means the rest of your days behind bars. Seldom smelling fresh air or seeing natural daylight. Everyday worrying whether you're going to get a shiv between the ribs and every night being some big hairy guy's bitch."

"Tell him about the teeth" another agent said.

"Oh yes" agent Summers said. "See, you've got nice teeth. Would be a pity to lose those." He shrugged. "But those will be one of the first things to go. They'll just smash them out. They don't like teeth. Frightened you might bite them. They like the soft feel of gums around their cocks, not teeth."

The third agent who hadn't yet spoken, got up from the table where he'd been perched and walked over to Oscar's chair.

"I'm sorry to be spooking you like this Oscar. I know I'd be freaking-out if I was hearing this stuff. But it's better you hear it from us now, than find out later, the hard way. You got to understand. It's not us doing this to you. We're not threatening you. We won't do anything to make these things happen – you know, losing your teeth and shit. All we are going to do is follow the law and present the evidence. That's all. The judge will sentence you, not us. And then, after that. Well, that's what happens. I wish it didn't. I'm not proud to be part of a system where such things can occur but" he shrugged. "I'd be lying if I said it didn't. Shit happens."

"But it doesn't have to" agent Summer said. "Just cooperate with us and we'll look after you. Join our team. Come on – make a choice. We're the winning team. What have you got to lose?

"Just his teeth" one of the agents said. They all laughed.

But Oscar did not talk. He did not cooperate and he did not give them Carlos. He said nothing but sat looking at them in silence. Finally the three agents fell silent, waiting for him. Watching him think and calculate. Watching him decide. Slowly, Oscar rose from his chair and held his arms out in front of him, ready for the handcuffs.

Those handcuffs actually became a fond memory when he was on the bus. Being shifted around the country from one county jail to another, as a federal prisoner, surrounded by State offenders, Oscar was forced to wear the black box. The US Marshalls who were in charge of prison transport, took Oscar's specially colored 'O.C.' prison file seriously and treated him accordingly. O.C. stood for Organized Crime and so Oscar was kept separate from the other prisoners and only loaded onto the bus after the others were all seated. Consequently all the others could see that he was wearing the box. Unlike regular handcuffs which are linked by a flexible chain and allow the wearer to move his arms and wrists, to hold things or even to scratch his nose, the box permits no movement. As the name implies, it is a black steel box, which replaces the chain joining the two wrist cuffs and holds the arms rigidly in front of the body, thus permitting no possible movement. Not only were Oscar's arms chained to his waist, in addition, he was shackled so that he could move only with short, shuffling steps.

The diesel therapy lasted for nearly two years, until his trial. From time to time, agent Summer would contact him at various federal institutions. Oscar would be shown into a nice comfortable office where a smiling agent Summer waited for him.

"Coffee Oscar? A soda maybe? Fruit juice?" he'd ask. "So how you keeping? You've been traveling a lot I see. You must know this country now better than I do myself. You're looking good I must say."

After a pause during which Oscar would just look at him without expression Summer would make his usual offer.

"It doesn't have to be like this Oscar. You know, all this traveling. You can stop it any time you want. Just play ball with us and we'll play ball with you."

After a while, still without saying a word, Oscar would stand and hold out his arms for the cuffs.

Eventually Oscar was sent for trial in Miami. As his attorney explained to him, the Feds decided against charging him in New York as the juries were notoriously more liberal than in Florida. In Miami however, with all the excesses of the Cocaine Cowboys, the shoot-outs in shopping malls and the public revulsion about the Marielito crime-wave, juries were less forgiving and a conviction, especially for a Cuban, was all but guaranteed.

Oscar's big-shot criminal attorney was officially handling the case on a pro-bono basis. "It's an opportunity for us to give back to Society, your honor" he gravely informed the judge. But even at five-hundred dollars an hour, which is what Carlos was secretly paying him, there was little he could do. As agent Summer had warned him, it was a 'slam-dunk' and Oscar was convicted on all charges including two under the Racketeer Influenced and Corrupt

Organizations Act, RICO, and one charge of running a Continuous Criminal Enterprise, CCE.

The Miami Herald announced that Oscar was facing one-hundred-twenty-five years in prison and the prosecution asked for Eighty but the judge, who was aware of Oscar's work for *National Geographic*, let him off with thirty.

Following the sentencing, agent Summer came to visit Oscar in the holding cell.

"I'm sorry it turned out like this Oscar" he said. "But I've got to tell you, I've got a kid brother who keeps messing-up, and I know I shouldn't, but I just keep covering for him. So I know where you're coming from. You protected your brother. I just hope he appreciates it. But Hell! I just wish we'd got him instead of you. Then we could have exposed that commie regime for what it really is."

Rising to his feet, the agent put out his hand. "Just want you to know, no hard feelings. We'll get off your back now. No more bus rides. No more black box. With a ticket for thirty, we can't get you into Danbury, but we'll recommend medium security. We won't push for hard time."

Oscar shook his hand. "Thanks" he said.

It was the first time he'd spoken in two years.

Summers kept his word and for the next twenty some years, Oscar served his time in Medium Security facilities. Of course such terms are relative. Medium security facilities are still surrounded by twenty foot high walls and fences, surmounted with evil coils of razor wire between the watch towers where armed guards patrol ceaselessly. But at least they are not like the Maximum Security facilities where daylight seldom penetrates and men often lose their teeth.

Oscar's artistic talents were soon noted and in most of the prisons where he stayed, the warden would have a signed and framed copy of one of his watercolors hanging in his office. Most of the Federal Institutions where he stayed were out in the open countryside, surrounded by rolling meadows and forests. Under the observation of snipers in the guard towers, Oscar was permitted to sit with his sketch pad in the forbidden areas close to the outer perimeter capturing the life outside. The dark, still silence within the nearby forest, the long meadow-grass bowing in the wind's caress, buttercups and hawthorn bushes in their seasons, all framed by the chain link fences and the coils of wire. He drew wild deer, peering nervously toward the compound and he painted wild ducks, flying in formation past the gun towers, but nothing he drew, however small and obscure, failed to include some visible reference to his prison.

Except for his art supplies, Oscar had few physical needs and in any event he was always financially secure. Though he gave away many of his drawings, to prison staff and fellow inmates, most of them were sent to a gallery in New York where his dealer maintained a bank account in Oscar's name. Prison commissaries – inmates' accounts for making purchases – were never allowed to hold more than one-hundred dollars at a time. Oscar's account was topped-up automatically by his New York dealer throughout the twenty-some years he was imprisoned. But other than that, Oscar received no word from Carlos and had no communication.

Consequently, when the day of his release finally arrived, Oscar had nowhere to go. He had no home, all his property had been seized by the Feds twenty years ago. He had no family; his parents were dead and his brother was out of touch. He was alone in the world.

After the paperwork was completed, all Oscar's possessions were returned to him and he signed for them, one by one. His wallet contained $300 in cash. His watch was a Rolex and still kept perfect time. He was then allowed to dress in the clothes he'd been wearing the day he was arrested.

"That is impressive" said the warden who'd come to personally escort him to the prison gates. "Your suit still fits you perfectly after twenty-five years." He patted his midriff, I wish I could still say that."

Standing in the prison gateway, the two men shook hands.

"Good luck Oscar. We will miss you … but don't come back!"

Walking towards the cab which would take him to the train station, wearing a long dark overcoat over his pinstripe suit, Oscar could not help but wonder what the future held for him.

Thirty-Five: Greenhaven, 2013

"Sorry Lady S." Police Chief Philippe Lacroix said. "There's just no way we can allow you to see him, at least not till Monday when he's due to appear in court."

"But Philippe, it's all my fault. I'm the one that got him so drunk. I should have taken his car keys and not let him drive."

"He's a grown man" Philippe said. "You're not his mother. Even if you were, it would make no difference. One of my officers is still in Hospital and three others are badly hurt. Did you see Sergeant Hartman yet? She's got a real shiner."

"Yes. George told me."

"So you can see it's more than just your regular DUI. City workers are still trying to fix the fire-hydrant he destroyed. Sergeant Hartman insisted on reporting for duty but two others are unfit for duty and, like I said, another officer is still in hospital. Anyway, Martinez is still in hospital himself. I'm afraid my officers had to resort to physical force in order to subdue him. We've even had to draw blood to test him for Phencyclidine, because of the ferocity of his attacks."

"Phencyclidine. What's that?"

"PCP. Angel Dust. One of those new street drugs that makes people act crazy with superhuman strength. Anyway, there's nothing to be done over the weekend, you'll have to wait for Monday.

Martinez was scheduled to appear in court at 11:00 on Monday morning and for the moment had retained Maurice Mayhew as his attorney of record. He had spent the whole weekend under armed guard in a secure unit of Miami's Jackson Memorial Hospital, handcuffed to the bed railings. With four broken ribs not to mention countless cuts and bruises, Martinez found breathing difficult and speaking even more so. Certainly Maurice was able to get very little information from him despite several visits to his bedside.

"I can't help you Orestes" he said "if you don't talk to me. You're not the first man to get drunk when out on a date with Lady Sanders. She must have hollow legs or something, the way she puts it away. She claims to be pure English but there must be some Irish in her to account for her endless drinking. Just give me your memories of the incident and leave it to me to get you out of here. But I need something from you. I can't work with nothing. I can't do magic.

It was at nine-thirty that same Monday morning that Sergeant Hartmann received the results of her DNA enquiry and it wasn't till 10:00 that she was able to share them with Chief Lacroix.

"Remember the body in Doyle's swimming pool?" she began.

The Chief nodded.

"Well, we've got the perfect match."

"With what?"

"Dr. Martinez's DNA is a perfect match for the DNA we picked-up at the crime scene."

"Remind me about the crime scene."

"If you remember, after we had removed the DNA traces of our own officers and the Doyles and their yardman, we were left with two distinct sets of DNA we could not account for. One set we found in the garden shed among the tools and also on the handle of the machete we assume was used to sever the victim's hands. The other set of DNA was all over the place and we assumed that it was the DNA of the victim. Well chief, as you're always telling us – 'never assume'. We were wrong. It wasn't the victim's DNA, it was the murderer's, or the murderer's accomplice."

"Explain."

"The DNA that we thought came from the body in the pool is the perfect match for Dr. Orestes Martinez. He must have been there that night and, since it wasn't his body in the pool, then he must have been one of the murderers."

"Unless he had an evil twin."

"OK. But we'll let Maurice Mayhew argue that one."

In court, Maurice Mayhew never raised the possibility of a guilty brother, twin or otherwise, but focused on his client's impeccable background, his ties to the community, his political ambitions and his determination to clear his good name.

"On the other hand my client does not dispute charges of being drunk. He admits to being extremely drunk that night, and he feels great shame and remorse. In addition to his own profound sense of embarrassment, his greatest regret is for the physical damage he has caused to the Greenhaven Law Officers in the execution of their duties. My client has the greatest respect for Law enforcement and intends to personally apologize to each individual officer as soon as he is released."

Approaching the magistrate Maurice said "Against my professional advice, your Honor. My client does not dispute any of the charges brought against him and pleads guilty to all of them. He has further expressed a desire to financially atone for any damage to city property and for any medical expenses incurred by the officers. I would submit, your honor, that such an obvious demonstration of remorse be reflected in the court's final sentence."

"The court hears you councilor and you make a very good point. All of this will be taken into consideration when the court convenes for sentencing at the end of next week. In the meantime, your client is released from custody."

"Your Honor." Chief Philippe Lacroix rose to his feet and approached the bench. "I'm afraid I must request an extension of custody as more serious charges are imminent."

"And what charges might those be Chief Lacroix?"

"May it please the court, we are preparing to charge the defendant, Dr. Orestes Martinez, with murder in the first degree."

"Who was murdered?' Maurice Mayhew leaped to his feet. "Where? When did this supposed murder take place?"

"The murder occurred on the night of Sunday, August 26, 2011."

"Where did this allegedly occur?"

"At 636 Canal Drive, here in Greenhaven."

"The Doyle's house?"

"Correct. The residence of Mr. and Mrs. Raymond Doyle."

"So who was murdered?"

"We do not yet know. At this time, the identity of the victim has not yet been established."

"How do we know there even was a victim?"

"We have photographs." Sergeant Hartmann handed over a folder of photographs of the pin-stripe body from the swimming pool. The magistrate was unable to conceal her disgust with the unpleasant nature of what she was seeing. Closing the folder with a slight grimace she returned it to the sergeant.

"The court hereby orders the continuing detention of Dr. Martinez in police custody for a further period of forty-eight hours, before appearing again in court. If formal charges of murder-one have not been brought, at that time, then Dr. Martinez will be free to go."

"My God" Lady Sanders said as she and George Attwood left the courthouse. "I can't believe it. That was the mysterious dead body in the pin-stripe suit. It was all over the papers in England when I was there last summer."

"The one half eaten by the alligator."

"And they're saying Orestes did that. But how? Why for goodness sake?"

"And whose body was it anyway?" George said.

"Why didn't you press formal charges in court?" Anna asked her boss when they returned to the police station.

"This is going to be a big case Anna. Maurice Mayhew is just small fry, he's just filling time. Martinez is going to be bringing in the big guns, from New York and DC. He's going to be lawyered-up, big time. We're going to have to do everything by the book. We've just bought ourselves forty-eight hours so let's use them properly. We're going to re-examine all the evidence from the murder site that we bagged two years ago. So far, everything we've tested carries Martinez's DNA. It's like he was rolling around touching everything. What I'm waiting for now is the blood match."

"On what"

"Remember there was a long broken shard of a Baccarat crystal Champagne flute, covered in blood. If we get a match from that … Dr. Martinez will be looking at Life."

Thirty-Six: No-Name Harbor, August, 2011

A couple of yachts with their sails furled, bobbed slowly in the middle of the small bay known as No-Name Harbor at the far end of Key Biscayne. One of the yachts showed no sign of life and no dingy was attached which suggested the owners were either ashore or elsewhere. On the second yacht, a young woman in a bikini lay on the foredeck, trying to catch what remained of the afternoon sun before it sank to the west, across Biscayne Bay and over the Mediterranean style roofs of Greenhaven. Attached to the dock was an unattended, all black Dartline 60 powerboat.

The young woman had turned her back when she removed her bikini top and then lay face down upon a towel so Oscar had not been able to glimpse her breasts. However, he was able to admire her tanned and rounded cheeks revealed by her Brazilian thong. Even though he had been out of prison for almost two weeks, only now was Oscar coming alive again. He still found himself stopping whenever he approached a door, waiting for a guard to open it for him. He was so used to wearing the same uniform, day after day, year after year, that he was still wearing the same pinstripe suit he was wearing when he'd left prison. He still had not adjusted to the brave new world of ubiquitous smart phones, "urls" and texting.

For twenty years he had switched everything off. He stopped smoking the day he was arrested, he deliberately repressed all thoughts of sex. He drank only water and ate only the food served in the canteen. He deliberately and consciously removed all desires from his life. If he desired nothing, then he would lack nothing, and nobody could ever take anything from him. But now he was a free man again, he was allowing himself to relax. During the previous week in Manhattan he had treated himself to several dinners in good restaurants and enjoyed some excellent wines and even a couple of cigars. He found himself increasingly aware of women's bodies and had even enjoyed a couple of nights with a fellow guest at the Plaza who was also visiting from out of town on business.

Oscar had been sitting at the Oak Bar, overlooking South Central Park when he noticed an attractive, red-headed woman in her mid-forties, sitting alone, further along the bar, engrossed in her cell-phone. Pulling a small sketch-pad from his suit pocket, Oscar started to draw her. It was around 4:30PM, just before the Happy-Hour crowd arrived and the bar was fairly empty. Sensing Oscar observing her so intently, the woman asked what he was doing. Embarrassed, he showed her his drawing and apologized.

"I'm so sorry. I should have asked you first."

He tore the page out of his book and gave it to her.

"This is beautiful" she said. "Could you sign it for me? And write, To Joy, in the Oak Bar of the Plaza Hotel."

Oscar invited her to join him at the bar and they both had a second drink while they introduced themselves and made some polite, but desultory small-talk.

"Do you draw nudes?" she suddenly asked.

He nodded.

"Would you like to draw me?"

He nodded. "Yes" he said.

A few days later, sitting at the bar of the Boater's Grill Restaurant, sipping on a Beck's beer while enjoying his cigar, Oscar felt strangely at peace with the world. In the same way that he would sit motionless but alert in a forest hide, waiting for a Florida Panther to emerge, so now he watched and waited for the girl on the yacht to roll over or stand up. The hunter, awaiting that magic millisecond glimpse of a nipple.

"Are you Oscar?" A muscular man in his early fifties, wearing a black polo shirt, white pants and blue canvas boat shoes had approached him from the other end of the bar and was holding out his hand in greeting.

"Yes I am" Oscar said, shaking hands. "And who are you?"

"My name's Ramon" the man said. "I'm your ride."

ooOoo

The first thing Oscar had done after arriving at Penn Station from the prison in Upper New York State was to visit his dealer, Howard Rosen, down in the Village.

"How are they selling?" he asked, after they had both caught-up with news.

"They're not" Howard said.

"What do you mean? Why not?"

"Because I've taken them off the market."

"But why?"

"Oscar. I have a bank account in your name with over two hundred and fifty grand in it. You haven't touched it. You don't need it. You've been in jail." He poured them both a drink. "Your drawings are increasing in value every day. Especially now they're off the market. Now that you're home we can market them properly. First we need to create a catalog, maybe a book: 'Nature through the bars" – something like that. Then we hold a retrospective. You'll do interviews. I tell you my friend this is going be big; this next phase of your life is going to be even bigger than the rest. I've got a writer friend who wants to write a book about you. Chapter One – Bay of Pigs. Chapter Two - Documentary Film maker; Chapter Three – Naughty Pirate; Chapter Four – Birdman of Alcatraz and Chapter Six – Revered Elder Statesman of New York Art World."

For the first time in so many, many years, Oscar laughed till tears flowed from his eyes.

ooOoo

The following day, Howard had taken Oscar to his banker and transferred his client account funds into Oscar's name. "You're a rich man again Oscar" he said. "And soon we're both going to become even richer."

Over lunch after leaving the bank, Oscar asked Howard who had been buying his paintings.

239

"I started-off with a lot of walk-ins" Howard said. "They saw the drawings in the window and liked them. Simple as that. When people asked about the artist or the background, I'd get a bit cagey. I mean I didn't want to scare them off and anyway – you know, I've got the gallery's reputation to think of. I don't want to be known as ConArt.com. Sorry to be so blunt."

"No offence"

"But as people started coming back and I could tell they were genuine collectors, I let them know more about the background. And then there was a nice little article in the *New York Times* which threw this whole romantic 'birdman of Alcatraz' type patina over it all. So sales increased and I started raising prices. And then, about a week after the NYT piece, this guy comes into the store and buys everything of yours. All fifteen drawings that I'd got left. Cash."

"Cash? Folding money?"

"Eighty thousand dollars."

"Who was he? Young feller. Mid-thirties maybe. Says he's buying on behalf of an institutional investor. Asks me to let him know whenever any more of your stuff comes on the market."

"Did you?"

"A couple of times. Just to test him. Doubled the price each time."

"He buy?"

"Both times. Not a murmur. Cash."

"You got a name?"

"I don't know how real it is, but here's the business card he gave me."

Oscar examined the card; it read 'Ramon Fernandez, Vice President, Corporate Acquisitions, AHCI Corp.'

"What's AHCI Corp.?" Oscar asked.

It's an Insurance company. It's part of the AHCU conglomerate."

"What's that?"

"Biggest Health Industry group in the country." Howard grinned. "And apparently one of your biggest fans."

"Indeed" Oscar said. "Very interesting. I think it's time I went to thank them."

Saying thank you was not so easy. The AHCU group was a vast, amorphous, corporate labyrinth of mirrors but Oscar was persistent. Holed-up in the Plaza he continued to phone for several days until he finally reached a department, deep in the Byzantine bureaucracy, which was familiar with the office of the Vice President of Corporate Acquisitions,. "We'll call you back" they said.

Oscar was once again sitting at the Oak Room bar in the late afternoon sipping on a very dry gin martini. His red-headed Joy had left the previous day, returning to her family in Houston, and Oscar was quietly savoring some of their more intimate memories when the barman approached him with a telephone.

"Mr. Enriquez? A phone call sir."

Oscar took the phone. "Hello. This is Oscar Enriquez."

"Next Sunday evening." It was a voice he did not recognize. "At sundown. The bar of the *Boater's Grill*, at No Name Harbor on Key Biscayne. You got it?"

"Yes" Oscar said. "I've got it." But by then the voice had hung up.

Thirty-Seven: The Tropicana, Havana, Cuba. 1989

It certainly was not the way he remembered it, back in the day when he and Camilo Cienfuegos would spend their evenings there. It most certainly was not the same as those magic days of his young manhood, before the Revolution. Back in those days, the bars and all the rooms were filled with sophisticated, smartly dressed and glamorous 'jet setters' from France, England and the United States. They had money to spend and were not shy about spending it. Against the background rhythms of salsa and the rumba, Carlos would hear a multitude of conversations in English or French and the constant sound of champagne corks popping. But today's visitors did not include any *Norteamericanos*, unless you include the Canadians – and Canadians didn't tip any better than the Europeans. True, there were plenty of tourists from England and France as well as other western European countries, but most of the visitors to the Tropicana these days were from eastern Europe and the Soviet Bloc. The fine dresses and smart suits were long gone, there was no more elegance and, even though the club was celebrating its fiftieth anniversary, there was little champagne to be found.

Worst of all, Carlos reflected, were the showgirls. True, they were still dressed in fishnet stockings and outrageous sequined bikinis, and they still balanced impossible wraparound headdresses piled high with pineapples, bananas, mangoes, grapes and peacock feathers. They still danced to the infectious beat of salsa and African music, but somehow with less enthusiasm and with less élan. Today's dancers were shorter and decidedly chubbier than the *"Las Diosas de Carne"*; the slim, towering Flesh Goddesses of his youth.

Even after the revolution, when the club was still being managed by Martin Fox, all the original dancers had stayed-on and Armando Romeu's orchestra still maintained the infectious Latin music of the Fifties. When Carlos passed his evenings here with Camilo, the elusive magical glamor still remained. But Martin Fox had fled to Miami soon after Camilo's death and Carlos' imprisonment. Since then the club had been run by the military bureaucracy as a way to attract foreign currency from the tourists. It had become more of a State theatre where the message was cultural. "Our object at the Tropicana is to promote Cuban culture and Revolutionary values", as one government spokesman said. "Our mission is to educate, not merely to entertain the bourgeoisie." A single ticket for the show was three times a Cuban's average monthly salary and provided a major source of government revenue - in addition to educating the foreign bourgeoisie.

As he looked around at the crowds of East European tourists dressed in leisure suits and flip-flops, while they ogled the chubby dancers gyrating beneath the stars, Carlos regretted coming this evening. You can't go home again, he thought. The past is another country.

But he'd known he would come here to the Tropicana, from the moment he first saw the tower of Moro Castle when he sailed his yacht into Havana's harbor. He sailed beneath the walls of *La Cabaña* where he had spent a year as the guest of Che Guevara and, when his crewmen finally moored the yacht in the inner harbor of Old Havana, it was beneath the ancient wall of Atares prison where he had received the first, though not the worst, of his beatings. If only to banish the nightmare memories these three castles evoked, Carlos focused his mind on better times. He tried to remember the Tropicana in the good old days. He needed to see if any of the magic remained. Besides, among the crowds of tourists, the Tropicana was a good place for discreet meetings and private discussions, and Carlos had a lot to discuss.

He had heard about Oscar's arrest and the seizure of all their cocaine, in the middle of the Atlantic while returning from Europe. Carlos immediately altered his destination from Miami to Havana. He had originally thought of making a more discreet arrival by mooring his yacht in Cardenas or Santa Lucia but the sheer ostentation of his vessel would make it conspicuous anywhere. Even in Monte Carlo it had attracted admiring glances. So he decided to brazen it out and moor it in the harbor of Old Havana. As soon as the customs officials bordered the boat, Carlos asked them to telephone Colonel Tony de la Guardia, his main contact at the Ministry of the Interior. La Guardia ordered a squad from the PNR, the Policía Nacional Revolucionaria, to mount a 24 hour guard on the boat and to issue entry visas to Carlos' yacht crew.

Carlos and the colonel shared a bottle of champagne below decks in one of the larger state-rooms. La Guardia was not surprised to hear the news about Oscar's arrest.

"Things are getting bad all over, my friend. I wouldn't be surprised if Pablo is behind it."

"Escobar? Why, what's the Medellin Cartel got to do with it?"

"Greed. Greed and jealousy. He hates the Cali Cartel and he hates you guys. You're his biggest competition and he'd love the DEA to finish you all off.. Let's face it, he's jealous of your relationship with us here in the military. According to Arnaldo, Escobar has been having private talks with Raul Castro. I tell you, even Arnaldo is getting worried. That fucking Escobar wants to take over everything."

General Arnaldo Ochoa was a much decorated and respected war hero and Castro had appointed him head of the Western Army with control over Havana. He was one of the most powerful men in Cuba he also ran Carlos' drug smuggling operation through the island. On 'behalf of the Cuban Government' he received two-thousand dollars for each kilo of cocaine that Carlos transshipped through Cuba. It was the memory of mutual friendship with Camilo Cienfuegos that had brought Carlos and Arnaldo together during a chance encounter at a military camp many years earlier. Even though Arnaldo had been a commander and Carlos had been a prisoner, the friendship had endured and eventually blossomed as a successful business partnership. But if a man like Arnaldo was becoming worried, things did not look good.

After sitting at the bar at the Tropicana for about an hour, nursing a weak Polish vodka, Carlos was joined by Ramon Fernandez who was his representative among the Cuban criminal fraternity. The young, muscular man who had served as Carlos' 'bitch' years before, had become softer and pudgier with age but he still had the arrogant swagger of his youth and these days his clothes were even flashier.

"Looks like that wife of yours is feeding you good" Carlos said, prodding him in the gut as he sat beside him at the bar. "I guess her *'Moros y Cristianos'* is better than the swill they fed us at the *Combinado del Este."*

"Everything is better than the shit they served us there. So anyway, how long are you back in town?" Ramon grinned at Carlos as the barman brought them both a Polish vodka. "I saw your boat down at the harbor. I guess you're keeping a low profile."

"How do you mean?"

"Great crowds down there staring at it. There's a whole team of PNR cops on duty, guarding it. You're going to make a lot of people very jealous with a boat like that. You want to be careful."

Carlos explained why he had decided to come to Havana and not Miami. "Sounds like they've been onto us for months. They've already started seizing all my property and freezing my accounts. I'm going to have to sell the yacht, it might be all I've got left. Maybe it's time I looked for a new profession."

"You'll bounce back" Ramon said. "This will all blow over and then it will be business as usual."

"I don't know" Carlos said. "Without Oscar handling all the logistics, it won't be the same and anyway it sounds like they've wrapped-up my whole organization. I don't know how many snitches they've got working against me. And then there's the business of Escobar. He's not a man you want as an enemy. You know me Ramon, I don't rattle easy but I tell you, that is one ruthless son-of-a-bitch. I'm serious. I think it's time for me to think of something else to do. Time to move on. What do you hear on the street?"

"Well" Ramon said slowly. "I don't know how this might appeal to you. But Medicare looks very promising."

"Medicare?" Carlos said, signaling the barman for another drink. "Tell me about it."

For the next hour Ramon explained how the US health industry worked.

He explained how the Medicare program was established in 1965 as part of President Johnson's Great Society to provide medical care for people over sixty-five years of age. Back in the more innocent sixties, most people knew their family doctor as a personal friend, and health-care fraud barely existed. The trouble was, most doctors didn't want to deal with Medicare patients and then have to wait weeks for the Federal bureaucracy to finally send a reimbursement check in the mail. So Medicare, looking out for its elderly patients, made it easier for them to receive care by approving more providers. The program made it simple for anyone who wanted to open an outpatient clinic or a medical supply company to get a Medicare National Provider Identifier, or NPI number — which was all you needed to start doing business. With this number, providers could start serving Medicare patients, then submit invoices and get paid by the Federal government. Many providers — like the ones that sold medical equipment — didn't even need licenses, and there were no education requirements. Medicare started direct-depositing payments into doctors', and providers' accounts almost as soon as bills were submitted. Before long, the situation changed and health-care workers were lining-up to get those Medicare patients in the door — and receive the steady payments. Uncle Sam's checks never bounced.

By coincidence, just a year after Medicare was created, the Federal Government introduced the Cuban Adjustment Act of 1966 which meant that any Cuban entering the USA would have the right of residency. By the time of the Mariel boatlift in 1980, Miami had thousands of new Cuban immigrants, many of them poor, many of them elderly and many of them grouped together in crowded apartments along Eighth Street or living in assisted living facilities. It was a situation begging to be exploited.

With very few background checks, the 'bad hombres' would apply for a Medicare NPI number and set-up as a health-service provider to start serving Medicare patients. By bribing doctors and nurses or the owners of assisted living facilities they would quickly assemble a list of genuine Medicare patients and then start billing the Federal government for health services or equipment that was either not needed or, in any event, not provided. Elderly Cuban patients who had little command of English and no understanding of the bureaucracy were extremely vulnerable to exploitation. And while the rewards were unbelievable, a successful 'provider' could easily pull-in one hundred thousand dollars each week, the risks were minimal. The Fed's policy was 'pay first, audit later' and it was many years before the bureaucracy even realized that a problem existed. The few occasions when the fraudsters were arrested, they would post bond and then return to Cuba for a comfortable retirement with money they had already repatriated.

"Interesting" Carlos said. "But I don't really see a role for me in all this. Seems a bit small-time and grubby."

"Exactly" Ramon said. "It is small time. It's a bunch of petty crooks doing one-off scams. But it doesn't have to be that way. Think how it could be if it was organized. There's not just millions to be made – there's billions!"

"Tell me more."

"I know plenty of the guys who've done it and come back here to retire. I know exactly how the system works. I know the paperwork, I know the jargon. I know the price of wheelchairs and walkers, I know which drugs are most commonly prescribed and I know what psychiatric care they sign-off on. I can train people over here so that within a day of arriving in Florida they can be applying for their NPI number."

Ramon leaned over and put his hand on Carlos' arm. "But I need somebody over there with the capital and the brains to organize them. To rent them places to live and office addresses to operate from. I need somebody to create the infrastructure, accumulate all the Social Security and Medicare numbers, develop a network of friendly doctors, hospitals and health-care providers we can work with so that the system carries-on even when the individual 'providers' are busted. This way, the system will endure and expand. The individual providers don't matter, they are replaceable. I can provide you with a steady stream of new, trained and enthusiastic recruits."

Ramon sipped at his drink while Carlos looked thoughtful. "You know the beauty of this – even when our guys get busted, it works in our favor. They bond-out, come back to Cuba, pay the military their cut and then retire in comfort. Can you imagine what a great recruiting tool that will be? We'll have no shortage of volunteers."

"All I need" he said, grinning. "is a partner who can blend into American society, a partner with the capital funds to set-up the system. I need a partner who's good at organizing. A partner I can trust."

There was a long thoughtful pause and then Carlos put his arm around him affectionately. "I taught you well Ramonito. I'm proud of you. I think this might prove interesting."

Carlos remained in Havana while waiting for more news from the US. He hired an attorney for Oscar but despite his high fees, he never seemed able to locate him. One by one his businesses and properties were seized and old colleagues and partners appeared before the Grand Jury and agreed to testify against him. It was obvious that Carlos faced a lifetime in prison if he was ever caught.

With the assistance of Colonel Tony de la Guardia he had managed to negotiate the sale of his yacht to a group of high-ranking military officers and he was later informed that Raul Castro himself was especially enamored of the twin staircases leading down to the main ballroom. In return for the yacht, Carlos did not actually receive any hard cash; he still had access to funds in Switzerland and the Cayman islands anyway. But he did receive something infinitely more valuable, the promise of whatever resources he might need from the Cuban government.

He conducted research on the Medicare program and interviewed many of Ramon's contacts who had successfully defrauded Medicare but, as the months passed, still he remained undecided. He was concerned that there was no news from Oscar. Had he flipped? Oscar was the only person who knew enough details about Carlos to really threaten him. But none of the Private Investigators and attorneys that Carlos hired in various States were ever able to catch more than a glimpse of Oscar as he was shuffled from one county jail to another. He just had to have faith in his brother. The two Castro brothers, Raul and Fidel, had survived all these years, successfully defying the United States government. Perhaps Carlos and Oscar could also survive. It was all a matter of trust, and brotherly love.

After months of indecision, Carlos was forced to act. His mentor and protector, General Arnaldo Ochoa was arrested in June 1989. Accused of disgracing the Communist Revolution by indulging in corruption and drug smuggling, he was subjected to a televised show trial and then executed by firing squad on July 13. Colonel Tony de la Guardia was executed a few days later. Pablo Escobar was obviously eliminating all competition and Carlos decided it was time to move on. His friends in the GAESA provided him with an exquisitely documented new identity and a new history that included impressive medical diplomas from Havana's top medical schools including a doctorate in clinical psychology from the Universidad de la Habana.

Within months, Carlos was living in the United States, embarking on an exciting new career in Health Care.

Thirty-Eight: Canal Drive, Greenhaven, August 2011

Growing up in Havana, the two Enriquez brothers were inseparable, but different. The eldest one, Carlos, was always the star. He was clever, charming and witty. From an early age he knew how to make everybody laugh and wherever he went, he was the center of attention. Despite not seeming to waste time studying, he always got top marks at school in addition to excelling in debating, boxing and baseball. If his father had not sent him off to school in Massachusetts, following the incident with the dancers at the Tropicana, Carlos was destined to become captain of the Belen baseball team as well as the school's lead debater. With such an elder brother, it was hard for Oscar to emerge from his shadow. Everything Carlos accomplished seemed so effortless while poor Oscar had to study hard to maintain his grades at school, had no skills at boxing and barely made it onto the school's rookie baseball team. While Carlos was never at a loss for words, Oscar was private and withdrawn, always conceding the limelight to his big brother.

Far from resenting or being jealous of his elder brother's starring role in life, Oscar adored and worshipped him and his only apparent goal in life was to win Carlos' approval. In return, Carlos loved his kid brother and always wanted to protect and defend him. Carlos would always help Oscar with his homework, particularly with his written work, helping him to articulate his ideas and to put his thoughts clearly into words. It was Carlos who first discovered Oscar's uncanny ability to draw and who encouraged him to develop this gift.

"It's all communication bro. It's getting your thoughts and ideas out and sharing them with other people. I do it with words, I've always been able to do that; to explain my thoughts in words. But that's all they are bro. Words. Ephemeral, once spoken, they're gone, nothing left but the wind. But you express yourself on paper, you have captured a moment in time; you have made your thoughts immortal. My words drift away and are forgotten but your drawings remain forever. I wish I had your gift bro."

Not everybody took the same attitude as Carlos. At school, both in Havana and later at Groton in Massachusetts, Oscar got bullied by the other boys who would make fun of his drawings and even rip them to pieces. So much in awe of his elder brother and feeling so inadequate by comparison, Oscar seldom stuck-up for himself or fought back against the bullies; he became increasingly withdrawn and private in his thoughts.

It was not till word of Carlos' arrest reached him in late 1959 that Oscar started to assert himself. Learning that his brother was no longer able to protect him and, at the same time, realizing that his parents were dependent on him, transformed Oscar from the passive dreamer into a positive actor. The training he received with the *Brigade 2506* simply completed the process and long before he arrived on Playa Larga in the Bay of Pigs, he had become a battle hardened, man of action, entirely without fear. The subsequent years, taking physical risks in the jungles of South America had toughened him even further though, unlike his brother, he remained a man of few words.

Unfortunately, the Federal prison System is not a sympathetic environment for a man of artistic temperament and the first day that Oscar sat in a prison yard with his pad and a pencil he immediately became an object of ridicule. He ignored their taunts and jeers for three straight days until somebody physically touched him and grabbed his pad. Even though there were at least twenty jeering prisoners standing around watching, not one of them was ever able to describe exactly what happened. All they could agree on is that Oscar rose suddenly and momentarily to his feet and somehow the other man appeared a few feet away, on his back with all four fingers on his left hand completely broken and useless. Oscar picked up the fallen sketch-pad and carried on drawing.

Similar scenes occurred at other prisons over the following decades, often motivated by jealousy as Oscar's artistic gifts were increasingly appreciated by prison administrators and he was granted many favors denied to other inmates. But when such attacks were made, Oscar's response was always identical; exceedingly swift and brutally efficient. His reputation spread rapidly through the system and it had been many years since anybody had been foolish enough to cross him. Otherwise Oscar was always friendly. He seldom spoke but he always had a smile of greeting for everybody. He would draw portraits for the inmates to send home to their families, and portraits of prison officials to hang in their offices. Oscar was entirely self-contained. He did not smoke, he drank nothing but water, he had no needs and no desires. He appeared to have no fear.

But today, sitting in the rear, leather seat of the Dartline 60 powerboat as it inched-out of No-Name Harbor and picked-up speed entering Biscayne Bay, Oscar, for the first time in several decades began to be afraid.

At first, he had felt good. Contact had finally been made, Ramon was expecting him and he seemed to know where they were going. Best of all, the powerful rumble of the twin outboard motors coming alive attracted the attention of the topless girl in her Brazilian thong and she sat up, uncovered, to watch them as they throbbed past her yacht. Oscar smiled and waved to her, she smiled and waved back, her perfect breasts swaying with the gesture.

Crossing Biscayne Bay, passing close to some of the remaining homes that had once formed the Stiltsville community, the Dartline's bow rose out of the water as Ramon pushed down on the throttle and the growl of the engines became a roar. In less than an hour, he would be meeting Carlos again, after more than twenty years and that was when he began to taste fear. How would it be? Had Carlos changed, again? Would Carlos blame him for getting busted and destroying the organization? Would Carlos want him back in his life? What is Carlos' life anyway? Married? Children? Might Oscar be an uncle? He'd like that.

Leaving the skyline of Miami behind them to the north they headed towards the sun which was sinking behind the Deering

Estates. Eventually they slowed the boat till it left no wake and they entered the Venetian Channel that meandered through the residential section of Greenhaven. After crossing the Alhambra Golf Course they eventually approached a long wooden dock belonging to a large private residence.

Even from a distance, as the powerful boat quietly chugged towards the landing stage, Oscar recognized his brother. Dressed in white flannel pants and a blue blazer over a white shirt, Carlos was beaming with pleasure as he caught the dock line that Ramon threw to him. Up on the dock, the two brothers embraced in a warm bear hug as they clasped each other without speaking. Finally Carlos released him enough to stand back and look at him.

"You look great, little brother. You haven't changed a bit."

Carlos pointed to Oscar's suit. "What's with the suit bro? You look like you're here for a job interview."

"It's what I was wearing in New York when they busted me."

"And it still fits you after all these years. Wow! I'm impressed. Anyway, maybe it is appropriate, maybe this could be kind of like a job interview." Carlos draped his arm across Oscar's shoulders. "Let's come up to the house and have something to drink. I've been waiting for this moment a long, long time."

Crossing a broad, perfectly manicured lawn, the two brothers walked past the swimming pool to where a group of comfortable patio chairs were grouped around a low table with a couple of champagne glasses on top. Opening a small cooler beside his chair, Carlos withdrew a bottle of champagne. "Krug. Clos du Mesnil" he said. "Only the very best for my little brother."

For the next hour, while they slowly finished the bottle, the two brothers discussed the events since they'd last been in contact. Oscar described the arrest in New York and was relieved that Carlos did not hold him in any way responsible. Apparently, they had been set-up and betrayed by Pablo Escobar and the Medellin Cartel. Oscar explained how the Feds had kept him on the move after his arrest, transferring him from one prison to another in an endless vicious cycle of diesel therapy.

"Well that explains why my guys could never locate you" Carlos said. "Shit. I paid them enough but they kept coming-up empty."

"Not much they could have done anyway" Oscar shrugged. "Let's face it, they had me cold. They had the drugs and they had the cash. As they said – it was a slam dunk."

"So you got the commissary money OK?"

"Yes. Thank you. That way I could pay for all my art supplies."

"But you hardly touched it. There were some months you didn't spend anything."

"There were some months I didn't need anything. Anyway Carlos, enough about me. I mean, let's face it, there's only so much you can say about prison. You just have to survive it. Tell me about you. How did you bounce back?"

Pulling a second bottle from the cooler, Carlos poured them both a glass and described sailing to Havana instead of Miami and selling the yacht while wondering what to do next.

"There was no way I could go back into the business. Not with Escobar after me. Somehow or other, Escobar had even got Raul Castro round his finger and persuaded him to execute Arnaldo Ochoa. I knew my days were numbered so I got a completely new ID, solid, government issued and I just vanished. Started a whole new life."

Carlos reached-over and squeezed Oscar's arm. "There was no way I could contact you directly little brother. When you've got Pablo Escobar and possibly the Castro brothers – not to mention the DEA all looking for you, you tend to get paranoid. As my brother and partner in crime, you would be the obvious place for them to look. All they had to do was wait and see how I made contact. Persuading the attorneys to defend you pro-bono was easy. It simply meant that the vast sums of money they were charging me was tax free. But beyond that, I could think of no way to support you until I came across that article in the *New York Times*. So I started buying-up all your art works. The perfect solution."

"Where are they now?"

"Who knows – maybe Ramon knows what happened to them. The important thing was it was the perfect way to send you money."

Carlos poured them both another glass.

"Anyway bro. Here we are again. No longer young, I grant you. But we're free men and we've still got plenty of life left. Escobar is dead. The Medellin Cartel is history. Fidel is in his dotage and Raul has other things to worry about. The DEA lost interest in us a long time ago. So here we are bro." Carlos leaned across to clink glasses. "The first day of the rest of our lives!"

Oscar clinked glasses and sank back in his chair with a beatific smile. Obviously the second bottle of Krug helped with his mood but most of all, after a lifetime of wanting his brother's approval, of wanting to be accepted as an equal – of needing to prove himself worthy of his brother's respect; Oscar finally was able to relax. He had done it. He had arrived.

Oscar looked around. The sun was setting but the patio and garden lights were obviously on some sort of timer and the beautiful landscape was bathed in a gentle glow, from the terrace all the way down to the wooden dock. "Fabulous place you've got here bro" he said.

"It's not actually mine" Carlos said. "It's a friend of mine who owns it. Said we should make ourselves at home."

Carlos did actually own a home nearby in Greenhaven, one that he'd owned since adopting his new identity. But until he had spoken with Oscar and sounded him out, he was uncomfortable introducing his brother into his real world. He needed to reconfirm his trust in Oscar first, make sure that he hadn't been turned. Knowing that his friends Raymond and Margaret would be leaving their home unattended for the long weekend, Carlos decided to use their elegant patio for the initial meeting with his brother.

"So come on bro." Oscar said. "Tell me about this new life. What's this giant Health Care Conglomerate I keep hearing about?"

ooOoo

Slowly Carlos explained the background to American Health Care United LLC. He began by repeating the conversation with Ramon in the bar of the Tropicana some twenty years previously. He spelled-out the mechanics of the Medicare system and how it could be so easily defrauded. While Oscar sat silently, listening intently, Carlos described the intimate workings of the Federal bureaucracy. Step by step he explained, in detail, how with his managerial and organizational skills he had elevated a small-time, mom-and-pop industry into a vast corporate conglomerate.

"I tell you bro." Carlos said, pouring yet another glass of Krug. "We should have got onto this scam years ago instead of risking our lives in South American jungles and dealing with murderous gangsters. This is risk-proof and far more lucrative than drugs. If only we'd known about this back in the day, you would never have needed to do all that time in the joint. I'm so sorry little brother that you wasted your life like that. Twenty years down the toilet when you could have been Vice President of a big health care corporation. Anyway bro. What do you say?"

Carlos grinned and pointed at Oscar's jacket. "You've already got the pin-stripe suit bro. You're all ready for your corporate office. What do you think? Ready to join me?"

After a long pause Oscar said "I'm not sure. That's a lot of information to digest."

Again there was a long pause. "I mean, you say that the past twenty years were down the toilet. But they weren't. I did that for you. I was protecting you – so it wasn't a waste. I mean I sometimes feel that the previous ten years running dope was a waste. If I hadn't done that I could be a successful film director by now, I could maybe have become a major photographer. Maybe have books of my works published by Rizzoli or Tashen."

He shrugged and paused again while he looked down at his feet. "I used to think about that a lot when I was alone in my cell at night. But you know, I joined-up with you and abandoned my professional career in order to help you. Because I thought you needed me. And I believed in you Carlos. You've always been my hero. That time that Manny Artime said you'd betrayed us to Che Guevara, I believed you and not him. I turned my back on all those Alpha 66 guys because I believed in you. They probably all think of me as a traitor as well – but I didn't care, because I believed in you. That's all that mattered. I sacrificed my professional career, my reputation and then over twenty years of my life – all because I've always believed in you. And all that time in prison, never hearing a word, not even knowing if you were alive or dead. I still believed in you. I believed you would be doing something great and worthwhile."

The two brothers were silent for a while. Carlos waiting and watchful. Oscar silent, brooding, again staring down at the ground.

"I didn't tell you much about Papi, did I?" Oscar finally began. "Well I guess you never really asked. You wouldn't have recognized him if you'd seen him. Mami never adapted to the US. She only left the apartment to go to church; she never really recovered from the exile and the Alzheimer symptoms were there early on. But Papi tried to adapt. He fought to keep his dignity. For a man who had owned so many rich estates and splendid houses all his life, to suddenly find himself in a rented, walk-up apartment with all the other little-old, landless exiles of Eighth Street …" Oscar's eyes were moist as he stared directly at his brother. "I don't know how he managed it, but somehow he still walked proudly."

There was another long silence while Oscar stared at the ground again; lost in his memory. "It was raining, the day of his funeral. Did you ever go to their grave? That cemetery on Eighth Street? We all stood there getting wet, as we lowered him into the earth, next to Mami. They'd always wanted to be buried in Cuba but I guess Eighth Street is as close as we can get now."

Oscar had never been a spontaneous talker and Carlos knew that his brother was trying to reorder and organize his thoughts before speaking, so he waited patiently.

"Artime came to the funeral you know. He stood next to me, in the rain. Smelling the musky, freshly-turned earth as we looked down into the grave." Oscar was obviously lost in the memory of that moment. "That's when he told me about you."

"What I said about Papi is not strictly true" Oscar began after a very long pause. "I said he walked proudly till the end. But in fact he didn't. He needed a walker to get around and in the end he needed a wheelchair. I know, because I pushed him."

"Oscar. I'm sorry. I'm sorry you had to do that all alone. I'm so sorry I wasn't there to help you look after them" Carlos blurted. "I can't tell you how much I would have preferred to be there – than the places I was being kept in."

Oscar did not respond immediately and when he continued it was as though Carlos had never spoken.

"Luckily I was making good money back then. The *National Geographic* paid well and I was able to buy them a little apartment. I was also able to buy Papi a walker and later-on a wheelchair so he could get around and visit with his friends. Otherwise he'd have been stuck in the apartment." Oscar raised his eyes to stare directly at his brother. "Maybe you didn't know, but somebody had got hold of their Medicare accounts and used them to rip-off the government. If I hadn't been around to cover their medical bills, they would have died in squalor."

There was a long strained silence while the two brothers sat staring at each other. "I've never questioned or regretted anything

Carlos. Giving-up my career, giving-up my freedom didn't matter because I believed in you."

Oscar was still holding his champagne flute in his hand but his fists were clenched so tightly with emotion that Carlos worried the glass would shatter.

"I felt so guilty and helpless all those years that you were held in Castro's jails while I was out free. I was building an exciting life as a film maker. I was visiting wonderful places and being paid to do so. But year after year I was so aware that your life was wasting away in some dark and awful prison. Your life had so much promise, you were a Senator, you were going to do wonderful things – and then it was all taken away from you."

"That's why I didn't mind going to prison for you. That's why I didn't see those twenty years as a waste. I was buying you your freedom, to make up for all those years that Castro had stolen from you. I was proud Carlos. I was proud to finally allow you to be you. All these years I thought you would be doing something worthwhile. Building a new and decent life. And now I find-out that I've sacrificed it all for nothing." He pointed to the bottle of Krug Champagne. "For this. For ripping-off poor, helpless old people – you lousy, worthless, scumbag bastard!"

Leaping to his feet, Oscar lunged across the low table and smashed the champagne flute into Carlos' face with such force that it shattered in a shower of blood and crystal shards.

"Oscar no!" Carlos yelled as he fell backwards, clutching at his face where blood spurted from the broken glass. Oscar was already across the table, sitting on Carlos' chest as he ground the broken glass into his face.

"I'm going to kill you, you bastard" Oscar yelled, grabbing the empty bottle of Krug by its neck and raising it above his shoulder in what would have been a fatal blow to Carlos' head. He held the heavy bottle high above him as he stared into his terrified brother's eyes. "I was so excited to see you this evening" he said, his voice back to normal. "You've broken my heart Carlos, you and your fucking Medicare. That's what killed Mami. You killed her with your Medicare scams. You killed our mother. You murdered her and wasted my life. And now you're going to die."

It was this desire to make his brother understand exactly why he was going to be killed, pausing in order to explain, that saved Carlos' life and cost Oscar his. The short pause gave Ramon just enough time to attach a silencer to his Glock-G pistol and to take careful aim, close-up, at the back of Oscar's head. Whatever remaining sound the two shots made was absorbed by the lush, tropical landscaping of the Doyle's neatly manicured backyard. Ramon's bullets were soft-nosed hollow points which expanded on exit, removing most of Oscar's face.

Shakely, Carlos stood up, gingerly picking pieces of glass from his face. "An inch higher and I would have lost my eye" he said. "give me your handkerchief, I need to staunch the blood."

"What do we do with him?" Ramon asked pointing to Oscar who lay half on his side. "Shall we dump him in the Bay?"

"Too risky. Too many people around. Then there'll be blood all over the boat. No. We'll leave him here."

"But what if they ID him and link him to you?"

"No photo ID will link him. Look, you've blown half his face away, even his jaw's gone. They'll never get dentals."

"What about DNA?"

"They weren't taking DNA when they arrested him back then. They won't have any DNA records of him on file. Empty all his pockets and cut his hands off."

"With what?"

"Look in that shed over there. They must have an axe or a machete. Even a goddam chainsaw."

While Ramon chopped away at the wrists of the corpse, Carlos cleared-up all the evidence. He placed the two bottles and his own unbroken champagne flute back in the cooler and, still holding the tissue against the bleeding slash across his cheek, began collecting all the broken pieces of glass. After Ramon dropped the two severed hands into the cooler and they had rearranged the patio furniture to its original position, the two men carried the cooler down to the boat and cast off. Even though they tried to be quiet, the sound of the two outboard motors cut through the silence of the night.

"We'll drop the hands in the Bay" Ramon said.

Startled by the unexpected sound of the powerful engines, the sleepy alligator hauled himself out of the canal and onto the bank. Looking for somewhere more peaceful to spend the night, he slowly slouched across the lawn towards the Doyle's swimming pool.

Afterword

This has been a work of fiction. The city of Greenhaven exists only in the author's imagination. Most of the characters in this novel exist only in the more bizarre regions of the author's mind and most of the action and events are entirely imaginary.

However, much of the Cuban section of the novel is based on historical fact. Some of the characters are obviously based on real people but any dialogue or action by historically real people, as described in the book, are the inventions of the writer.

The author is eternally grateful for the historical research provided by Hugh Thomas and his wonderful book 'Cuba: A History' which provided a solid foundation to this novel. He is also indebted to Grayston L. Lynch's Decision for Disaster, and also Vicente Blanco-Capote (2503) and Andrés Pruna for personally sharing their vivid memories of the Bay of Pigs invasion. Any inaccuracies in the historical record are entirely the fault of this writer.

Finally, the author would like to thank Charles W. Throckmorton, Esq. for the wonderful lyrics to Marisleysis.

THE GREENHAVEN TRILOGY

The Greenhaven Trilogy is a series of novels set in a genteel South Florida city called Greenhaven. Each of the three novels takes place in the present time and features the same group of local residents. Regular characters include the City Mayor, the Chief of Police, the director of the local museum and a brash, international real estate developer.

Although the trilogy's setting is contemporaneous, each individual novel includes a backstory set in the distant past, which is ostensibly unrelated to modern Greenhaven. It is only as the historic theme develops, that its relevance to the contemporary story becomes all too apparent. As the titles might suggest, each of the novels is also a murder mystery; the first two in the series begin with a dead body on the first page while the final volume concludes with a dead body on the last page.

Volume One **_Death by Water_** is subtitled '_The Cuban Connection_' and it explores how the growing Cuban influence is changing and affecting the culture and politics of modern South Florida. The historic backstory describes Castro's revolution and the effect it had on one of the island's wealthiest families. While one brother languished in Cuba's jails for eighteen years, his younger brother fought at the Bay of Pigs. The trials of the Cuban diaspora is seen through the eyes of the once wealthy parents, learning to adjust to a life of privation on Miami's Calle Ocho. The book opens with a dead body floating in a Greenhaven swimming pool, but the identity of the body and that of his killer is not revealed until the final page.

Volume Two '**_Death on the Eighth_**' is subtitled '_The Flagler Connection_' and it opens with the discovery of a dead body near the eighth hole of the city golf course. In addition to discovering who murdered the well-known victim and why, the story also revolves around the battle to preserve the golf course from a rapacious developer who wants to turn it into a monstrous, multistory multiplex. The historic backstory traces the history of Miami from the time that Henry Flagler first created the 'Magic City' with the arrival of his railroad. The story-line traces the Spanish American war in Cuba, through the brothels and gambling joints of Miami's Colored town, to the wild drug and sexual excesses of Stiltsville out on Biscayne Bay. Eventually we learn how all these sordid beginnings gave birth to the genteel City of Greenhaven.

Volume Three '***Dead Naked***' is subtitled '*The Russian Connection*' and it opens and ends on a nude beach. The beach is just north of Greenhaven, near the City of Sunny Isles which is known as 'Little Moscow' because of all the Russian real estate investments. In addition to the modern characters who appeared in the previous books, some of the historic characters also reappear. The main story follows the eventual demise of the brash developer who was introduced in the first and who dominated the second volume. The historic backstory begins with an anti-Jewish pogrom in nineteenth century Tsarist Russia followed by descriptions of New York gangs at the turn of the century and the development of South Florida before Henry Flagler arrived with his railroad.

In addition to solving the mystery of the various murders, and following the amusing interplay of the main characters, the books should be enjoyed for their detailed historic research with particular emphasis on the evolution of South Florida.

Each of the three novels is a standalone book and they can be read in any order. However, the chronological order is recommended, since so many of the trilogy's political and romantic themes find a satisfactory resolution in the final volume.